OUTREMER

A NOVEL

Nabil Saleh

Quartet Books

To my wife, Nada

Acknowledgements

I would like to express my deep gratitude to
Antoine Kiwan who closely followed the development
of the story, bestowing his advice all along; to
Cecil Hourani, Robert Irwin and Omar Hamza who graciously
read the manuscript and contributed to its improvement
with their knowledgeable comments; to my editor, Zelfa
Hourani, whose discerning eye none of the shortcomings
of the manuscript escaped, and to Talal Farah for the
books he generously lent me.

My special thanks go to Jean Vanderpump for her patience,
her pertinent comments and suggestions, and for her keen
interest in the inception of the book – all of which was
particularly encouraging and contributive.

First published in Great Britain by Quartet Books Limited in 1998
A member of the Namara Group
27 Goodge Street
London W1P 2LD

A catalogue record for this book is available from the British Library

ISBN 0 7043 8103 6

Phototypeset in Great Britain by FSH Group, London
Printed and bound by CPD Wales, Ebbw Vale

Contents

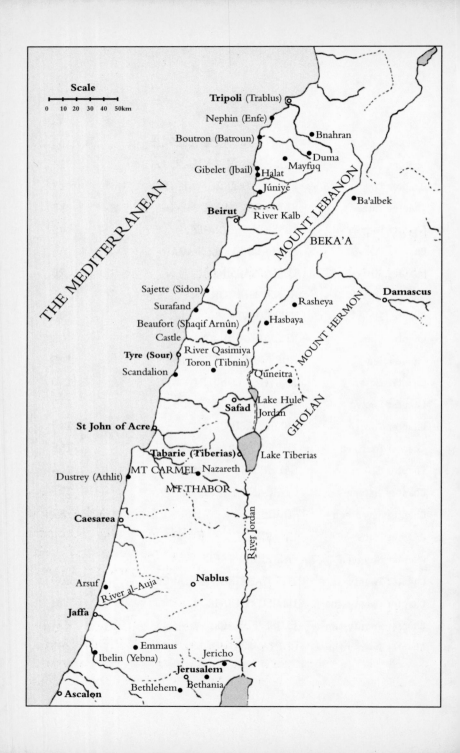

PROLOGUE

ESCAPE FROM MONTSÉGUR — 1244

> *God will be avenged on
> those whose rapacity
> has closed the roads and ports
> which lead to Acre and Syria*
> Southern troubadour

'Good evening, friend, may I join you?'

Without waiting for an answer, a shadowy figure materialized in the shape of a little man with shifty eyes and a forced smile, who came and sat on the bench opposite Guillaume Maurel in the inn at Arles, a safe haven for Cathars.

When the innkeeper brought them each a bowl of soup, the stranger made the sign of the cross without taking his eyes off his silent fellow guest. Immediately Maurel realized that he was being put to the test and, without looking at the man, crossed himself. It was not the right time for a Cathar to uphold his belief and scorn the cross for being the instrument of Christ's torture.

Still not satisfied, the man asked, 'Where have you come from...what is your destination? Who knows,' he carried on, 'we may be travelling in the same direction.'

The reply came quickly. 'I left Aix-en-Provence early this morning and my next destination is Montpellier.' There was no doubt whatsoever in Maurel's mind that the persistent stranger was a spy of the Inquisition. 'You see,' he continued, feeling compelled to add, 'I am going to my sister's and her family for a joyful reunion — they are to baptize their first child — a boy,' he declared in undisguised triumph.

His smile cool more menacing than any uttered threat, the stranger replied curtly, 'A coincidence indeed. Montpellier is where I am going; we will be travelling together after all.'

Maurel had no alternative. The two men made plans for an early departure the next morning, while the remaining guests, a couple of travellers, ate their thick soup, their eyes fixed on the bowls in front of them. They must have undergone the same questioning and escaped arousing suspicion. The last thing they wanted to do was to interfere in this conversation.

Alone in his room, Maurel went over in his mind the ways in which he could rid himself of the unwelcome companion-to-be. A hurried departure was out of the question, as it would immediately convert mere suspicion into certainty. Killing the man on the spot would throw suspicion on to the innkeeper and his wife, and their inn would then no longer be safe for fugitive Cathars. The only solution would be to set off together and for Maurel to improvise *en route*. Still worried, he closed his eyes in search of rest, but was unable to drive out of his mind the memories of the dramatic circumstances which had brought him there, three days after the fall of Montségur...

...He was there again, at the top of a rocky peak, 1,200 metres high, where the castle of Montségur, refuge of the Cathars, looked down with contempt upon the besieging Catholic troops, sent from the north by the French King to fight the southern heretics. There was every reason to rely on the impregnability of the fortified castle, which had become the capital of Catharism following the surrender of Béziers, Carcassonne and nearly all the towns and villages which counted Cathars among their inhabitants. The only reasonably negotiable road from the valley to the castle was heavily guarded and impossible to get through, while the steep faces of the rocky peak made sure that no one could enter that way.

Montségur seemed to him impregnable, unless food and water became scarce, although that situation was many months away. The highest in the Cathar religious hierarchy, the *Perfecti*, had obtained ample supplies for the place in anticipation of a long siege, though that was deemed very unlikely, for the Count of Toulouse, friend of the heretics and opponent of the King of France's hegemony, would come to the rescue.

As an additional measure of security, the *Perfecti* had hired some hundred and fifty mercenaries headed by Pierre-Roger de Mirepoix. Knights and soldiers living in the castle with their noisy families made a striking contrast to the quiet *Perfecti* and to the *Credentes*, the Believers, who formed the congregation of the faithful, and led humble lives as weavers, glovers, farmers and merchants in their village which lay just outside the castle. Understandably, men of arms and Believers remained a little worried about the siege despite all the reassuring factors, but that was not how the *Perfecti* saw it;

death was looked upon as a deliverance from their earthly bodies which are the creation of the Devil and imprison their souls until they are able to reunite with the impeccable Spirit through several reincarnations...As he recollected these holy men and their horrific fate, Maurel shivered with reverential admiration.

At sunset, one day in the previous October, he and de Mirepoix had climbed the ladder leading to the parapet for a last inspection before turning in for an early night; this was customary too for all the inhabitants of the castle and villages, they slept at sunset and woke at sunrise.

Despite the difference between their stations and ages, they had been brought together by a mutual respect for the courage and boldness each had displayed on one occasion or another. Often they stood together at the same point with no words exchanged, no speech needed for the one to understand the other.

Having completed his round and reported to his superior that all the sentries were at their posts, he had leant over the battlement at the south-east corner. From this privileged and dominating position he could see the small tower located some two hundred metres to the east and built at the edge of the chasm. With just a handful of soldiers manning it, the tower served as an advance defence for the castle and for the small Cathar village which lay trapped on terraces between the castle's south-west wall and the void, surrounded only by a wooden fence. In the case of imminent danger, the inhabitants of the village and the *Perfecti* lodged in the humble cottages corbelled out on the other side of the mountain, had to run to the safety of the more secure castle walls...

He had gazed at that village, then at the rocky area which started immediately below and extended in a sheer drop for about six hundred metres, completely surrounding the peak and in turn followed by a forest of small trees; he then became absorbed in the contemplation of the last rays of the sun, disappearing as if a giant hand had stretched out to tuck them tidily away for the next day.

He, Guillaume Maurel, a Believer, was a man of twenty-five years, short but athletically built. Coming from this mountainous region, he knew all the footpaths which led to the valley below and farther away, and he acted as a guide to the *Perfecti* when their duties called them outside the stronghold. The travels of the *Perfecti* were made for the purpose of taking the *consolamentum* to the dying, for business or for any other good reason, and he was there to guide the traveller safely to his destination. His thoughts had suddenly been interrupted by de Mirepoix's voice.

'Am I right to put my child, Esquieu, and my wife in danger?' The trace of a smile had unexpectedly touched the older man's lips as he continued, 'Now I could myself be branded an infidel, a heretic – not by the Saracens, but by my own race.' The irony of the situation had brushed aside any dispirited ideas.

Maurel had actually been aware that his companion had no reason to be unduly concerned. It was well known that the professional soldier was not a Cathar. He had sympathy for the sect, as indeed most of the inhabitants of the Languedoc used to have, but that was before the King of France and the Pope launched their armed crusade against those whom they called heretics. After decades of persecution, which often ended by burning alive those Cathars who did not recant, not only had the sympathy of non-Cathars towards the members of the sect dwindled considerably, but also the number of informers against them had risen alarmingly.

The feudal lords of the south had chosen de Mirepoix to

protect the Cathars in their stronghold of Montségur for a handsome reward, which he had accepted. No one could have reproached him for practising his trade at a time when kings, popes and lesser lords all resorted to mercenaries to fight their wars for them.

'This peak is the safeguard of our belief, our country, our independence, our language, and each of these concepts is worth dying for. But that will not be necessary unless the King's people have grown wings, and that we will *never* see.' He, Maurel, was quick to reassure him, as if wanting to add another dimension to what might be going on in his companion's mind. De Mirepoix had looked at him, but had not uttered a word. He had been preoccupied, expecting a message from the Count of Toulouse to be sent by the lighting of a large fire on a faraway mountain facing Montségur as soon as night fell.

At that time of the year, darkness quickly followed sunset and he had barely finished his last words, when a fire could be seen from afar. De Mirepoix did not hide his joy and was happy to talk and give him the good news. 'A rescue operation is on its way. Soon our attackers will be forced to leave the region lest they are caught in a trap.' That was the message conveyed by the fire.

Feeling comforted, they had climbed down the ladder and returned to their night quarters. De Mirepoix had rejoined his wife and son in the overcrowded keep, while Maurel had gone back to one of the shacks built all around the castle courtyard. These shacks were needed for the hundreds of people who had flocked there in much greater numbers than the castle's capacity.

Being unmarried, he had shared his small quarters with another soldier of nearly the same age by the name of Arnaud de Foix. Before going to sleep he had thought, *'Another night, another day.'* But that was not to be.

A little before dawn, as those besieged had discovered only too late, twenty Basque mercenaries of the King's army had silently climbed the steep south-east side of the peak, using pitons and ropes. They had advanced slowly but surely; all their movements were calculated so that they did not need to communicate with each other, assistance being extended even before requested. Like a top troupe of acrobats, they had moved together in harmony. Rocks and bushes were not obstacles but aids which propelled them towards the top.

The climbing party had eventually reached the small tower positioned outside the east walls of the castle, but still some seventy metres below the fortress. The sentries were quickly overpowered and the remaining soldiers, who were asleep, taken prisoner. The attackers immediately shut themselves inside the tower; ropes and cables were made fast, then unrolled towards the valley to assist the large armed party there waiting to follow, climb the peak and occupy a perilously narrow strip.

Before long, the sentries on the castle's east *chemin de ronde* had heard some unexpected agitation coming from the direction of the tower and lost no time in sounding the alarm. The inhabitants of the two villages, the *Perfecti* and the Believers, anxiously woke up and hurriedly left their mattresses. Some of them were still in their night apparel and a few took with them their precious possessions; these did not amount to much, often just a copy of the Gospel of St John or some other sacred book. Total confusion reigned.

When everyone had found protection within the walls, the two gates of the castle were barricaded, the bartizans manned and all the soldiers, including him, Maurel, hurriedly rejoined their assigned defence posts on the wall walks. They were ready to fight and repel the intruders.

Silence had followed the turmoil, while everyone tried to

see or guess what was going on at the tower. At daybreak, the extent of the catastrophe became clearer; not only was the tower occupied by enemy soldiers but what was worse, those under siege could plainly see a number of the King's men climbing towards the top, although with some difficulty despite the use of ropes and cables. That was not all: after the first crashing and banging, several war machines came into view, being pushed and pulled towards the top. The outsize parts of what appeared to be a giant mangonel or catapult left the besieged speechless, through astonishment, fear, even admiration. The soldiers fighting on the Cathar side could not consider a sortie due to their small numbers and because the assailants had the protection of the outer tower and their bowmen lying in wait behind its crenellations. The few ballistae and trebuchets available to the defendants for hurling stones could do nothing against the terrible onslaught. The best tactic was to stay put and pray for a miracle.

The King's war machines, most particularly the now assembled mangonel, had gone into action as soon as the soldiers succeeded in rushing the barbican only a few metres from the castle. This formidable weapon, the mangonel − so news rapidly reached the castle − was the Bishop of Albi's contribution to the crusade.

Stones and other missiles had rained down on the castle, cracking the keep terraces, smashing the crenellations and making the curtain walls impossible to defend, while in what was left of the courtyard, the roofs of the light shacks were being torn open, taking away the meagre protection they had offered. Everywhere was overcrowded, refugees side by side with wounded, and nearly every missile which landed claimed a new victim.

All the besieged women, whether of the nobility, *Perfectae*, Believers or soldiers' mistresses, had been bustling around, helping the wounded and the dying. Some had even operated the trebuchet on the high wall facing the fort, only to fall, one after the other, crushed by the huge stones propelled by the Bishop of Albi's mangonel.

Despite the devastation and terrible hardship that had been endured by those still alive within the castle walls, the deadly siege was to continue for a further five months, when it became clear that unconditional surrender was going to be unavoidable. Negotiations and a truce followed, a white flag was raised. The victorious soldiers had entered the fortress through the now wide-open gates, immediately followed by the Dominican friars in charge of eliminating heresy from the Languedoc. The friars had set up a Court of Justice and the prisoners were brought before them in groups of ten. No tribunal had been needed to give the Cathars a week or so to give themselves up, as all of them were prisoners and so treated as heretics. Those who recanted and those who denied being Cathars had been taken back to a makeshift jail. Most *Perfecti*, whether men or women, reasserted their Catharism and prepared themselves for the atrocious death of being burnt alive at the stake. Barely minutes passed between the time one wretched group appeared before the Inquisitors and when sentence was passed.

In the confusion during the first hours following the surrender, the elderly Cathar Bishop, Bertran Marty, had taken Maurel aside, as well as de Mirepoix, Arnaud de Foix and another Cathar by the name of Renaud de Laurac. He had addressed first the defeated commander.

'De Mirepoix, you have served the Cathars with honour although you are not one of us; you will not be inconvenienced more than necessary by the Inquisitors. As for you,' he had turned towards the others, 'I am going to entrust you with a vital mission. You are among the handful of our people who know where our treasure is buried. I want you to remember its exact location and to pass that information on to your first-born child or, failing that, to your next of kin, and for him to do the same until better times come.' Bishop Marty had remained silent for a few seconds before resuming. 'Another mission I want you to undertake is to protect our Church by destroying its enemies whenever you have the occasion. By punishing the persecutors and their descendants, further persecution will be prevented. Don't turn your anger against scoundrels and petty criminals who denounce their neighbours out of fear, or harm our brothers and sisters in some way or other. Strike those who exercise real power, and strike their descendants. De Mirepoix knows how to get you out of the castle. Go prepare yourselves, leave me; I must meditate and pray before I am delivered from this body which keeps my soul prisoner.'

Before daybreak, unnoticed by the King's sentries and guards who were discharging their duties with great laxity as the prisoners had nowhere to go, de Mirepoix had guided them to an underground passage located below the old keep. Its access was concealed under the water cistern and the passage opened into a chasm. De Mirepoix and Bishop Marty were the only ones who knew of its existence. Not for one second had de Mirepoix contemplated escaping through that way, for it would have meant abandoning his wife and young son who could not have made such a perilous descent.

Being experienced highlanders, they had quickly climbed down with the aid of ropes they had brought with them, and soon they were in the valley. Under cover of the half-light at a relatively safe distance from the enemy, they had stopped and divided all the money they had equally, and hugged each other for a long moment. They then quickly went their separate ways to increase their chances of avoiding soldiers and spies who were everywhere. Because they were highly trained guides, escorting the Brethren who needed to travel, their prospect of escape was very good. And it was highly probable that they would not see each other again after that.

He, Maurel, knew all the refuges and inns to use on his flight to Lombardy, for that had been his destination. He had not known then precisely where he would settle, but Lombardy was where he had felt he would be safe, for that part of the Italian peninsula had never shown any eagerness for implementing the Pope's decrees against religious heresies.

After walking for two exhausting days and nights, he had finally reached the outskirts of Perpignan. He had not entered the town, but gone straight to a farm belonging to a couple who were Cathar sympathizers. Here he was able to wash, eat and sleep, but not before telling his appalled hosts of the dramatic events which had taken place at Montségur. All three had only been able to guess at the tragedy which must have followed; a tragedy culminating, as always, in the immolation by fire of the *Perfecti* and unrepentant Cathars, innocent human beings consumed by the flames for their belief.

At first light the next morning, he had left his hosts and set out in the direction of Arles. Entering the town a day later he lost no time in seeking out this inn run by a married couple. Here he was able to relax, for the wife, although a Cathar, was married to a man who covered for her. He was given a room and a bucket of water for his ablutions. He could have had something to eat in the privacy of his own room, but as that would have attracted attention, he joined the other guests downstairs, looking forward to a quiet evening and a nice supper. This had been his expectation when he approached by the unwelcome and inquisitive guest...

With his head still full of recent events, Maurel had a sleepless night, dreading the journey ahead with his unprepossessing companion.

On their way to Montpellier, and far from any habitation, Maurel suggested a halt; the landscape was hilly and somewhat rocky with not a soul to be seen. They sat down beneath a pine tree and started on the provisions supplied by the innkeeper. A bottle of wine focused the attention of Maurel's companion, who helped himself and then passed it to the Cathar who only pretended to drink. Finally the spy, having greedily consumed all the wine meant for two, fell into a heavy sleep. This was just the moment Maurel was waiting for. Drawing a highlander's knife from beneath his shirt, he cut the man's throat from ear to ear as he used to do to animals wounded during hunting. Without losing a moment or having a single thought of regret, he took the opposite direction to Montpellier. He could not afford hesitation or scruples, too much was at stake; not only he himself, whom he could sacrifice, but more importantly his secret and the mission entrusted to him.

Several days later, he reached the Larche Pass in the Alps of Provence. It was bitterly cold, he was covered in snow which never stopped and soon it would be dark. Unless he found refuge before then, he was sure he would die of frostbite. If he survived until the next day, he could then be on his way to Lombardy – to safety and freedom. As he struggled on through the gathering darkness, Maurel made up his mind to settle in Milan, if he ever reached there...

God in His mercy had decreed not to let Maurel die in that desolate place with no prospect whatsoever of receiving the *consolamentum*. Exhausted, about to abandon his fight for survival and lie down in the thick snow to await deliverance by death, he imagined his body buried beneath a white blanket only to be discovered years later. Engrossed in these sombre thoughts, he caught sight of a faint light in the distance. Painfully and slowly he climbed on, towards a wood cabin he could make out on the edge of a valley. Summoning up his last forces he dragged himself along to this final hope. He was just able to knock on the door before falling to the ground unconscious.

Some time later, he did not know how long – it could have been hours or even a day or two – he woke to find himself lying on a bed of straw on the floor of a cowshed, except that the animals he could see close to him were goats. At the same time the large figure of a man entered the shed and welcomed him with a warm, comforting smile.

Maurel felt completely reassured when he was addressed in Piedmontese, a dialect he understood and spoke, having learnt the language in the course of his many trips to Lombardy. He realized he was safe among people who did not want forcibly to save his soul at the expense of burning his flesh and bones.

A more mundane and more immediate thought flashed through his mind. Was he still in possession of the money and valuables hidden close to his chest? Without letting the other man see, he felt for and found his purse and fingered it under his shirt. Greatly relieved, Maurel beamed at his saviour who offered him a piece of cheese, a loaf of bread and a jug of wine. He ate and drank these offerings and gratefully went back to sleep.

CHAPTER ONE

THE MISSION — MILAN, 1268

'Aimeric, I wouldn't mind a little walk. Will you accompany me?'

Guillaume Maurel's son, a good-looking twenty-year-old, reluctantly put aside his book and looked at his mother Blanche, hoping that she might give him a reason not to interrupt his reading; but instead she encouraged him to go out and get some fresh air.

'If you wish, father. Give me a few moments...Agnes,' he shouted to their faithful servant as he was getting ready. 'My cloak.' Disappointed, Agnes slowly carried out what was expected of her. She hated it when the house was not full of people and conversation was lacking. Were all the members of the family present, she would have enjoyed listening to a lively discussion and, who knows, maybe an argument developing, although that was not something which occurred often in Guillaume Maurel's peaceful household.

Twenty-four years after his flight from the hell of Montségur and the spies of the Inquisition, Maurel was now a prosperous draper established in Milan, a city of 200,000 inhabitants, with a great many churches and more than a thousand shops.

He had made a small fortune buying material from his fellow Cathars and selling them raw wool purchased from sheep farmers. He had married the devout, sensitive – and still impressively beautiful – Blanche, daughter of Mabille and Loup de Durfort, an eminent member of his Church. Their only child, Aimeric, unlike his father, was literate, with a sensitive and delicate nature that he had taken from his mother. He was not particularly fond of violent games involving the handling of weapons. This his father had eventually managed to teach him, though with some difficulty, but Aimeric was, nevertheless, full of that courage and determination which came with reflection, not precipitation.

At the age of nearly fifty, Maurel could have been deemed an old man by his contemporaries; he had, however, kept all the vigour of his youth and, whenever asked, did not hesitate a second to take one of the *Perfecti* back to the Languedoc to console a dying member of the community or to conduct ordinary business transactions.

Much the same as his parents, Aimeric was a devout Cathar; so when the elders of their Church gathered to spend an evening round the fire, he would listen intently to the account of the persecution that the Languedoc had suffered, shed a tear or two and clench his fists. Maurel would watch his reactions with a smile of approval and profound relief, for he had in the course of the years witnessed so many youngsters leaving behind the faith of their parents and reverting to Catholicism or becoming unbelievers. Aimeric was not that sort of person and his father intuitively knew he could be relied upon for the plan he bore in mind for him.

And so on that chilly day in November 1268, Maurel and Aimeric, well wrapped in cloaks, left the modest house that Guillaume had stubbornly refused to exchange for somewhere more in keeping with the level of prosperity he had acquired in exile. They made their way to one of the city gates through the tangled network of tiny branching streets and alleys, where dozens of children swarmed amidst the passing carts full of goods, exciting the animals and irritating the pedestrians.

They took the stroll to talk more freely, away from the watchful eyes and acute hearing of Agnes. Although their servant was a good Cathar, what the father had to tell the son was to be heard by no one else, not even Blanche, at least for the time being, for what he was about to say the heart of a mother would find hard to bear. Leaving the city's walls behind they immediately found themselves in the quiet countryside. Suddenly Maurel paused, forcing his son to stop, and looked at him with profound tenderness.

'Aimeric, my dear son, I want you to keep for ever in a corner of your mind what I told you at the age of fourteen about the treasure of our Church. Always remember its location, but don't divulge it to anyone – not even to your future life's companion. Only when a council of our highest *Perfecti* assembles and summons those holders of the secret still alive to appear before it, is the location of the treasure to be disclosed – and to that council alone.' He remained silent for a moment, then carried on. 'All our mighty protectors have been annihilated by the Pope of Rome and by Charles of

Anjou. Soon no place will be safe for us, not even Milan. I'm concerned for our safety, and…there's something else.'

Here Maurel hesitated and looked intently at his son whose curiosity was aroused.

'Listen carefully, Aimeric. There's another matter I want to tell you about. Years ago I was entrusted with a mission that remains unfulfilled for several reasons. Some could be due to my own shortcomings.'

'I don't believe for a second that you could fail in fulfilling any mission entrusted to you.'

His father looked at him with affection and continued. 'You must feel completely free to accept or reject what I'm going to put to you, for it will have no chance of success unless you believe in the mission and are prepared to risk your life for it. I don't expect a rushed answer. Take your time to think about what you're going to hear. Believe me, son, whatever the answer, I will accept it without any argument.'

'Father, have I ever questioned your decisions or your plans for me? Tell me what you want. Order me to do it and I will.'

'This time it is different, for it is your life that could be at stake. I expect you to leave your dear mother and me and sail to the Holy Land, to St John of Acre more precisely. You would meet my old friend Arnaud de Foix there. You remember who he is, don't you?

'Yes, I do, as if I have met him many times over.'

'After the time of our escape together from the slaughter at Montségur,' Maurel carried on, 'Arnaud made his way to the Holy Land. Now that most of the Kingdom of Jerusalem is in the hands of the infidels, he has established a shop in Acre, the capital of what remains of that kingdom. He makes swords which are greatly sought after. As you can guess, you would not be going there on a pilgrimage; your mission would be to avenge our brothers and sisters murdered by the forces of darkness, our faith slain by fanaticism and our country, the beloved Languedoc, raped by barbarian northerners.'

'Just tell me, father, what I have to do.'

Slowly and solemnly, the reply came. 'You will have to kill a man, the descendant of an evil family. He is the son of Guy of Montfort, brother of Simon of Montfort. Simon and Guy, as you know, were the foremost persecutors of the Cathars. Simon was justly killed by our people fifty years ago and Guy a few years later. The name of the House continues to shine, however, and that we can't tolerate. The target is Philip of Montfort, Prince of Tyre. How you will manage that, I don't know; what I know for certain is that Arnaud will be ready to assist you in every way possible. Philip of Montfort is probably the most powerful lord of the Kingdom of Jerusalem. He rules over the fief of Tyre on the Syrian coast, but it shouldn't be impossible for someone like you to approach him, using some pretext or other. That is, of course, should you decide, by your own free will, to fulfil what your father was not able to achieve. Think it over, but don't discuss it with your mother yet. It would be too cruel to present her prematurely with the dilemma of having to choose between her duty as a Cathar and her love as a mother. If, in a day or two, however, you tell me that the task is beyond your capacity, we'll discuss it no more and you will, at least, have spared your mother unnecessary anguish. On the other hand, should you assent to the matter, we will always have enough time to tell her.'

Aimeric remained silent for a long moment, then announced firmly with an air of determination, 'Father, I'm ready to go to to wherever you intend to send me. I'm prepared to do whatever you instruct me and whatever my faith, the faith that you and my mother have taught me since childhood, dictates to me.'

Maurel put his arms round him, too moved to speak. Father

and son retraced their steps to the house through the maze of alleys, courtyards and dwellings, lost in their thoughts, with probably the same preoccupation in mind. How would Blanche react to the news that her only son was about to leave the comforts of a loving home for a mission from which he had practically no chance of returning alive?

Ashen-faced, Blanche listened to plans for the projected voyage. At Aimeric's insistence Maurel had left it to him to announce the news to his mother, to prevent her blaming his father for putting the life of their only son at risk, and so he had taken the initiative and the responsibility upon himself.

Blanche, looking more determined than ever, rose from her chair, put her arms round her son's neck and looked him straight in the eyes. 'I am the daughter of Loup and Mabille de Durfort. Both they and their parents were slaughtered by the soldiers of the King of France, hungry for conquest, and by the Pope's Inquisitors, blinded by fanaticism. I also want to avenge them and all the brothers and sisters who fell innocent victims of murderous insanity. If my son is the humble instrument of God's vengeance, how can I question His decree?'

The two men were astounded; they had not expected such a reaction. They listened in silence to Blanche's emotional tirade and, after a special moment in which the three of them were in complete spiritual communion, Maurel disclosed to the others that the plan to kill Philip of Montfort was not his alone. All the *Perfecti* of Lombardy and Sicily had deliberated in council and notified him of their decision, expecting him to devise a workable plan.

The *Perfecti* had forbidden Maurel to undertake the assignment himself, as they could not afford to lose him. After all, he was a most reliable guide and his continued presence among them was of vital importance. When Maurel suggested to the Council that his son be the instrument of their decision, he was asked to approach Aimeric himself; not just to test his reaction, but most of all to avoid putting pressure on him out of respect for the Council. All those involved in the plan recognized that its chance of success rested on the faith of whoever agreed to carry it out.

That evening, the Maurels silently ate the dinner Blanche had prepared and Agnes had served before she was asked to retire to her room. They were all lost in thoughts revolving around Aimeric's impending journey, a journey fraught with danger, and around the mission which could cost him his life.

Maurel, always a pragmatic man, formed in his mind a list of all the things his son would need during his travels. This allowed him momentarily to empty his head of the guilt tormenting him for being the direct cause of the mortal risk to which his son would be exposed. There was another matter for Maurel to address, the entrusting of the exact location of the Cathar treasure to some person in whom he had the greatest confidence now that Aimeric might never return from the Holy Land.

Blanche prepared herself to mourn her only child and, in her mind and heart, a time of sorrow had already set upon her. She was in no doubt whatsoever that once Aimeric turned to wave farewell, having torn himself away from her last embrace, nothing short of a miracle would bring him back. With youth's casual attitude towards death, which was not seen as a fate to be concerned about, and an already total commitment to an objective he had known nothing about until that morning, Aimeric devised and discarded one plan after another, striving for the one that could lead to success.

At last Maurel broke the silence, as if thinking aloud.

'Your sea journey ought to start at Venice, as it is now protecting St John of Acre after Genoa was beaten in the war they fought for more than twenty years in the streets of Acre.

'With divine grace,' he went on, turning to his son, 'you will escape the dangers of the sea voyage, but you will be met with greater menaces. The infidels are at the doors of what is left of a mighty kingdom and there is the mission to accomplish. Maurel sighed deeply and started giving directions. 'Arnaud's workshop is in rue de la Carcasserie close to the port. He's well known and I'm told that you will find him in Acre with no difficulty at all. He lives above the shop and you can stay with him. He will introduce you as his nephew.'

'From what I have heard from you since childhood, this man is to be trusted completely.'

'Absolutely. Arnaud was, and has remained, one of us. He'll assist you with your mission and will muster all the means at his disposal for its success, even at the cost of his own life; he is the Cathars' representative in the Holy Land. Of course he doesn't present himself as such, for persecution is always around the corner for us. Rather he is a skilled craftsman who makes wonderful swords. A Crusader knight of any standing is compelled to be the proud owner of a blade coming from his workshop.'

Blanche, who had remained silent while the two men were talking, intervened.

'For sure you have a plan; so why don't you disclose it to our son?'

'No definite plan is yet available — at least not to my knowledge,' replied Maurel feeling that he had to offer his wife some reassurance. 'All I know is that Arnaud has sent a verbal message with a brother from Languedoc to the *Perfecti* advising them that he has managed to infiltrate a spy into Montfort's court. He himself is too well known to risk leaving Acre for Tyre, hence he has requested assistance, precisely for what, I do not know. What I *do* know for sure is that Arnaud is far from being a fool; he must have a plan in mind. Be reassured our son will not be alone in a faraway hostile country. Quite the contrary. He'll be given all the assistance he needs by our brethren and will be helped by the whole community from Languedoc which is, and must remain, unaware of the mission. He will not have to do anything dangerous unless he has a good chance of escaping unharmed.'

Despite the reassuring words, none of the Maurels could sleep that night, least of all Aimeric's father.

CHAPTER TWO

VENICE TO ACRE — SPRING, 1269

In the inn overlooking the port of Venice, where a hundred galleys could anchor at any one time, bearing witness to Venice as the greatest naval power of the thirteenth century, Aimeric Maurel looked through the small window of the room he had rented while awaiting permission to board the *Santo Stefano* bound for Acre. The *Santo Stefano* was a big cog, which bore a single large square sail. She had two castles, fore and aft, enabling her to defend herself sufficiently and repel any attack by pirates or Italian competitors.

Those enemies represented greater danger to the Venetian flag than Mameluke warships which did not normally venture far from the Syrian or Egyptian coasts and were, furthermore, poorly equipped and undermanned. In the face of an ever present threat, Venice took no chances; by law, all sailors had to be armed and all ships had to sail carrying a party of soldiers.

With some difficulty and notwithstanding tips judiciously distributed, Aimeric had found lodging in the city of the doges; he had been told all inns and rentable rooms were already taken up by merchants and pilgrims, either awaiting orders to embark or recent arrivals off galleys back from foreign places. The word to board the *Santo Stefano* would pass from one inn to another and from house to house as soon as her cargo of timber, metal and alum was secured in the hold and when all the crewmen had been accounted for.

Having time to spare, Aimeric enjoyed the hurly-burly of the port from his window on the second floor of the inn. All sorts of people bustled around the quay: a few turbaned men in Oriental, colourful garb and a few bare-chested black slaves stood out from the crowd; porters unloaded sacks of spices from the bilges of the ships, leaving behind an exotic perfume which made those present dream of mysterious places. Other porters loaded a galley about to depart with whatever goods the trade-minded Venetians were able to sell abroad. Wooden boxes surreptitiously taken on board could well contain arms and ammunition, the export of which was supposedly prohibited by the Serenissima Republic lest they fell into enemy hands.

Our young Cathar had been in Venice for a full ten days and had already visited St Mark's Basilica, the Church of San Giacomo di Rialto and the Arsenal and leisurely sailed on the waterways which streaked through the city and were its lifeline. He had shown interest in the Doge's Palace and the wooden Rialto bridge which opened in the middle to allow boats to pass through. He had even witnessed an execution carried out on the piazzetta where a scaffold had been erected between two columns looted from Constantinople, one supporting the statue of the lion of St Mark, the other the statue of St Theodore. At least the executed man had not been charged with heresy, but accused of a murder he had confessed to.

Having exhausted most of what the city had to offer an inquisitive traveller, Aimeric chose to remain in his room for longer and to resume his observations. From his post he came to notice a youth of about fifteen sitting on a low wall, watching intently the activity taking place in front of him. When for three consecutive days the youth was to be found at the same place in pursuit of the same occupation, Aimeric's curiosity was aroused. He came out of the inn and casually approached the young observer. Drawing nearer, he perceived a trace of sadness in the otherwise attentive eyes of the slender but well-built and well-groomed young man.

'My name is Aimeric Maurel. What is yours?' he asked.

Shaken from his dream, the youth politely replied, 'Marco, son of Nicolo Polo.'

'Are you so fascinated by the sea and by the activities on the quay that you don't miss one single day of your guard duty?' asked the older man with a broad smile as a prelude to the conversation he hoped to strike up.

'My father and my uncle sailed for Constantinople many months ago, the first stop before venturing into Tartar territory,' came the reply. 'Soon the sea will bring them back to me. One day it will also take me to faraway countries, because they have promised to take me with them on their next expedition.'

'And what do they do, if I may ask?'

'They trade with mighty emirs and sultans. I shall do the same one day and I will tell the whole world about the marvels I encounter during my travels.'

Aimeric smiled at the youth's boasting and told him, 'Acre is my final destination; my journey will start whenever the *San Stefano* is ready to sail, which could be any moment now. I don't believe I will see any marvels at Acre; I am told half the town has been destroyed because of the wars which have raged for years between people of the same race and creed, while the enemy is at the city gates, waiting for the right moment to raze its walls to the ground and put its inhabitants to the sword.'

'Why, then, do you intend to go and live in such a place?' asked the young Venetian, with concern in his voice.

'My uncle, an artisan, is getting old; he is not married and has no one to help him. He wants me to join him and learn his art, which is making swords.'

The two new friends chatted a while and came to know each other a little better. At a certain point in their animated conversation, Marco remained silent for a moment, as if struck by a sudden idea, then spoke up. 'We have a neighbour, a merchant, who is booked on the same sailing. His destination is also Acre. I heard him say that he does need a travelling companion and that he is prepared to pay him handsomely. I am sure you could be that person. Come on, follow me.'

Without waiting for a reply, the young lad promptly led the way through a maze of narrow alleys. Aimeric dutifully followed, intrigued by the offer and equally interested in the money. After a brisk walk of some minutes, the two companions apparently reached their destination, for Marco paused in front of a two-storeyed house adorned with ogival windows and a recessed balcony surrounded by an amazing lacework of stone. The two of them approached the front door through a courtyard, unusual in this pile-dwelling city; indeed, it was small, but had enough room for some cypress trees and a large flowerbed to complete the feeling of opulence conveyed by the whole building.

'We would like to visit Signor Favretto, if that is not too much trouble,' declared the self-assured Marco to the smartly dressed doorman who answered the door and appeared to know him.

The man bowed his head in acknowledgement and led the two unannounced visitors into a large ante-room furnished only with a massive table and two straight-backed chairs. At the rear, a flight of stairs led to the top floor. From the ante-room they were invited to enter Signor Favretto's study, another large room, with walls covered in a beautiful blue silk material and containing dark oak furniture embellished with colourful *objets d'art*, softening the atmosphere of severity. From behind his desk, Signor Carlo Favretto, a heavily-built man in his late thirties, greeted them with a smile, invited them to sit down in the armchairs facing him and asked Marco for any news about his father and uncle.

'Having been made aware of the object of the visit, the Venetian merchant showed a keen interest in what Marco suggested. He offered his guests wine in coloured glasses and fruit on a sumptuous silver tray brought in by another servant – this one a turbaned black man wearing rich multicoloured livery – and for about an hour discreetly questioned Aimeric to get to know him a little more. Apparently satisfied, or more probably having no better alternative, he confirmed Marco's offer, but this time mentioned the sum of money he was prepared to pay a travelling companion. Nothing much was said about what would be expected from such an assignment and no questions were asked by Aimeric, who was only too glad to accept the offer, having little to lose, as he would in any event be stuck in a confined place with nothing to do for three long weeks, and much to gain from the prospect of a little savings to start him off in a foreign land.

The deal struck, Aimeric and Marco left their host with the

understanding that the two travelling companions would meet on the day of sailing, at the inn where the Cathar was staying, conveniently close to the port.

The following days were spent by the two friends happy being together, despite the age difference. When word came from the *Santo Stefano*'s captain that his ship would leave port the next day, subject to favourable winds and waters, Aimeric bade farewell to his Venetian friend, clasping him to his bosom; they promised to meet up again whenever and wherever that might be. Aimeric next concentrated on the final preparations for his journey. Not for one moment during his stay in Venice, far from family influence, had he questioned the nature of his mission or its relevance. Not only was he ready to carry it out for the sake of his faith and to avenge his forefathers, but he was also prepared to conduct a normal life in the meantime, convinced that this would make him a better man for whatever lay ahead. His persuasion and belief were firmly rooted in his mind and were not the product of implanted ideas.

At sunrise on the day itself, Signor Favretto, accompanied by two servants carrying his luggage, called for Aimeric at the inn. The small party headed for the quay to board the ship which would be their living quarters for the coming weeks; with the help of money generously distributed, the two travellers were given a small private cabin on the deck. It barely provided enough room for two narrow bunks and for the luggage that the servants stowed away as best as they could. Their duty accomplished, their master dismissed them. Kissing his hand they disembarked.

From the deck, amidst the pushing and shoving of a multitude of pilgrims and fellow travellers, Aimeric and Signor Favretto gazed at the final stages of the preparation before sailing. The crossbowmen assigned to the ship took up position on the top of the castles, colourful flags and banners were hoisted, the sail was raised and the moorings cast off. From the shore, a priest blessed the ship and her occupants. The crowd were able to see him officiate, but could not hear a word of his prayer because of the shouts and cheers of those on the quay.

When the cog reached the high seas, Signor Favretto confided to his young companion. 'I am a jeweller and a banker. I carry precious stones and pieces of jewellery on me in a purse that does not leave me day or night. I, however, have to sleep some time, and it is precisely at these moments that I expect you to show vigilance. We will sleep in turn.'

The Venetian, probably sensing that a word about the high-level contacts he had in the Holy Land might provide him with an additional protection and a better standing in his companion's eyes, carried on. 'The precious merchandise I have is intended for the Venetian Consul General in Acre, the barons of that city and the nobility of Tyre and Sidon. I will be staying at the Consul General's *palazzo,* which is in the Venetian district, by the port, next to the Church of St Mark. You can find me there in case you are in any sort of trouble. One never knows what to expect in a foreign country.

'Oh, by the way, if I am not at the Consul's, try the castle of the Grand Master of the Templars. You probably saw the small box in my cabin; it contains bills of exchange that I am entrusted to remit to the Templars. I do not believe that these papers will tempt any thief, but we must keep our eyes open in case.

'You may have asked yourself why it is that with all my connections I have not hired a person I already know to accompany me on this trip, or asked one of my servants to attend to me. Instead it is to you, a perfect stranger, that I have given my trust.'

Indeed, Aimeric had been turning over these questions in

his mind. Signor Favretto obliged by providing the answers.

'This ship will call at Bari and Crete before her final port of destination. A word said ahead of my planned journey, an indiscreet remark uttered by one of my servants or, worse, a conspiracy between one of my people and known criminals, and I could end up murdered just before Bari with two or more passengers jumping ship at the first port of call. That is the reason why Marco picked you up – a stranger in Venice, with no connections.'

With more boastful confidence afforded by the Venetian, Aimeric became convinced that his temporary employer and his powerful associations could well be useful to get him close to the court at Tyre; so he decided to reveal as much as was necessary to keep in contact with his employer upon their arrival in Acre. With feigned admiration and modesty, he said, 'With your permission, I will call on you to pay my respects once you have settled; still, if you ever have any need for me ahead of my visit, you only have to send word to my uncle's workshop in rue de la Carcasserie and I will respond immediately. By the way, my uncle's name is Arnaud de Foix and he makes swords; he will be more than happy to be of service to you.'

Satisfied with the impression he believed he had made on his young interlocutor, Signor Favretto condescendingly put an end to their conversation. 'Whenever I need you, I will certainly know where to find you.

If Signor Favretto was really in such a hurry to leave his young companion, it was because a day or two after sailing he had met two characters Aimeric immediately decided looked shady, and it was their company that the Venetian was eagerly awaiting. Actually, his two new acquaintances showed him great respect and offered a variety of services ranging from cooking him a proper meal to introducing him to powerful people in the Holy Land. That was not all; they presented to him a young and beautiful girl who, they said, had been entrusted to their care by her parents for the journey until they reached Acre, where she would be joining her aunt, a nun.

Margherita was very attractive indeed, so it was no wonder Signor Favretto was bewitched by her, the more so after he saw her laugh and blush while listening to his witty stories, some of which were a little *risqué*. He was bored and desired her company, which he found highly enjoyable; who knows, she might even agree to join him in his cabin.

He opened up to Aimeric who, taking his minding task seriously, begged him not to let anyone too close to him or into his cabin. Aimeric went so far as to request a day or two to enable to him to make enquiries about the two characters. Magnanimously the other agreed.

Almeric interrogated members of the crew and fellow travellers and was soon able to report to his anxious employer what he had unearthed.

'These two are well known by some on this ship; they have often made the journey to and from Acre. What they do is to dupe fallen women, promising them a new life in the Holy Land, only for them to find out that they are expected to increase the number of Acre's prostitutes, already very high. These poor creatures have no one to turn to in a foreign country; they will have to do what they are told. In truth Margherita's aunt, the alleged nun, is most probably an ageing prostitute running a bordello.

'These two "gentlemen" are accompanying four other girls whose fate will be the same as Margherita's; they don't even stay idle during their journeys, but use their charges as bait to trick and rob unwary travellers.'

'I had my suspicions,' said Signor Favretto, unabashed. 'That is why I asked you to investigate.' Thereafter, piqued, he did not talk to Aimeric for a whole day; but because of his good heart his sulk did not last longer and they resumed their friendly relationship.

The rest of the three-week journey passed with no noticeable incident. At last, one morning a sailor, perched dangerously on the top of the mast, shouted, 'Land, land.' All the passengers rushed on to the deck in great excitement.

Skilfully the pilot sailed at a distance of three miles from the tall and graceful Gothic Church of St Andrew, steering clear of the reef as high as that building and keeping the ship heading directly towards the Tower of the Flies which stood at the harbour entrance. Once inside, the *Santo Stefano* made a majestic slow cruise to her berth, her sail folded.

The sentinels at the tower signalled the arrival of the ship; thereafter church bells began to ring and all sorts of people converged on the port to meet friends, families, acquaintances, future customers of the city's shopkeepers or future victims of confidence tricksters; they all mingled in the crowd with mere onlookers. St Mark's flag, floating high on the mast, indicated that the ship belonged to the city of the doges, benefiting from commercial privileges, and while her cargo was being unloaded on to the crammed quays, the pilgrims and most of the other passengers knelt down for a prayer of thanksgiving.

The nobility and persons of importance were the first to be taken off the ship, among them Signor Favretto, once more using his purse for the same privilege. He had put his arms round Aimeric, bidding him farewell, and had given him the promised sum of money for his good services, and a little more. They had renewed their promise to meet again.

When it was Aimeric's turn to leave the ship he was amazed to see the extent of the destruction in the areas close to the port. He soon received the sad confirmation that the ruined houses were not the doing of the Mamelukes, but the result of the wars between Venetians and Genoese and between Tyre and Acre. Aimeric completed customs formalities, normally extremely meticulous, in a relatively short time, for he had few bags, and they did not occupy the attention of the customs staff for very long.

By the time he had finished with official haggling, the party of welcomers had already subsided, most of them having followed the nobility and rich travellers. So when the young Cathar looked around, his eye soon fell on a man the same age as his father and stocky like him. The man gazed back; something inside Aimeric told him that he was in the presence of Arnaud de Foix, who must have been summoned to the port by the bells ringing and by the ship's flag. He was moved at the sight of the man he had heard so much about and also by the thought of their forthcoming task. Getting close to the person he believed was here to meet him he said in Italian, the language commonly used in Outremer – Crusader states in Palestine – 'You have the greetings of your brethren in exile.'

Arnaud opened his arms and hugged him, barely able to restrain his tears. Then, with no words exchanged, he helped his young guest carry his possessions and they turned their backs on the port. They passed the brothel district close to that area, as in most port cities, then the vaulted and smelly souk where, to the astonishment of the newly arrived, they came across several individuals wearing Oriental garb.

Arnaud jokingly answered Aimeric's inquiring look.

'Trade has no boundaries,' he said, before pursuing his explanations in a more serious tone. 'This is the land of wonder. People of different creeds may be at war; they nevertheless buy and sell from each other. Mind you, not all these Orientals are Moslems or even genuine Orientals; some are Christians who belong to the Oriental Church, some are Jews, some are what we call here *Poulains*, meaning Euro-Asiatics, and a few are Europeans who have adopted the local way of life. Among the latter, some have taken more than one wife and others bath every day, not worried about diseases which could penetrate their bodies through their open pores.'

Aimeric was speculating whether the word wonder as used by his mentor was appropriate, when he noticed that the passers-by did not greet each other. Instead, they either kept their eyes averted or viewed everyone else with barely hidden suspicion. That, he came to understand later on, was one of the consequences of war between people of the same race and creed, in addition to the general atmosphere of fear which emanated from a besieged town where everyone kept to himself, not knowing when the stronger would have to sacrifice the weaker to save his own life or when a business acquaintance would be coming back with a drawn sword.

The two companions finally reached Arnaud's workshop, which was located at the edge of the souk in order to reduce the danger of a blaze spreading from the strong fire he needed for his craft to the hundreds of shops there. The workshop, a relatively vast area, was built of stone specifically to avoid its catching fire from a mere spark; it also served as a kitchen and living room in winter. The storey above the ground floor was made of wood and divided into two rooms. In good weather the cooking took place in a small courtyard behind the building, where a well serviced all their needs.

'The whole area is poor in minerals, except for Beirut's iron mines which belong to the Ibelins, the Lords of that City,' Arnaud explained as he showed Aimeric his workshop. 'No other exploitable iron is to be found here, so what I need for my work is mostly imported. The swords I make are much sought after; if you are interested, I will teach you my craft.'

Then, realizing that his young guest had not come all that way to be an apprentice, he quickly added, 'That is, of course, if you have the time.'

Arnaud remained lost in thought for a moment, struck by the passing idea of the immense difficulty of the mission entrusted to them; then pulling himself together he said jokingly, 'Would you believe that for highly important customers I send my blades to Damascus, ... yes, to Damascus, to have them either decorated with inlay work or ornamented with precious stones. Would anyone not living in this land ever believe that?'

Aimeric smiled. 'As far I could venture without being presumptuous, having been here only for a few hours, I would describe this land as a place full of surprises. I doubt I will have the time to benefit from your teaching, but I will certainly watch you at work whenever I have the opportunity.'

It was a little before noon and still chilly at that time of the year, so the two Cathars sat indoors on a bench in a corner of the workshop–cum–kitchen. Aimeric talked about his father, his mother, and other people of his host's generation. The latter listened avidly, asking for more details; rejoicing when he was told that a brother or sister he knew was still alive and grieving whenever told of the demise of an old companion. When all courtesies were done with, a long pause ensued, as if a time for reflection were needed before getting on to a most serious subject. The silence was finally broken by Arnaud.

'Your dear father and I have confronted many dangers; we are lucky still to be alive. Renaud de Laurac who ran away with us from Montségur did not have such luck; he died in mysterious circumstances in Sicily, shortly after our escape. I came to know the sad news through a fellow countryman, not a member of our Church, who came here on a pilgrimage.' He sighed and carried on.

'Now it is you who will have to face deadly danger. I didn't expect Guillaume's only son to be entrusted with the mission. Oh, don't misunderstand me; I am, in a way, very happy to see you here, but at the same time I don't want to see you come to any harm and my dear old friend to grieve more than his fair share. We have done our bit.' He sighed again.

Aimeric reassured him that he had come to him of his own free will and with a full knowledge of the perils ahead. 'Be assured,' he added, 'I am neither foolish nor suicidal. I deeply and strongly believe in my assignment and I will discharge it with God's blessing and your help. That will surely make the odds in favour of my staying alive. I beg you to tell me the plan, if there is one.'

'I don't have one yet, rather the start of something vague which could develop into a plan. Let me explain. Tomorrow you will meet Shams who takes care of me and my household; she belongs to a religious sect which is neither Christian nor Islamic. Like us, the adherents to that sect believe in the reincarnation of the soul and, like us, the sect's members are divided into two classes: those who have wisdom and know the intricacies of their religion and those who have no knowledge of the true meaning of their religion.' Noting that Aimeric seemed to be completely rapt by his explanations, he added the following details. 'Similarities between the dogma of the two doctrines are even more striking; they believe, like us, that asceticism can liberate the soul from this corrupt and ungodly world.'

'How interesting this is and how lucky you are in having met this woman; I am dying to make her acquaintance,' exclaimed Aimeric with the ardour of youth.

Arnaud smiled. 'Wait. You've heard an account of only a part of the situation. Shams has a younger brother by the name of Abdallah, a fine, courageous young man; I managed to introduce him into the court at Tyre. One day I sent him to that city to deliver a sword made to order for the Knight of Picquigny, whose confidence he gained. With my encouragement and support, Abdallah has remained in the Knight's service. He has befriended another servant there by the name of Touma. A Syrian Christian, that one. Touma attends to the person of the Prince of Montfort himself. Abdallah has convinced his friend to report to him on all his eyes see and his ears hear at the court and in Tyre and then, of course, my man repeats to me all he has learnt from his source. What's more, Shams's brother is not a fool; he knows pretty well how to distinguish gossip from valuable information.'

'But that is a wonderful beginning.'

'That seems also to be the end,' said Arnaud mournfully.

'Why is that?'

There was more regret and sadness in his voice. 'Because I haven't seen or heard from Abdallah for a whole six months; nor has his sister. We don't know whether he is dead or alive. It could be that he is afraid to continue our business together. You can imagine the state Shams is in, not knowing what has befallen the brother she loves so much.'

'Then I have to go Tyre and find out for myself.'

Arnaud, although very pleased with his young companion's enthusiasm, voiced what reason dictated. 'You must wait a little longer, until your face becomes familiar here. You have, in addition, to find a motive for visiting Tyre. Don't forget, Acre and Tyre are not the best of neighbours; truly they are at peace now, but there was a lot of bloodshed not long ago and a lot of resentment and suspicion remains. Most frightening of all is the enemy at our gates. The Mamelukes of Sultan Baybars roam through the countryside; you never know when or where they will strike, despite the truce concluded last year. Drums of war beat and beat; they will not stop until we are all thrown into the sea.'

CHAPTER THREE

BAYBARS, THE MAMELUKE SULTAN

The one who takes command must be endowed with vigilance
Qadi Muhiddine reporting a saying of Baybars

'O great Sultan, Master of the Earth! I am but your slave who expects justice from the most just of all.'

The mature woman who uttered these words fought her way through the crowd and the guards to be the first to present her case to Baybars, the mighty Mameluke Sultan.

'What is it, woman? Speak up.' He signalled her to approach, which she did and dropped to her knees, without showing any fear, only the determination of one convinced of her rights and with nothing to lose.

'For five whole years I was kept prisoner in the city of Tyre; I managed to buy back my freedom, but left behind a nine-year-old daughter. I didn't have enough money for her freedom, too, so I did something my heart couldn't accept: I left her – but I worked for her rescue. The good people of Damascus gave me the amount needed for her release.

'I went back to Tyre and paid the sum they had asked, took my girl and left the city which was witness to our calamity for so long. When we were close to Safed, an armed party of Knights Hospitallers intercepted us and snatched my daughter from me. The only hope I have to get her back once again is in your justice and your distaste for seeing Moslems abused.'

When the poor woman had finished her story, Baybars went into a great rage against those who traded on the truce he had granted them. He at once dictated to a secretary a stern letter intended for the Prince of Tyre and for the Grand Master of the Hospital, demanding that the girl be reunited with her mother without delay. The letter also stated that three runaway slaves, who earlier took refuge in Tyre, must be handed over to their master.

It was the beginning of the month of Ramadan of the year AH 667 (AD May 1269); the Sultan of Egypt and Syria, the Mameluke Baybars, had taken up residence in his Damascus fortress which he had reached after a four-day ride from Cairo.

Baybars' visit to Damascus was not welcomed by the inhabitants of what had been the city of the Umayyads, far from it. As soon he set foot in the town, fear enwrapped the entire Northern Province. No man, whether a dignitary or a civil servant, felt safe; no one knew what words he might or might not have said or what deed he might or might not have done would reach the Sultan's ear. No Qadi could sleep through an entire night, for he would not know which one of the judgments he had rendered (indeed not always justifiable) would be brought to the attention of the man nicknamed The Crossbowman and The Panther. As for ordinary people, all they had to expect were more taxes, more forced labour and more drafting into the army.

Earlier the same morning, the much feared Sultan had inspected the fortress garrison. At the appointed time he had appeared at the fortress gate leading to the large bailey, accompanied by the haunting sound of drumbeats. He was about forty years old, powerfully built, his blue eyes an indication of his Kipchak Turk origin. He wore a loose purple garment with a slot in front and his head was covered by a black turban embroidered with gold thread. By his side hung a sword; immediately behind him a slave held an ornamental yellow umbrella over his master's head. Following the slave walked bearers of more swords, spears and crossbows, each one of them wearing the cloth and turban reserved for his function.

Baybars had mounted a magnificent grey horse presented to him by the corporation of the city's silk-weavers upon his arrival and, seated motionless, he watched the soldiers marching on parade in front of him in ranks of five.

When the inspection ended, the Sultan had returned to the fortress and held court in the grand hall, on a dais erected for the purpose, sitting up on a pile of cushions attended by his *Atabak* (chief minister) Al-Hilli and by the Qadi Muhiddine, who acted as his personal secretary and historiographer. The dignitaries had stepped forward in small groups and, once in the presence of Baybars, were awestruck. They had thrown themselves on to their knees, kissing the ground he had walked upon, incapable of looking at his face, far less of speaking. He had done nothing to put them at ease and alleviate their fear, quite the contrary. From time to time he had uttered one or two words which might have had no real meaning for most, but were understood by those they were intended for. The recipient of the Sultan's message had then become paralysed by more fear, while he could only marvel at the amount of information the Sultan was getting about the important and even the trivial events which were taking place in the Province. Indeed, Baybars relied on the most efficient secret service of the time, a service which seldom failed him; how could it be otherwise – the smallest mistake, the slightest failing and the culprit could be either beheaded or crucified.

This successor of Saladin had none of the magnanimity and gentlemanliness of the latter, whose House the Mamelukes had supplanted. He ruled by the sword and, with his ferocious ways, Baybars had succeeded where others had failed or could not bring about a conclusion. For now the Franks held only a narrow strip of the coast extending from Acre to Latakia and their princes and princesses had begged him for a truce; this he had found expedient to grant for the time being. In view of the present circumstances, he believed he should not provoke the nations of the Franks and, in particular, the King of France who, as reported to Baybars by his spies, was preparing another crusade which no one knew when or where to expect.

Before that looming danger, a number of Crusaders' cities and fortified castles had fallen to the Mamelukes, yet the jewel in Baybars' victorious crown was arrogant Antioch which he had stormed a year before to the day; its men had been put to the sword, its women and children sold into slavery at a low price as there had been so many, and its wealth plundered and distributed to the victors. The Sultan could be proud of his achievement so far; nevertheless, he had sworn not to rest until the last infidel had left the eastern Mediterranean shores.

He was, however, too clever to be fanatically blind and lose sight of his immediate interest. He realized that he still needed the Franks, to be sure, not on his territory – but for their skills as merchants, endowed with an adventurous spirit that had taken them to distant countries over treacherous waters aboard unreliable boats. He needed their raw materials, so essential for his war effort and still available despite the knowledge of the likely use he would make of them and despite the renewed threats of excommunication voiced by the religious authorities against those who traded with Islam. Hence Baybars' contempt for the Franks knew no bounds; however, that did not prevent him from having a good relationship and a treaty with the Emperor of Constantinople, himself a Christian but of the Greek Orthodox faith, or from corresponding with Charles of Anjou, King of Naples and Sicily, and vigorously pursuing trade enterprises with Venice.

When the last dignitaries had retired, having affirmed their allegiance to Baybars, the petitioners were brought close to the dais by the soldiers in attendance. Among them was the woman whose tragic story had incensed Baybars and made him demand that the girl be handed over to her mother and the three runaway slaves to their master.

A few days passed after which there came a reply turning down the Sultan's demand. What infuriated him was that his claim had been rejected on account of the christening of those he wanted back. With no time to loose Baybars summoned the recently appointed judges of the various schools and put a question to them.

'Is there anything in the law which would prevent me from laying waste the enemy's harvest and cutting down and burning his trees?'

'If, in his great wisdom, the Sultan deems that his planned action will weaken the enemy of Islam, it follows that the law is no obstacle. The Prophet, peace be on him, ordered the cutting down of the vineyards of Taef's inhabitants and that was the cause of them adhering to Islam. On another occasion, during the Banu al-Nadeer war, he gave the order to cut down a variety of date palms known as *asfar*,' came the scholars' unanimous reply.

His conscience at peace, Baybars, at the head of a light contingent of soldiers, took the road to Toron, a fortified town he had occupied four years earlier and which lay some fourteen miles from Tyre as the crow flies. At Toron he was joined by his chief minister and by Emir Jamal al-din who, with more soldiers, had taken different routes to reach there.

From his temporary headquarters, the Mameluke sent his troops to the countryside close to Tyre, with orders to inflict as much damage as possible: to burn anything growing, in particular the sugar-cane plantations, one of the main sources of the city's income. Terror struck the inhabitants of Tyre, Sidon and Acre and the hamlets surrounding them. All the residents of the countryside rushed to the towns in search of protection. Fortifications were strengthened and new defences erected. Everyone, even the animals, alerted by their sense of the looming danger, was on tenterhooks, not knowing where and when the Mameluke would strike first.

After a few days of unbearable tension, accompanied by the wanton destruction of properties, Philip of Montfort sent three emissaries to the Sultan with a message of peace and a reminder of the recent truce signed by them both. Listening to the Prince's message, Baybars could no longer control his anger and ordered that the emissaries be put in shackles.

'Your master has had the temerity to remind me of a truce that he himself has broken more than once,' he ranted and raved at them, 'as if I were the only one bound by its terms. He gives refuge to runaway slaves, keeps a young girl apart from her mother and pockets the money he has received for her freedom. Moreover, your master has forced them to accept baptism, making of them apostates. In the recent past he has refused the exchange of his Moslem prisoners for the Christians in my gaols for the most selfish and ruthless reason – his unwillingness to lose the benefit of free manpower.

'Above all, he broke his solemn word that we had both agreed to storm Acre at the same time, I by land and he by sea. When I presented myself at the walls of that city, he didn't appear, neither on land nor on the waters. What kind of truce do you dare remind me of? Do you expect me to stay idle while you tear up and trample on our agreement?'

The destruction persisted another week until a party of knights left Tyre under the mantle of darkness and, in a daring raid, captured a Mameluke emir and his retinue who had foolishly strayed from their lines. Baybars was in no position to sacrifice such an important prisoner; furthermore, word was still arriving about a new crusade on its way towards Outremer – or maybe Egypt was its destination? Only God knew! Baybars could not take a chance; he had to go back to Cairo and be ready to repel any attack. Negotiations for the release of Montfort's emissaries against the release of the emir were successfully concluded. The little girl and the runaway slaves, being small fry, were not part of the peace discussions and were soon forgotten.

The truce reconfirmed, Baybars struck camp and headed southwards, leaving behind the decreasing yet still obsessive sound of beating drums. The besieged population gave a cry of relief: it was saved.

One question, however, remained on everyone's lips: *'How long will the respite last?'*

CHAPTER FOUR

MISSION ENDANGERED

'I am unable to keep it to myself any longer. O esteemed brother, tell me, I beg of you, do you agonize as I do over questions which remain unanswered?'

A few weeks after his arrival at Acre and as part of his daily routine, Aimeric Maurel had joined Arnaud de Foix in his workshop where he was busy lending devotion and love to his craft. After watching him in silence for a time, Aimeric uttered this anguished cry.

'Questions about what?' asked Arnaud de Foix, putting down his hammer and looking at his young companion with a mixture of curiosity and concern.

'I don't know. About everything...whether I deserve the confidence my father and the elders have in me and whether I can, or want to, carry out the mission I am entrusted with...I feel my head is about to explode.'

'Is it doubting the relevance of the mission that puts you in such a confused state?'

The young Cathar looked away and hung his head, ashamed.

Arnaud did not need more to realize the torment Aimeric was in; he sent away Abdel Malek, his young apprentice, and took Aimeric by the arm, prompting him to sit down on a bench beside him.

'You haven't seen what your father and I witnessed. The endless persecution, the torture, the burning at the stake, people set against people and families divided...'

'No, I haven't seen any of that but, believe me, I have relived it since I was a child, and I suffered then as I suffer now,' Aimeric interjected.

'We who escaped,' Arnaud continued, apparently unaware of the interruption, 'were condemned to a bitter exile. True, we didn't lose our lives, and we have been able to lead a decent life since. But away from our beloved Languedoc we forgot what joy meant, for there is no joy for those who have been pulled from their roots...'

'Don't you think that I also feel constant pain, knowing how much my parents and my brethren have endured?' exclaimed Aimeric. 'But should we allow the past to keep on haunting us? Forgive me, esteemed brother, if I open my heart to you, but I have no one else to turn to for advice. Don't believe for a moment,' he hurriedly added, 'that I am satisfied with the answers which jostle my mind; it's just the questions which are certain, the answers are not. One day I wake up free of any doubts and then, a moment later, I am besieged with them.'

The older man tried to revive Aimeric's flagging resolution.

'The horrendous ordeal suffered by our people, all the crimes committed against us, they can't go unnoticed or unpunished just because they took place a long time ago. Someone should pay for the fathers' sins; not in a spirit of revenge alone, but mainly to prevent the perpetration of similar atrocities against people of different creeds. What befell us in the past shouldn't be given any opportunity whatsoever to repeat itself.'

Aimeric missed none of Arnaud's words and was deeply impressed by his steely determination. Thoughts of his father's suffering and the martyrdom of his mother's parents flashed through his mind. He felt utterly ashamed of himself, the more so that he had not been completely candid with his host.

When he had stepped ashore at Acre, the Mameluke siege of Tyre had barely been lifted; fear, which enwrapped the entire Holy Land, could still be sensed in the air that one breathed, and the feeling of imminent danger had not yet dissipated.

A couple of days later, Arnaud had introduced him to Shams as his nephew. The young man had been agreeably surprised to see a woman in her mid-thirties, with a beautiful face that she uncovered when at work, and a slender body discernible under her long robe. He was intrigued by what he had learned from his host about her religion and the similarities it seemed to bear to Cathar tenets. Afterwards, he seized every opportunity to interrogate her about her beliefs, using Italian, the language that she hesitatingly spoke but understood perfectly well. To his astonishment, he discovered that she knew very little, being a simple person and not having been taught the intricacies of her religion. In actual fact, what Aimeric had become interested in was Shams's body, not her soul. Seeing her move about the house day after day made the blood pound through his veins; whenever she was at work he followed her from one place to another, and when she had finished her duties he engaged her in often futile conversation, with the aim of delaying their separation. In other words, Aimeric believed himself to be in love. Having grown up in an austere home amidst a strict environment, he had not had the opportunity to mix intimately with the opposite sex; he had known nothing of the pleasures of the flesh, but was eager and willing to learn. The hot weather, the intensity of the colours of nature, the quick-temperedness of the people and the deadly danger at the city's gates: all these elements, put together, had made him feel daring.

Unfortunately for Aimeric, Shams was not prepared to be his teacher. She had enough experience to see the admiration and desire in the young man's eyes, but she was also an honest, married woman with no want of cleverness. She liked working for Arnaud and realized that if Aimeric's shy pursuit of her were allowed to continue, a time would come when open persistence could replace timidity and that would have made the situation unbearable.

With this about to happen, Shams had devised an innocent plan. She hadn't missed noticing Aimeric's basic probity of character and therefore took the decision to make him ashamed of allowing his imagination to run wild. She decided to present her family to him and, thereafter, the image of her that he produced in his mind would have to include her husband, Gerios, and their only daughter, Zeinab. Surely, after that, the young man would be able to control his feelings and everything would be back in order once more.

And so, one Sunday afternoon, Shams had taken Gerios and their daughter to pay a courtesy visit to Arnaud's house, ostensibly for the purpose of welcoming the newly arrived nephew. When they arrived they were directed across the courtyard to two benches beside the well. Zeinab, a young girl of sixteen, had big dark eyes and an alluring body. Like her mother,

her head and the lower part of her face were covered by a thin white veil; her eyes, her forehead and even the locks of dark hair crowning it, were left uncovered. The veil, supposedly intended to enhance modesty, had the opposite effect, for the impression conveyed had been suggestively sensuous, particularly when the veil had slipped from its contrived position disclosing for a moment a peach complexion before being rearranged with calculated delay. No sooner was Aimeric able to have a good look at Zeinab than he became enthralled by her, only having eyes for his new infatuation.

By listening to the conversation translated for him by Arnaud, but mostly from questioning him after the guests had left, Aimeric gathered the information he was seeking about Zeinab and her parents.

Gerios came from the town of Gibelet (ancient Byblos, or Jbail as commonly named by the locals). He belonged to the Christian sect of Maronites, who had been persecuted by the Byzantines because they believed in the one will of Christ; later on they recanted and joined the Church of Rome. He used to peddle small items carried on the back of his mule and to visit villages and isolated farms of Mount Lebanon. Fate took him away from his usual path to a village of the Gharb Mountain where young Shams lived with her Druze family. A few more visits and Shams eloped with Gerios. Her family was still set against her because she had married outside her religion; all, that was, except her younger brother, Abdallah, who was glad to see her happy. When death threats were made against the couple and taken seriously, they decided to settle in one of the cities under the rule of the Franks and as far as possible from Shams's family.

Fearing for his life, Gerios was prevented from roaming through the countryside looking for customers, so he opened a small shop in Acre, the capital of the Kingdom of Jerusalem, or what was left of it. The shop was stocked with all kind of goods, from threads to saucepans, that the newly arrived pilgrims and visitors to the town might need. Shams for her part started serving food on an open kitchen stall, very popular with passers-by and the many single men who formed the bulk of the inhabitants of the town. When Zeinab became old enough to help her mother, the latter agreed to take charge of Arnaud's household, a task she did in the early mornings before going back to her cooking.

As the days passed, Aimeric believed himself to be madly in love. Shams had been right in her calculations and the young man was not obsessed with her any more. It was as if she had never been part of his dreams and imagination. When she realized the change in him, Shams had felt relieved and just a little dejected at the same time.

Aimeric, however, instead of the feeling of joy which normally accompanied an amorous state, had been over-whelmed by intense remorse. Day or night, he could not remove the image of this newly found passion from his mind, and now that he was away from his family and from the climate of frustration and desire for revenge, his mission had started to lose its importance, and even its relevance. Conscience-stricken, he had been wondering whether he was a coward who had lost heart when getting close to his intended victim, or whether love had triumphed over creed and other feelings. All the same, Aimeric was an unhappy young man who was judging himself with the utmost severity.

Unable to endure alone the confused state of his mind, he had partly confided in Arnaud, the only person whom he thought might help him get free of his mortal indecision and regain his self-esteem.

He had been right in his expectations. His mission had recovered the importance it had when he took it on, yet his recent obsession, his undeclared love for Zeinab, was still a burden to him. He had to share his other secret with someone so that he could talk about her with confidence and say her name out aloud. He had practically no choice but to unburden himself once more to Arnaud. This he did one evening and the reaction was immediate.

'Actually, your behaviour of late has worried me. First I put it down to homesickness, then to those questions and doubts about the mission. Now I understand better and I can see that you harbour more than one preoccupation. About Zeinab, allow me a word of warning. With the local people here, one has to be very careful; courting is tolerated only with the view of marrying and, even then, under strict supervision. I don't believe you want to commit yourself yet, you have to get more acquainted with the girl; although, as I explained, that is easier said than done. Above all, we have an objective to attain and that objective doesn't allow you to be tied down to or to endanger the person you love.'

It was as if Aimeric had heard only part of Arnaud's words of advice and warning.

'But you like Zeinab and you like her parents, don't you? Surely there must be a way to see her without antagonizing local feeling.'

The older man smiled with indulgence and reassured his lovesick companion. 'Yes, I presume there must be many ways, for since the world began young lovers, longing for a private tryst, have shown cunning and ingenuity enough to make a monk blush with envy. It is your good luck that you don't need to make the effort of using your imagination to see Zeinab. All you have to do is to buy food at her mother's kitchen stall; the daughter is around all the time.'

There was another reason for Arnaud's understanding that could never be disclosed. How could he tell this young man so madly in love – or anyone else – that he had lost his heart to Shams the moment she had entered his house? Even the woman at the centre of his deep devotion was unaware of his feelings and would remain so. Arnaud would never tarnish her name or bring shame on her.

He remained silent for a while then, in a more serious tone, said, 'Don't allow your heart to take control of your life. You shouldn't forget that this body of yours stands between your soul and pure spirit, between light and darkness. There are much more important things to manage in a meaningful life. I do hope that you agree with me about the order of priority, otherwise I cannot see the point of continuing this conversation or for you to remain here away from your parents.'

Arnaud's stern words shook Aimeric of his dream. Suddenly he realized how disloyal and ungrateful he had been to his parents, to his faith and to his host. Taking the latter's hand, he kissed it and solemnly pronounced, 'I promise you I will endeavour to complete what I came to do, even if I have to pay the heaviest price for that. I make this promise with full consent and knowledge of the danger ahead, and of the sacrifice awaiting me. Just one small favour I beg in return: don't forbid my seeing Zeinab. I promise that it will not interfere with my duty.'

Arnaud gave another quick smile, adding, 'A final word of advice. Start learning Arabic so that you can communicate with your beloved one without the need of an interpreter!'

Thereafter, whenever Aimeric had the occasion, he ate at Shams's kitchen stall, sitting on one of the low stools intended for new arrivals who have yet to adopt local ways, while the native customers and old hands sat cross-legged on the ground. All of them took advantage of the shade provided by the branches of a venerable fig tree growing nearby while consuming Shams's cooking or, if too poor for that, inhaling with delight the aromas wafting from the food as an acompaniment to a meagre piece of bread.

Zeinab busied around and blushed whenever she sensed Aimeric's amorous glances following her every move. In return, and whenever his attention was drawn away from her, she cast a furtive look at him.

She opened her heart to her mother and found her very understanding, even encouraging. With unhappy days around the corner and deadly danger at the city gates, Shams looked favourably at the prospect of the union of her only daughter with a young Frank. If the situation became intolerable for non-Moslems in the Holy Land, the young couple could always start a new life in any country of Christendom without feeling completely out of place. Hence Shams watched with indulgence the long-range courting which would remain just that until Aimeric declared his intentions.

Faithful to the promise made to Arnaud, Aimeric did not spend entire hours at a time dreaming of his love when not able to see her; for the sake of his cover, he started spending first a couple of hours a day, then much more, in his host's workshop, watching him busy at his craft. Soon the young man became enthralled with the transformation taking place in front of him. He was fascinated by the sight of the hammer striking the iron on the anvil amid a shower of flying sparks, whilst the apprentice, Abdel Malek, made sure that the fire was revived when needed. Then followed the operation of quenching, with its mysterious effects. No less absorbing a spectacle was the making of grips and pommels. The latter, when the sword was intended for a great baron, might be of jasper or rock crystal carved by a jeweller, another brother in religion.

Aimeric's other occupation was to stroll along the streets, particularly those close to the sea, the idea being that his face would become familiar and that he would collect from travellers and sailors any information he could about the court at Tyre, and especially about the movements of Philip of Montfort. One day during August, he decided to visit Signor Favretto and found him at the Venetian Consul's *palazzo*, freshly awakened from a siesta and warmly welcoming. The jeweller-cum-banker took his young friend in his arms.

'My dear travelling companion, I am delighted to see you again. Believe me, had you not come to me today, I would have sent for you before long. Other than that I wanted to see you again, I have a new proposal for you.' Signor Favretto leant towards Aimeric and, looking left and right, whispered, 'What you are going to hear is still a secret; please keep it to yourself. Hugh of Antioch-Lusignan, King of Cyprus, will soon be crowned King of Jerusalem; the ceremony will take place at Tyre basilica next month. I want you to accompany me to that city a few days in advance of the event. You see,' he added in an even softer voice, 'I intend to take there what is left of my collection of jewels and gems. It is indeed an extremely fortunate and unexpected occasion to clear my stock. Knights, noblemen and women will compete with one another for the most beautiful ring, the most sparkling brooch or pendant. The clergy has to be catered for and will display the same eagerness for buying the most expensive ornaments. I need someone to keep an eye on my merchandise and to keep me company. I know no better man than you; I beg you to accept.'

While Signor Favretto went on with his monologue, a joyful hope filled Aimeric's heart; could the proposal he had just heard be the opening that he and his older associate were waiting for? This had to be a sort of miraculous sign telling him, no, commanding him, to accomplish the mission.

Aimeric hid his feelings and controlled his voice, simply saying, 'I will be honoured and glad once more to be your companion.'

In the two weeks to their departure, Aimeric used his spare time to continue studying the Arabic language he desperately needed to learn in order to communicate with Zeinab when the time came.

On the date set for their departure to Tyre, the two Franks boarded a small sailing vessel. A sea journey was much safer than one by land, where roaming Mamelukes might at any time conduct an unexpected raid, despite the prevailing truce; recent events bore witness to the ever-looming danger.

One sailor and a *raiss* (skipper) manned the boat which carried, besides the two companions, a group of three Jews, recognizable by their clothes. After a day's journey the boat reached the northern harbour at Tyre, just before the mighty chain was stretched between the two lofty towers which guarded the entrance to the port from sunset to sunrise. Smoothly she entered the calmer waters of the harbour under an archway and anchored there, protected on three sides by the massive walls of the city. The passengers disembarked, all of them setting off in the direction of the Venetian quarter situated in the eastern part of the port area where the Jewish community was housed and where the two companions' inn was. The two groups took leave of each other in a civil fashion.

That night while the Venetian was asleep in the room they were sharing, the young Cathar's mind could not rest. Now that he was close to his target, strangely enough it seemed more remote than ever. It appeared so out of reach that doubts beset him once more; there was no question about the justice of the cause, but what about its feasibility? And how was he going to approach Abdallah? How was he going to transform him from a mere informer into an accomplice for an execution? All these questions assailed Aimeric's mind until he fell into an agitated sleep.

The following day, Signor Favretto and Aimeric started their round together, visiting princes and princesses, bishops and knights. With the prospect of the coming coronation, not a guarded secret any more, jewels and gems were indeed in great demand as the Venetian had expected. Among the households visited was that of the Knight of Picquigny, Abdallah's master. While Signor Favretto presented his collection to the Knight and his lady, Abdallah was pointed out to the enquiring Aimeric who surreptitiously showed him a ring in the form of a tiny sword, given to him by Arnaud for identification purposes, and told him where he was staying. Both men agreed to meet on the beach the following day, very early in the morning, before their employers had left their beds.

At the agreed time and place, a less-than-reassured Abdallah and an eager-to-know Aimeric strolled on the white sandy beach, away from inquisitive listeners. The heat would soon become unbearable, but at that early hour it was still possible to enjoy the walk, if only the two men had not been greatly preoccupied with their thoughts. The young Cathar opened the conversation.

'Your sister Shams sends you her greetings. She is most anxious to have news of you and longs to see you in Acre, since she herself can't make the journey here. My uncle Arnaud has told me about the services you render so efficiently and is keen to have fresh information about the court. Tell me what news you have learnt from Touma.'

An embarrassed Abdallah answered, 'Touma is avoiding me. I don't know whether he has had second thoughts and regrets his acquaintance with me, or wants more money. What I can do is to sound him out; that will be done, I promise.'

'Fair enough, but why leave your sister and my uncle with no news for so long?'

'The journey to Acre takes too long and I decided not to neglect my duties unless I had something important to report;

besides, the tense climate which persists between the two Frankish cities may raise questions. I beg you to ask your uncle and my sister to forgive my shortcomings. I understand that you will stay for the ceremony of the coronation; that is enough time for me to see Touma and come back to you. Now, will you excuse me; I have to rush back before my master awakens.'

Abdallah turned down an offer of money and hurriedly departed, leaving Aimeric pondering whether the reason for his lack of co-operation was what he has just heard or a disaffection due to a newly felt fear. Or was it, perhaps, a sudden fondness for his master and his fellow Franks?

On 24 September 1269, the basilica at Tyre was invaded by a joyous crowd from the early morning; only the area close to the altar was left unoccupied, for the good reason that a row of soldiers prevented the attendants from taking over that part which was being reserved for dignitaries from all quarters, all eager to watch the King of Cyprus being crowned King of Jerusalem. The expected ceremony was more than a mere formality; it gave a new lease of life to what, at one point, looked like a doomed kingdom. It was the culmination of a wise policy which made Venetians and Genoese came together, Acre and Tyre make peace and Margaret of Antioch-Lusignan, Outremer's most celebrated beauty and sister of Hugh III, marry John, the elder son of Philip of Montfort who was, until that alliance, profoundly suspicious of Hugh's ambitions.

As usual, Signor Favretto bribed his way and that of his companion to a spot from which they could enjoy the best view of the ceremony. Aimeric was most anxious to hear the *Te Deum* signalling the start of the service – for the sole reason that he would finally be able to see that seed of an unholy and cursed family, Philip of Montfort, his intended victim.

In the meantime, the two visitors admired the vast basilica which rose to the heavens and whose porticos were supported by noble, rose-granite columns, unknown in Syria and brought from Egypt during the Byzantine era.

After a long delay which made the standing crowd weary and seething with impatience, the choir started singing praise to God, accompanied by the organ; the altarboys came out from the sacristy bearing lighted candles and, in a half circle around the altar, led the dignitaries following to their allocated seats. Only then was Aimeric able to catch sight of Montfort, a man of mature age, slim and very erect, with piercing eyes which, to the young Cathar, seemed to linger over him; but he promptly dismissed the idea as a figment of his imagination. How could anyone know about his dark intentions?

Song and music died down and King Hugh made his appearance in the company of the Bishop of Lydda, acting for the Patriarch. Wearing his white ermine cloak decorated with the royal emblems, the King had on his head the royal crown of Cyprus which would be replaced for the ceremony by the royal crown of Jerusalem, and he held in his hand the sceptre of his rank.

After the lengthy solemn service, the newly crowned King left the basilica with great pomp and ceremony, accentuated by the organ's triumphant musical resonance, and took his place under the canopy erected outside for him to receive homage. After those of the high clergy and the nobles had come the turns of the various delegations. Kept afar by the soldiers in attendance, Aimeric was able to distinguish among the ones paying homage the three Jews who had made the journey from Acre on the same boat as him. He learnt from the gossip flying around that they represented their community and had made the trip to show their allegiance to the new ruler of the kingdom.

At that sight, a strange thought entered Aimeric's mind, a thought that had never occurred to him before, unable, as he was, to see any but the sufferings of his own Church. These people had been, and still were, persecuted much the same as the people of his own faith. Did any one of them harbour the same hatred and longing for vengeance as he did, or ought to? Could the Bishop, who had just finished officiating, be the target of any of those who had suffered in the name of religious fanaticism? Could Montfort, the most powerful Catholic prince of the Kingdom, be another of their targets? Quickly Aimeric dismissed these absurd ideas which had no foundation whatsoever except, maybe, in an unconscious hope that someone else would carry out what he had come to accomplish. But who would do that? None of the Jews or Samaritans he had encountered since he set foot in the Holy Land seemed capable of any violent act. They were either scholars lost in endless religious discussions, or gentle, industrious people absorbed in their daily work as dyers, tanners or small craftsmen.

It was certain that none of the three elderly men of that delegation would fall on the nobleman, or on anyone else. On the other hand, could anyone imagine *him* in the role of executioner? He smiled inwardly at the first thought and felt dispirited at the second. He did not understand what was happening to him; why did he allow his imagination to run wild instead of concentrating on his mission?

The poor man did not realize that he was bewitched by love, a demanding and intrusive emotion he had never felt before. He was also under the spell of the mythical and mystical Orient where nothing seemed, or indeed was, certain or final, and where questions were asked but no one answer was provided, with the result that minds became blurred and resolve weakened.

Aimeric shook his head, attracting the attention of the Venetian who looked at him enquiringly; he pretended to be tired and restless, so they both headed for their room at the inn. One obsession remained in Aimeric's mind and that was an irresistible desire to talk to the Jews he had just watched dutifully paying homage to the Catholic king. He needed to understand this other reaction to religious persecution.

Fate dictated that his wish was promptly answered, for during the night Signor Favretto's temperature rose to a worrying level, most probably due to his long stay outside in the burning sun. A concerned Aimeric asked the assistance of the innkeeper, who sent a boy to the nearby Jewish quarter to fetch a doctor. To the young man's surprise, who should enter the room but one of the three Jews from Acre, seen again at the basilica. Before long, his presence was explained. He introduced himself as Samuel of Scandalion, a physician from Acre acting for the physician of Tyre who was himself in bed with a temperature.

Samuel tended to the sick man, applying fresh compresses to his forehead until his temperature went down. He then prescribed that he rest, drink a lot of water and nothing else but a clear soup. Before leaving, he promised to come back the next morning to make sure Favretto was on the mend. Aimeric had never seen anything like the treatment given to his companion, with such success and kindness. The few times he had been in contact with Frankish physicians he had found them pompous, ignorant and often dangerous. He awaited Samuel's promised visit with eagerness.

The physician arrived early and found his patient in high spirits and in good health. On the point of leaving, he was asked by the young Cathar whether he could walk with him a few steps. The two of them took the direction of the physician's lodgings.

Encouraged by the civility of his older companion, Aimeric explained, 'Forgive me for intruding on you like this, but I am very interested in the way you administered your skill; I never in my life thought that a physician could be other than overbearing and most of the time inefficient. Please don't be offended and bear with me; you will soon realize that you are far from being included in my judgement. Tell me, I beg of you. How is it that your way of proceeding is so irreconcilable with the one practised in my country?'

'Well, now. Which is this country of yours?'

'I am from Milan; there I have seen and heard of many more people being killed, than cured, under the knife or axe of a "man of science" or after drinking a potion of his preparation. When I saw with my own eyes the way and the manner in which you treated my companion, I felt that I must know more.'

The physician felt torn between two feelings: caution, that told him not to be too obliging to someone he had only just met, and being moved by the touching enthusiasm of his young companion for knowledge. Eventually, the latter feeling won.

'The little I know I have found in the teachings of Hippocrates, Galen and Ibn Sina, then by carefully following the practice of my old masters, all of them Orientals.

'You see,' he carried on, 'science has no boundaries and knows no discrimination; the mighty Frankish nobles and the dreaded Moslem sultans and emirs, they all put their faith and health in the hands of Oriental physicians, whether Christians, Moslems or Jews.'

'That is amazing. I have already realized that old enemies do business together; what I didn't know is that they also trust each other with their lives. Why do they call themselves enemies?'

Samuel responded with a twinkle in his eye. 'I assume you haven't been here long enough. Soon you will become familiar with local behaviour and will realize that friends and enemies alternate according to circumstances which change swiftly and frequently. Enemies of today are allies tomorrow against a common foe. That is the way it is here.'

Aimeric remained silent for a moment then, mustering all his courage, asked, 'Would you accept me as your student? I am prepared to pay for my tuition.'

Besides a newly acquired interest in medical science as he saw it practised and depicted by Samuel, Americ had quickly calculated that if he acquired the art of healing, all doors would be opened before him, far more than before a blacksmith, however talented he might be. He would learn not only how to cure, but also how to dispose of undesirables with no suspicious trace being left behind. For his part, Samuel had already appraised the potential in the young man and was making plans to teach him, medicine, Jewish philosophy and the right meaning of religious precepts. Who could tell, his future pupil might one day convert to Judaism.

Following a moment of reflection, the physician replied, 'The study of medicine isn't solely about how to heal and how to ease pain; it also includes learning about nutrition, logic and mathematics, knowing by heart Ibn Sina's *Canon of Medicine* and other treatises on medicinal herbs and the art of healing. An apprentice physician should have a strong stomach, be able to bear the sight of blood and stand the dissection of corpses.'

The last part of his discourse was made in a low voice and still in the same tone he concluded, 'You should know that you will have to perform at least one dissection, even if that offends your religious beliefs and is forbidden by man-made law. Are you prepared to engage in the arduous way I have just described?'

'Yes, I am, if you are my teacher.'

Samuel was unable to refrain from a smile at this less than indirect compliment. He simply said, while taking his leave,

'Come and visit me whenever you return to Acre; you will find me in my house on Montmusart.'

Aimeric returned to the inn to find the Venetian bored and in a bad mood, but with no temperature. He urged Signor Favretto to stay in bed for the day with the promise that he would go round the customers who had yet to pay for the purchases they had made. Signor Favretto, who had quickly regained his good humour after Aimeric's promise, warned him, 'Some of those customers might want to give back the pieces of jewellery they affected to buy; take what you are given and don't argue. These people never intended to buy anything; all they want is to be able to flaunt a wealth they don't have. Others might give you a portion of the amount they owe; take any money given to you. The day will come when I shall make them all pay their dues one way or another.'

Aimeric started his round by visiting the household of the Knight of Picquigny in the hope of seeing Abdallah. Taking advantage of the truce concluded with the Mamelukes, the Knight was out on a hunting expedition arranged by a friendly Moslem Emir; his Lady, however, received the young Cathar and handed him a purse of gold bezants, owed to the Venetian. Abdallah was ordered to show the visitor out. That was the occasion that Aimeric had been waiting for, an opportunity for the two of them to talk. He was happy to hear that Touma, the Syrian servant, was still willing to inform on Montfort's court, and Abdallah was ready to convey to Arnaud any information acquired. The young Druze gave a solemn promise to make the trip to Acre whenever he was aware of any planned journey by Montfort outside the walls of Tyre.

Having not yet developed a plan as to how he would discharge his mission, Aimeric showed his approval of the informants' renewed commitments. For the time being, the only choice he had was to keep them busy until a plan could be elaborated. With a clear conscience, Aimeric contemplated his return to Acre; his heart was full of joy at the prospect of seeing his loved one again. A few days later the two Franks were back in the capital of the remnants of the Kingdom of Jerusalem.

CHAPTER FIVE

BAYBARS STRIKES AGAIN

While the Holy Land was engrossed in the endless festivities that followed the crowning of the King of Jerusalem, a mere title by now, oblivious to the grim present and unwilling to give a thought to the horrors of the future, the Franks' implacable enemy, Sultan Baybars, devised a new plan to rid the eastern Mediterranean shores of the intruders. During the autumn of 667 of the Hegira year (AD 1269) he arrived without warning at his Egyptian palace, built and fortified within the walls of the huge citadel standing on the Moqattam plateau, outside the city of Cairo. The construction of the citadel had been started by Saladin and pursued by those who succeeded him, but had never been fully completed. Included in this fortress, besides the palace, were a library, large stables, plus accommodation for the staff. Within its walls with their overlooking towers there was enough room for thousands of soldiers to have their quarters.

Surrounded by his usual retinue, the leading emirs he had summoned to his court and the impressive paraphernalia that had become part of the royal ceremonial, Baybars reclined on his formal throne, a stately bed inlaid with precious stones. On each side of him upon piled cushions sat the high-ranking emirs, while flanking the end of their lines less important dignitaries settled on the carpeted floor.

Each of those present was recognizable by his apparel. The prominent ones wore tunics lined with red satin and adorned with expensive fur on the lapels, cuffs and the lower part, their belts of either gold or silver were studded with jade and other stones and on their heads were gold-tasselled skullcaps covered with a veil upon which hung two pieces of white silk bearing the Sultan's name. Lesser dignitaries were entitled to fewer ornaments, while the learned men wore the attire of their respective functions. The ceremonial at the Mameluke court was as well regulated as it was grandiose. The former slave who had usurped power in Cairo and Damascus needed to show that his court had a long-established ritual. The strength and prosperity of the present ruling class might be newly acquired, but at least they seemed to relate to an entrenched system.

Baybars dictated to a secretary, who was taking notes on his knees, a letter addressed to Charles of Anjou, King of Naples and Sicily, and brother of King Louis IX of France, who was to be proclaimed a saint by the Catholic Church. The message was a reply to an earlier appeal to the Sultan to spare the Franks of the coast and turn his sword away from them. The tone of the response was conciliatory, a characteristic unusual for Baybars. The reason for this had much to do with the information that he kept receiving about a new crusade to be headed by Louis IX, already under preparation and whose destination might be anywhere in the east. None the less, faithful to his reputation, the Sultan added ominous words when sending out the following message:

> The Franks on these shores that are foreign to them have destroyed themselves; the lesser among them disobey what their lords have agreed and all of them call on their faraway brothers to come and rescue them from a danger yet imaginary because of the prevailing truce.

The letter was passed to Charles of Anjou's emissary, a few feet away from the throne. With him was another man who hid his face beneath the hood of his cloak. The latter was summoned by Baybars to approach; he obeyed the command, shifting along on his knees, only to be admonished by the Sultan. 'Why do you hide? I know who you are; you're a covert observer from Rome; go report to your master what you've just heard.'

Everyone present was struck by the amount of intelligence that the Sultan obtained from his spies, and while the audience remained lost in wonder and amazement for a long moment, the Mameluke enjoyed the effect of his rebuke. Then, unexpectedly, he chose to pray in the Dhahiri mosque that he had had built in the poor Al-Husseiniyya district on the outskirts of the town, using for its dome wood retrieved from the razed fortress of Jaffa. The magnificent mosque was not regarded by the wretched inhabitants of the neighbourhood as an arrogant reminder of their miserable lives; on the contrary, for them, the choice of the mosque's site, the adjoining *madrassa* (school) and the mausoleum the Sultan had built for himself, were matters of great pride.

Having performed his devotions, Baybars returned to his palace, accompanied by the mosque's imam, and there held another audience, this time reserved for his familiars and for a handful of the most powerful emirs. He let those present know of his decision to go on a pilgrimage to the Holy Cities of Mecca and Medina. Astounded by the unexpected announcement, they listened to the Sultan's instructions for the journey. 'We will leave in five days' time; you will all accompany me with your men–at–arms. Preparations must be conducted in the utmost secrecy. No one, no one, I repeat, should be made aware of my destination. If there is any leak the person responsible will pay the heaviest price. You are warned.'

After that chilling threat, not a soul dared mention anything about the intended pilgrimage, except for the Sultan's chamberlain, who was heard saying, 'I wish that my master would take me with him.' These words were reported to Baybars who commanded that the unfortunate man's tongue be cut out. The sentence was carried out immediately and thereafter not only did mention of the journey remain strictly forbidden, but the chamberlain's name and even his existence were obliterated.

Eventually, the Sultan's large cortège reached its first objective, Mecca, where the Mameluke performed the ritual of the pilgrimage. He generously distributed alms and clothes to the inhabitants, while a Hanafi Qadi instructed him on the meaning of the elaborate series of rites. Although genuinely absorbed in his devotions, the Sultan was otherwise preoccupied. He issued orders that large contingents, not the usual limited number of scouts, patrol the two Holy Cities. Soon the real reason for the hastily prepared pilgrimage, the extreme secrecy which surrounded the intended journey and the seemingly exaggerated measures of security put in place once there, became evident. Baybars' spies had passed on to him information about a plan of the Mongols' to attack Mecca and Medina. Already a Mongol advance party, sent by Abaga, the Ilkhan of Persia, was wandering around the two Holy Cities. When the Sultan's presence in the Hejaz became known, the Mongols withdrew – never to return.

It was not a simple raid that Baybars had aborted, but a plan drawn up between Abaga and the Franks of the coast; the latter had been expecting a large military expedition led by King James of Aragon to come to their rescue. However, that was not to happen, for the King's fleet ran into a storm shortly after leaving Barcelona, forcing the King to return home. Nevertheless, a small squadron under the command of James's two illegitimate sons reached Acre. Once there, and despite the limited numbers of the new arrivals, it was decided that the strategy devised with the Mongols should go ahead; but Baybars had had knowledge of the plot, thanks to the excellence of his agents and unwise leaks from Frankish quarters.

The Mameluke had succeeded so far in thwarting an important element of the plan against him; but because it was not his nature to leave the remaining elements to chance, he took the decision to do battle with Acre without delay. Well aware how thick its walls were and how determined and desperate were its inhabitants, he devised a ruse of war which relied on the inexperience and arrogance of those recently landed Franks.

Moving swiftly towards the coast at the head of an army of some fifteen thousand men, Baybars reached the Meshiya hillocks which kept him out of sight of the Franks, but which were close enough for him to storm the city of Acre if his ruse turned out well. He summoned the two emirs of Ain Jalout and Safed to his tent and issued orders:

Take three thousand men to beneath the walls of Acre. Burn all that is green and whatever is dry; destroy villages and hamlets; taunt the knights and deride them until they cannot take your provocation any more and leave the security of their walls to fight you. Allah willing, they will chase you. If this happens, feign a hasty retreat which will bring them towards me for their destruction and leave the city at my mercy.

Dutifully the two emirs followed their instructions, bringing total chaos on the plain surrounding Acre. The devastation went unpunished, which had the effect of incensing the two princes of Aragon and their retinues. They showered the Templars and the Hospitallers with scorn and abuse, demanding immediate retaliation, but the veterans were wary, sensing deception, and steadfastly refused to lead the army away from the town.

Eventually, wisdom prevailed at the Franks' quarters and Baybars' stratagem failed. He did not, however, leave the area empty-handed; he returned to Damascus, preceded by severed Frankish heads carried on pikes. These trophies had been won when a Frankish regiment, on its way back from a raid beyond the castle of Montfort, had sent scouts in vanguard to avoid falling into a trap. They reported to the regiment's commanders the activity on the plain of Acre, and an argument developed among the latter: one party was of the view that they should slip unobserved through the orchards back into Acre; the other, which prevailed, was to attack the Moslem soldiers. Most of the Franks were slaughtered, while the town's inhabitants helplessly watched the blood-bath.

After the fight had subsided and the Mamelukes had returned to their camp, the wounded were carried to a makeshift hospital in the Templars' quarter. Those people of the town who could be of any assistance hurried to provide succour for their fallen brothers. Physicians were badly needed, which explained why, when Samuel of Scandalion presented himself to the Templars offering his services, no one, not even the most bigoted among them, turned him away. Whether a knight or a villein, the life of every wounded soldier had to be saved, irrespective of who did the saving; any sign of religious intolerance would be a dangerous, empty gesture at a time when a deadly enemy was at the gates. The Jewish physician was accompanied by Aimeric Maurel.

Aimeric's attendance was the result of the new passion that he had fully committed himself to shortly after disembarking from the boat which had bought him and Signor Favretto back from Tyre. Naturally his first move had been to give Arnaud a detailed account of his journey. Although eager to rush to the kitchen stall to catch a glimpse of Zeinab, he did not, for his upbringing would never have allowed him to be forgetful of his duties. Both Cathars had agreed that no more could be done for the time being, except wait for Abdallah to show himself

Aimeric had been somewhat relieved by the respite and, at the same time, disturbed by a guilty feeling precisely because of that relief. Aware of Aimeric's haste to see the young Syrian girl, Arnaud had teasingly kept asking the same questions over and over, and when the young Cathar told him about his intention to learn the art of medicine from Samuel of Scandalion, he had laughingly said, 'So, now it is no longer the making of blades that you are interested in, but how to heal the wounds they inflict. Could it also be that you have forgotten all of Acre's other attractions?'

Realizing that Arnaud was only being playful, Aimeric had hastily taken his leave, shaking his head in vehement denial. He had raced towards the kitchen stall, his heart pounding in his chest so fast that he had had to stop and try to get his breath back. When he was a few metres away from his objective he had been able see the slender figure of his beloved one bustling around. His heart had started beating even more rapidly than when he had been running and his face was flushed. He had not been able to wait to regain his composure but had immediately advanced towards Zeinab. As soon as she saw him she had impulsively turned her back, hidden her face in her hands and rushed into her father's shop, leaving a bewildered Aimeric wondering whether he should be pleased or feel insulted. A moment later Shams had appeared with a large smile and greeted the young man kindly without losing her usual dignified demeanour; Gerios had followed, leaving the store to greet him with the same cordiality but more exuberance. There was no doubt the young Frank was a welcome guest among Zeinab's family, and that had made him feel happy. That day, the object of his love had failed to reappear outside, yet it did not seem to be of great consequence, except for the disappointment not seeing her; none the less, he knew in his heart that his love was shared by Zeinab and blessed by her parents.

After a few days spent between Arnaud's workshop and the adoring contemplation of Zeinab, Aimeric had mustered all his courage to visit the venerable Samuel at his house on Montmusart. There had been no difficulty in finding the place and convincing the old man to start teaching him the art of healing.

That explains why, after the latest Frankish disaster under the walls of Acre, he was attentively watching the physician dress the wounds, apply poultices and comfort the dying – he even participated in the acts of healing, directed and carefully watched by his teacher. Another of his duties was to mix herbs, dried flowers and plants, or to pound medicinal grains in a small mortar, always following the instructions of the physician who, from time to time, consulted his copy of lbn Batlan's *Tacuinum* that never left his side.

Aimeric was also in charge of receiving and recording the last wishes of the dying, as everyone else, including the officiating priests, were too busy trying to cure mortal bodies or save sinful souls. Most of the pitiful creatures waiting to die were destitute, their only possessions being their clothes and the weapons that had not been abandoned on the battlefield; one or two were better off and had either a few gold bezants or a bag of spices, salt or pepper they had intended taking back to their home countries, which they would now never see again.

One of the knights who seemed to be mortally wounded was being attended by the young Cathar, who sensed a mysterious voice telling him not to leave the badly hurt man. Bending close to his ear, he asked him his name and the answer came out with great difficulty.

'Jacques de Castre from Roquefixade.'

Aimeric's heart sank; Roquefixade was a small village close to Montségur, and most of its inhabitants belonged – or rather had belonged – to the Cathar Church. Could it be that this unfortunate fallen warrior was himself a brethren in faith? He did not know what to do or what to say. On the one hand he was tempted to give comfort to the dying man by telling him his name and that of his father's village; on the other hand, this information would have given away what he should keep hidden for the sake of his mission. Finally, compassion won and, after making sure that no one else was close enough to overhear, especially not a priest, he mentioned the names of his father and de Foix, and talked about the Languedoc he himself had never seen but had heard so much about. The two men shed tears; then, in a whisper from the knight's lips came the repeated word *convenensa*. Jacques de Castre was without any doubt a Cathar, for he was telling his compassionate carer that he had passed the convention with the Cathar Church by which he would request, and would not be refused, the *consolamentum* at the hour of his death. A very apprehensive Aimeric made sure that he could not be seen or heard, then rapidly in a low voice recited the prayer for the occasion; he lay his hand on the dying man and invoked the Divine Spirit. As it would have been dangerous to attract attention to himself by overstaying with one patient, he then moved on to take care of other wounded, leaving behind a man much quieter in his mind.

At the end of a long, emotional and exhausting day, the young student was sent home by Samuel, who had decided to spend the night with his patients. The physician had literally to push him out of the door.

'I need you tomorrow, fresh and alert. For that you should have a good night's sleep; for my part, I am an old man who habitually closes his eyes for just an hour or two a night. Go!'

Reluctantly, Aimeric left for home, but only after he had brought the wounded knight to the attention of the physician.

He found Arnaud in his workshop by the fire, lost in thought and contemplating the dancing flames. More sorrow appeared on his face after he was told of the presence of the mortally wounded Cathar in the city and a sigh escaped from his lips. His young companion could not fail to notice the despair in his voice as he said, mostly to himself, 'Are we all doomed to die far away from our beloved country?'

CHAPTER SIX

THE ASSASSINS

'Keep out of the way of he who bears in his hand the death of the enemies of Islam.'

The menacing shout, cried out at regular intervals, came from a very strange procession making its way from the high ground of Jabal Bahra. This mountain ran parallel to the northern part of the Syrian coast, in the direction of the valley near the town of Hama where Sultan Baybars had established his camp after his victory on the plain of Acre.

The central figure in the procession was Najm al-Din, the ninety-year-old Overlord of the Ismaili sect, who was being carried on a litter by two strong adults. Beside him walked his son Shams al–Din, and all were preceded by the crier, a giant of a man who held an axe with a long shaft encased in silver, to which several knives were affixed. The old man and his son were on their way to make a complete submission to the Mameluke.

With his customary opportunism and political flair, Baybars had hitherto reasoned that the Franks on the coast should be given a false sense of security for the time being, until it became clear where the new crusade instigated by King Louis IX, would be landing. He had taken the decision to subdue the Ismailis who had, in the past, allied themselves with the Crusaders and the Mongols and made a nominal submission to him.

The Ismailis had succeeded in the mid–twelfth century in acquiring or building a number of fortresses, some of them perched on top of almost inaccessible peaks. Among their fortresses were Qadmus, Kahf, Ulayqa and Masyaf, which was the headquarters of the Ismaili Overlord.

The sect resorted to political murder whenever its independence or existence seemed endangered; this extreme measure was carried out by self-sacrificing devotees, identified as *fidais*. Seldom did the targeted victim escape his fate, for his proposed murderer was the least troubled by his own safety. He would strike at the first opportunity, unconcerned whether he himself would be killed. To survive without completing an assignment would have been shameful.

The motivation of these young people, prepared to pay with their lives for the success of their assignments, remained a mystery. One explanation was that the leader of the sect would select young Ismailis in whom he saw future *fidais* and accustom them to the use of hashish. Then under the influence of the drug they would be taken to a secret 'garden of paradise' where they would taste many kinds of earthly pleasures, ranging from intimate encounters with beautiful girls to the consumption of intoxicants and more drugs. Back in the real world, they would have one desire only – to regain that lost paradise. That, they would be promised, on condition that they blindly obeyed whatever orders were given to them. Hence the name 'Hashashin' (Assassins) from the Arabic word *hashish* was given to members of the sect.

Another explanation for the deeds of the self-sacrificing young men took into account their religious fanaticism and fierce sense of independence, which made them believe that he who died for his faith and land, would abide forever in paradise, the celestial one this time.

Whatever the motivation for the extreme zeal of the Assassins may have been, the result was the same. They were feared by Franks and Moslems alike, and at one time they were able to collect tributes from both and keep a neutral stance between the warring factions by the use of different ways and means, including assassination.

Alas the strength of the sect had declined; levies were being continually extorted from it by the Hospitallers, the military religious order which possessed the fortress of the Krak des Chevaliers at the southern end of Jabal Bahra. To slaughter the Grand Master of the Order would be to no avail, for another master would immediately be elected – with even more dire consequences. Moreover, Sultan Baybars had started to exact taxes on the gifts and tributes still sent to the Assassins by a number of kings and princes who saw them as a guarantee for longer life.

An even greater danger was the prospect of being wiped out by the Mameluke, who did not seem to tolerate any longer the sect's freedom to choose and change alliances in keeping with prevailing circumstances. With unceasing plots hatched by the Crusaders of the coast and the Mongols of the hinterland, the Ismailis could one day have been tempted to take an active role in one of those conspiracies.

Ismaili concern appeared well founded, for immediately after his triumphal entrance into Damascus, Baybars took his army to the vicinity of Hama and established camp, expecting all neighbouring lords and princes to come forward and give allegiance to him. The Lord of Hama and the Lord of Sahyun from further north dutifully turned up and prostrated themselves before the Mameluke, who bestowed upon each of them a magnificent ceremonial robe and a fine sword.

On the other hand, neither Najm al-Din nor his son Shams al-Din had shown up at the Sultan's camp; the excuse they had sent with a messenger was severe weather. Indeed, falls of snow heavier than any in living memory had made all roads impassable, and snow was still falling. The Sultan, however, was not duped by their excuse, which he rightly interpreted as another message telling him that if the two Ismailis were stranded in their stronghold owing to bad weather conditions, then he too was unable to reach them for the same reason.

Fury mounted in Baybars at the affront received, yet he prudently took the decision to refrain from any hasty action before the night had passed. Early next morning he summoned the Lord of Sahyun to his tent and ordered him to bring to him the Ismaili, Sarim al-Din, Lord of Ulayqa, another Assassin stronghold. Sarim al-Din was the son-in-law of Najm al-Din but, unlike the elderly Ismaili, he was prepared to be compliant and swear allegiance to the Mameluke whatever the price exacted from him and from his people might be, for what counted for this opportunist was for himself to be recognized as the Overlord of the sect. Already aware of Sarim al-Din's disposition of mind, but knowing as well that he did not command the same respect as his father-in-law, Baybars had until now neglected his advances, not willing to lose the chances of winning over Najm al-Din in person. Now, however, he had just one course of action left, owing to these stands of defiance which could not be allowed to remain unpunished.

Baybars's intention was to split the Ismaili community before he delivered his blows. As expected, Sarit al-Din presented himself to the Mameluke's camp with a fair number of lesser Ismaili sheikhs who had realized that resistance was beyond the bounds of possibility and convinced themselves that peace now, even with harsh conditions, was better than to fight a desperate battle and risk annihilation. During a grand ceremony, the Sultan dismissed Najm al-Din and his son from office and appointed Sarim al-Din to be the Overlord of the sect, covering him with a ceremonial cloak as a sign of his new function.

Having made sure that this one fairly influential Ismaili section would not assist those who defied him, Baybars had sent his soldiers and an armed party familiar with the area to the castle of Masyaf, the Ismaili religious seat. Those besieged had soon realized that any resistance was useless; the water in their cisterns was frozen and their storehouses nearly empty. The fortified castle had surrendered without putting up a fight.

Neither Najm al-Din nor his son were in Masyaf at the time of its fall; but before long they had heard of the disaster, realized that all was lost and had started their humiliating, long march, punctuated by the already familiar crier's warning, 'Keep out of the way of he who bears in his hand the death of the enemies of Islam.'

It had not escaped Baybars when he heard the crier's shouts, and if it had his entourage would have informed him, that the intended warning was about the death of kings, totally inappropriate in the circumstances, not the enemies of Islam.

As the cortège drew nearer, Najm al-Din was helped out of the litter and entered the camp in the sole company of his son on whom he leant heavily. In the presence of the Sultan, both went on their knees, the son giving a helping hand to his father. On the latter's instructions, a shirt and a ring were put at the Mameluke's feet; the old man, still on his knees, spoke. 'My Lord, the shirt is mine, and as a shirt is closer to one's body than any other garment, so I long to be closer to you than any other lords and obediently to serve you. The ring is also my ring; just as you put it on and take it off your finger whenever it pleases you, so I will be as docile and compliant. My Lord, I beg a few more moments of your time and implore you to come out of your tent with us to receive another proof of my absolute surrender to your will.'

Intrigued, the Sultan stepped out of his shelter wrapped in a heavy cloak, for the weather was still appalling. He was followed by the two Ismailis who respectfully directed his view towards one of the high hills surrounding the camp. There, in orderly lines by a sheer and deep ravine, stood some fifty scantily clad men.

Shivering from the cold and from the number of his years, Najm al-Ddin explained, 'All the men my Lord sees up there are prepared to sacrifice their lives without asking a single question.'

At this point, the old man sent a signal with his hand in the direction of the *fidais*; immediately, the one closest to the chasm jumped to certain death. Another sign and the next *fidai* leapt, also to his death. He then turned to the Sultan, who was stunned but did not allow his feelings to show. 'These *fidais* are now yours; if my Lord condescends to send the same signal, he will be obeyed the same way my Lord has just witnessed.'

Baybars waved his hand twice as recommended and two more Ismailis forfeited their lives; he abruptly went back to his tent, signalling to the father and son to follow him inside. 'Your mistakes of the past are forgiven, Lord Najm al-Din; go back to your people. I appoint you as my deputy, but you will have to exercise your duties jointly with Sarim al-Din. You will pay to the Treasury the annual sum of 120,000 Dirhams. The amount due from Sarim al-Din is 12,000 dirhams. You, Shams al-Din, you will remain in my court.'

The Mameluke dismissed the two Ismailis with these words, 'As for the *fidais*, be assured that from now on not a single one of them will die in vain or for bravado. Death, it will be, but only for the Sultan's cause.' The chilling words suggested that Baybars already had in mind more than one deadly assignment for the *fidais*.

CHAPTER SEVEN

AFTER THE TURMOIL

Some sort of normality had returned to life in Acre, following Baybars' latest deadly incursion beneath the city walls and the carnage which could have been easily averted with a little wisdom. The relatives and comrades of those who had died such an atrocious death at the hand of the Mamelukes were, to this day, in mourning and the wounded under care. No witness of this latest butchery could erase from his mind the image of the mounted knights and the foot soldiers being mercilessly beheaded as soon as they fell – whether they were dead or still breathing. None of the city's inhabitants could ever forget the nerve-shattering sound of a hundred drums being beaten continuously. The general mood was downcast and dispirited, made worse by a harsh never-ending winter. Come sunset, not a soul was to be seen in the streets.

A shadowy figure slipped at night from the Venetian district in the direction of the Patriarch's Tower, some five hundred metres away, unseen by anyone. Passing the quays and along the coast, it reached its objective, a shabby house located at the foot of the Tower. A knock on the door in the agreed manner and the nocturnal visitor was let in by a middle-aged Arab, revealed in a candle's flickering light. The light also revealed that the latecomer was none other than Signor Favretto, who was then led by his host to a small room, bare except for a worn carpet and a few discoloured cushions. The Venetian addressed the Arab in his own tongue, calling him by his name, 'Salamu 'alaykum, ya Ahmed,' and received greetings in return. Both men sat cross-legged on the floor, shivering from the cold, as no fire was available. After a suitable time devoted to civilities, they engaged in closely argued negotiations.

'No doubt at all, the goods can be delivered within six months,' emphasized the Venetian.

'That is satisfactory, on condition that delivery takes place at the port of Jaffa.'

'That can also be done. The skipper, however, will certainly refuse to enter the harbour and will anchor his ship off the shore; you will have to arrange for several short boat trips to transport the cargo.'

It became clear from the discussion that Signor Favretto was engaged in the process of concluding a business transaction with the enemy. Worse was to come when the subject of their deal was divulged as being steel and timber which would certainly be used for the rearmament of the Mamelukes.

Eventually the two men reached agreement, at which point they relaxed slightly, but Ahmed still did not know the measure of Signor Favretto, who caught him off guard.

'I am taking great risks and so will the skipper and the crew; that deserves some compensation, does it not?'

Exhausted and exasperated by these negotiating tactics, Ahmed replied with a deep sigh, 'Your prices are too high and they are seldom all that we pay in the end. Before delivery there is inevitably an extra here or hidden costs there. What else can we do but yield to your harsh conditions? You are aware of that, for you realize how badly we need your services.' Then, as if talking to himself, he quoted an Arab proverb, '*The man who needs fire will hold it in his hands.*'

The Venetian was unmoved by the charge and the tone of disgust, and imperturbably pursued the bargaining exercise until all the terms were to his liking. Then, business completed, one after the other they left the grim meeting place.

Signor Favretto retraced his steps in the dark towards the Consul General's *palazzo*, unaware of another shadowy figure following him from a distance and taking cover in darker corners whenever likely to be seen in the light of the moon, which at times materialized from beneath shifting clouds. When convinced that his quarry had no other plan for the night except to return to his accommodation, the pursuer turned his back, heading towards one of the houses in the red-light district. Inside, he was soon revealed as one of the two shady characters who had made the boat journey from Venice with the man he had just been following, and that his old accomplice was also there with the young girl Margherita and another, much older woman.

'Well, Pietro, what did you see?' asked the man who had opened the door and answered to the name of Sergio.

'We did well to persevere with our surveillance of the man. Our pompous jeweller is a fraud; he deals with the Moslems, most probably selling them arms. Otherwise, why should he meet with one of them in the middle of the night and in great secrecy?'

'Well, well, this is more than we expected; we won't need Margherita's charms after all to relieve him of his superfluous gold. What do you think about that, my lovely?' As he talked, Sergio stroked the girl's hair; she looked at him meekly while the older woman giggled. Taking a sheet of paper and a quill pen, he elaborately wrote a few words on Margherita's behalf, gave them time to dry, then folded the paper and sealed it. He stood up, putting an end to this rather unsavoury gathering.

'That's enough for tonight; let's have some sleep. Tomorrow we'll see how much our man will sing.'

During that same night another reunion, this one totally innocent, took place at Gerios' lodging, which was one vast room above his shop. Gathered round the man on the carpeted floor were Shams, Zeinab and Elias, Gerios' eldest brother, who was also a Maronite priest or *Bouna*. He addressed Gerios while the others listened respectfully.

'Dear brother, we were so worried when news of the Sultan's attack reached us. I immediately left Jbail and came here to take you back with me to your birthplace – it's peaceful, and close to mountains populated by your brethren, not by infidels. *Ajallek'* (apology to you), 'O sister. I don't intend to demean your former people or you, whom I consider one of us by virtue of your marriage to my brother, and also because I myself gave you baptism. Sell your shop, Gerios, and all of you come with me.'

Zeinab, not allowed to speak her mind in front of grown-up males, looked desperately at her mother, seeking assistance. She could not stand the prospect of moving away from the man she loved and who, she was certain, felt the same towards her; but she also could not voice her feelings and, anyhow, would never dared to. Gerios, too, furtively glanced at his wife for moral support; she pretended to ignore any of the appeals for help. Shams hated the mere idea of moving further away from her brother Abdallah, whom she dearly loved and who was her only relative not after her blood. Although Abdallah was in Tyre and not Acre, she knew that he was reachable whenever it became necessary. Besides that, she loathed the prospect of getting too close to Gerios' relatives, and in particular to Elias's wife; yet she was astute enough not to antagonize her brother-in-law. So she remained silent, as if unconcerned about his proposal, counting on her husband to do the talking she expected him to.

Gerios was no fool and was able to read what was passing through Shams's mind and to perceive her unwillingness to leave Acre. There was also the undeclared love between his daughter and Aimeric which should be allowed to blossom into marriage. What a triumph it would be to see Zeinab wedded to such a fine young man, a Frank.

'My dear brother,' he said, 'I am deeply touched by your concern for our safety. However, I don't believe that there is imminent danger here or that there is any safer place somewhere else. You see, my business is doing well.' He touched wood before proceeding. 'With Shams's kitchen stall as well, I can provide enough for my family. I don't want to start a new life and a new business at my age. If, however, the situation becomes unbearable, we will have no better refuge than a home with you, dear brother.' Finishing with these words, Gerios stood up and went over to his brother and they hugged one another. Shams and Zeinab surreptitiously looked at each other, quite relieved.

The following morning, Signor Favretto received a letter bearing Margherita's name. He still remembered the young girl with tenderness, a feeling which rapidly disintegrated as soon as he finished reading the message. The girl told him to come to her place for them to discuss matters in relation to the business he had conducted the night before at the house next to the Patriarch's Tower.

He was at one and the same time disappointed, puzzled and worried. Disappointed by the girl for her attempt to blackmail him, because, as he guessed rightly, that was what the letter amounted to; puzzled because he did not know how she had found out about his business with Ahmed and how much information she actually possessed; and, finally, worried, as his dealings with the Moslems, if exposed, would create an uproar among the masses and affect their morale. He had no problem regarding his accountability towards the authorities, as he held a licence issued by the High Court at Acre allowing him to trade with the Sultan and his subjects. Notwithstanding the legality of the actual situation, which obviously Margherita and those who stood behind her ignored, Signor Favretto would have much preferred not to make his business public. He discussed the whole matter with the Consul General and both agreed on a plan of action.

Without wasting time, the Venetian headed for Arnaud's workshop, hoping to find Aimeric there. He wanted him to be present when he visited Margherita, for part of the plan was to accept her invitation, but not to be on his own with her lest he fell into the trap of a different kind of blackmail. When Aimeric was found and told about what was required from him, he agreed to oblige, eager to please his powerful travelling companion; but first he had to warn Samuel, who was expecting him that morning for another lesson in medicine, not to wait for him. Signor Favretto offered to accompany Aimeric, so the two men set off in the direction of Montmusart and to the physician's house. He welcomed them with his customary affability and invited them into his home. They felt it more civil not to show their impatience to leave; they explained the object of their visit as soon as they could after the necessary social exchanges.

'My dear gentlemen, Aimeric's absence has not come at a bad moment, for I have just received an unexpected visit from the greatest Jewish scholar of our age. Come, come, allow me to introduce you to him, my religious mentor.'

They all went into another room to meet a man of an advanced age, who was presented to the two Gentiles as Moshe ben Nahman from Spain. Impressed by the words Samuel had used to introduce his guest, but nevertheless in a hurry, they took their leave of the two Jews after a short exchange of compliments.

At the door, Samuel told a delighted Aimeric, 'I have good news for you. The knight you recommended to my care, but whom you nevertheless continued to look after, having little confidence in my art...' the physician chuckled, eyes twinkling and with a teasing smile, '...this Jacques de Castre has recovered from his wounds rather miraculously and will be leaving his sick-bed at any time now.'

Finally the two Franks met up with Margherita, and her disappointment at not seeing Signor Favretto alone was plainly visible. Despite her frustration, she played the role allocated to her perfectly well. With an expression of alarm she addressed her intended victim.

'O Signor Favretto, I am so glad that you accepted my invitation; I haven't forgotten either your kindness during our journey or your generosity after we reached our destination, when you helped me get rid of my two tormentors.'

This was rather embarrassing for the Venetian, for he had neglected to inform Aimeric of his later contact with the girl. No reaction, however, came from the young Cathar, who was concerned not to cause him further embarrassment. Unaware of the effect of the minor revelation she had made, the girl carried through her act before the two men, who remained silent.

'Now fate wants me to repay part of my debt to you. Yesterday, late at night, I overheard our two lodgers – my aunt and I must take in paying guests to survive, mention your name. I went as close as I could without being noticed and I heard them refer to your dealings with the Moslems and their firm intention to denounce you to the authorities. They seemed very resolved and determined to do what they consider their duty. I don't want my benefactor to go to jail, so I made my presence known, went on my knees and begged them not to utter a word about you to a living soul. After hours of adjuration and imploration, they agreed not to divulge what they know on one condition, that each one of them gets a hundred gold bezants. If I'd had that sum, I would have paid it myself and spared my benefactor any worry, but I am a very poor girl, living by the goodness of people like yourself, so I had to approach you and ask you to buy their silence.'

Signor Favretto and Aimeric listened to the girl's monologue without interrupting her once; as a matter of fact, the former was savouring in advance the moment he would take the initiative and dramatically confound his would-be blackmailer.

Margherita had ended her prepared speech, wiping away a tear or two, and now she expected to see his self-importance collapse. What she heard from him was quite the reverse.

'My dear girl, I am most obliged to you for having put in all that effort just for my sake. Rest assured that I conduct my business in the most irreproachable and open way. Our Consul General knows the details of all my dealings with the Christians and the Moslems, inside and out. When I took leave of him this morning I left with him your letter. Tell your two miserable lodgers that if I ever hear from them or see them again, they will be put in irons to rot in the *palazzo* jail in the company of all those who helped them. This warning is not from me, but from the Consul General himself. Oh, another thing. If ever one word is reported about any of my dealings and comes to my attention, I will immediately assume that the source of the leak is in his house.'

Wrapped in his dignity and followed by Aimeric, lost for words after the performance he had just witnessed, Signor Favretto left a totally bewildered Margherita. The Cathar went back to the workshop with a handsome reward from the Venetian, and the promise to stay in touch. He reported to Arnaud Samuel's good news about the Knight being out of danger. 'Do you think it a good idea to invite him to spend his convalescence with us?'

There was no hesitation in his answer. 'That is not only a generous idea, for the poor man must be all on his own with no family and no friend, it could also turn out to be one of expedience; go to him and offer hospitality in your name and mine.'

Aimeric reflected for a moment. 'I wonder whether we can fully trust him.'

'Do you mean, can we tell him about our mission?' Arnaud asked bluntly. 'Rest assured that if he comes to stay with us, we will soon be able to form a judgement about him; don't worry before time.' He smiled as he continued, 'I don't believe you have spent enough time here to become familiar with the local aphorism: If you haven't travelled, played games for money or traded with a person, you can't pretend to know that person.'

Jacques de Castre gratefully accepted the offer of hospitality. His health improved day by day due to the care provided by Aimeric and the attention from his two hosts, and he was soon able to walk around the house. Reassured about the knight's progress as the first rays of the sun appeared Aimeric would leave home for his daily lesson. At times he would listen avidly to the physician as he passed on to him the teachings of prestigious old masters in medicine, philosophy, religion or mathematics, while at other times they would go and visit the sick together. With such training, the young Cathar's education made strides on both theoretical and practical levels.

What had started as a formal association developed into a warm friendship between the teacher and the student, who found real pleasure in each other's company. Aimeric came to know the physician as a humane person, dedicated to alleviate suffering regardless of the social and financial circumstances of his patients, even when he was certain that he would not be paid for his care and dedication. He had never seen him lose his temper, and on the rare occasions when he witnessed him in animated discussion the subject had been religion and philosophy. He had, as Aimeric came to realize, a tremendous respect for Maimonides' legacy and he despaired at the attacks of his critics. At such times, he engaged in endless analysis that often remained unfathomable to the student. What mattered was that the pupil was keen to learn and was making good progress.

One day, returning home after an exhausting training session devoted to visiting patients, Aimeric found a letter waiting for him, brought by a newly arrived pilgrim who had agreed to deliver it against a reward to be paid by the receiver. Apprehensively he examined the missive for some time, afraid to open it lest it contained bad news. When he finally found the resolve to confront the contents of the message, it bore comforting news; his parents were in good health. The young Cathar read the letter to his two companions who had started to show signs of impatience, though as he did he omitted passages which were too personal or sentimental. When he finished reading they all remained silent, each letting his mind travel back to the loved ones and the place left behind.

After that, Arnaud broke the silence and, as if intent on arousing the Knight, cunningly declared, 'Here we are, the three of us, three people against whom, with their parents, their relatives and their Church, abominable deeds have been committed; we are separated from our dearest ones and exiled from our country and yet we continue to live normally, as if persecution is our lot and resignation our fate.'

De Castre was goaded into protest. 'I have never submitted to what you call our fate or resigned myself to be down-trodden; I am ready to fight the oppressor and die for my faith, just like my parents who willingly walked on to the pyre, ordered by the Whore of Rome.'

Arnaud was encouraged by what he had heard. 'Let us examine what we can do together to incite the old spirit and revive hope.' He added, as if talking to himself, 'Amazing how a small religious community such as the Ismaili is able to command deadly fear and respect...Maybe we should learn from them one or two of their methods...Do you know that a Montfort is a short distance from here, as Lord of Tyre?'

'Of course, I know that. The idea of killing him has been with me since I reached this land, but the beast is well protected because he fears assassination from more than one quarter. Tell me, has the idea ever crossed your mind?'

'To tell you the truth, once or twice,' replied Arnaud, 'but now that you have mentioned it, I believe it deserves more reflection. We will talk about all that later; we all need rest.'

Arnaud was relieved now that a brother, a man of war with such resolve, had joined them. Yet the relief he felt stirred up inside him not only a tormenting sense of guilt prompted by self-inflicted incrimination of a shaming pusillanimity, but also, what was more damaging, the feeling that his religious faith was gradually slipping away from him.

CHAPTER EIGHT

TWO CONVERTS

*They will destroy the walls of Tyre
and pull down her towers*
Ezekiel 26.4

Nasir and Hasan, both in their early twenties, entered Tyre from the land side entrance through four gates, one after the other, each surrounded by a high outer wall manned by soldiers. A few moments before, the two young Arabs had left the rich suburb of the fortified city where they had spent the night in a small café by the sea. The hospitality provided by the café's owner had been spartan: a supper of grilled fish, and a corner for the night in the open air, except for a roof of dried palm leaves. Fortunately, it was spring and the weather had been mild; and atmospheric conditions seemed to be the least worry of the two young men.

Once in Tyre, they had asked directions to the Church of St Michael, and on the way there they marvelled at the bulk of the fortifications, the strength of the buildings and the cleanliness of the streets. The city was not large and they soon reached the church. Nasir banged on the door several times, each time louder than before, until finally, when they despaired of receiving an answer, a passer-by advised them to try an adjacent cottage which was the presbytery. Here they were more lucky: an old priest half-opened the door.

'What do you want?,' he enquired rather rudely.

Nasir, replied, 'If you are Father Joseph, we have a message for you from Father Julian.'

'You mean Father Julian from Antioch, the priest in charge of the Church of St Symeon?' yelled the old man in a state of great agitation.

'Yes, except that the poor man was murdered and the church burnt to the ground when the Sultan stormed Antioch.' Again it was Nasir who answered, apparently in charge.

The two young men were immediately invited inside the presbytery and bombarded with a hundred questions.

'Tell me what happened. How did the poor man die? What was your relationship with him and how is it that you are here?'

The agitation of the old priest was understandable. After the fall of the northern city to the Mamelukes nearly two years before, news from survivors was scarce, so Nasir gave their anxious host a full account concerning the message that he and his companion had been entrusted with.

'My lord, my name is Nasir and my brother here is Hasan; we are from the city of Antioch, where we were living peacefully under Frankish rule. Our modest house is, or more accurately was, in the vicinity of the Church of St Symeon and that is how we came to know and respect Father Julian. During the whole time we were neighbours, this man of God showed us nothing but kindness and generosity; he was respectful of our religion and never tried to convince us to forsake it.

'During the siege he sent for me and my brother and told us that the city was about to fall, that none of the Franks could expect to remain alive or free after the mayhem which would necessarily follow its sack, and that in all probability his church would not survive and all its treasure would be either looted or destroyed. He said that none was more precious than that which he was going to entrust us with − it was dearer than his own life, or any life.

'While he was speaking to us, Father Julian removed from a sumptuous reliquary the bones of the right hand of St John the Baptist, equally revered by us as Yahya. He wrapped them in a piece of linen and handed over to us the bundle and a sum of money, with instructions to look for you in Tyre and deliver the relic to you should he be slaughtered or enslaved.'

'Tell me what happened next,' interrupted Father Joseph.

The two brothers showed every indication of being ashamed of themselves and chastened; then Nasir, the more articulate one, continued his account. 'After the fall of the city, what the poor priest expected effectively took place. He was murdered on the altar by the mob and the church levelled to the ground.'

'What did you do with the relic after these horrible crimes?' There was a suspicious tone in the old man' s voice that he could not conceal.

The two Arabs looked even more embarrassed and mortified.

'Antioch was in ruins; we had to reconstruct our lives and

find a new livelihood. Forgive us, but we forgot all about the relic until one day...'

Nasir cut short this apologetic explanation and kneeling with his arms open in a dramatic gesture, burst out, 'Until one day a miracle took place. Bear with me and all will be perfectly clear. Our beloved mother fell very ill and was on the very threshold of death, despite the best care we could provide for her. We and all the family were in total despair, not knowing what we could do more than we had already done. One day, my brother Hasan, the very one here in your presence, stood up as if moved, not by his will or limbs, but by an irresistible power. He took the Holy relic from the chest where it had lain forgotten and brought it to our mother who was about to die, the poor soul. He placed it upon her breast and urged me to take the following oath with him: "Lord St John of the Christians, if you cure our mother, not only will your relic be given back to the church but we, ourselves, will convert and accept baptism."

'In a matter of hours our dear mother was attending to the household chores as if she had never been in mortal danger. That was a miracle, I tell you, and we are here to perform our vow.'

'Where is the relic now? Is it with you?'

Their answer greatly heartened the excited priest. 'Yes, it is with us.'

Obeying Nasir's commanding gesture, Hasan retrieved from beneath his robe a small bundle of dirty material which he placed on the floor and carefully unfolded. Into view came the bones of a hand.

The priest prostrated himself before the relic and uttered a prayer. Getting up, he asked his visitors, 'Is there anything else you were enjoined to give me?'

'Oh yes. There are these documents handed over to us at the same time as the relic.'

Another silent command from Nasir prompted Hasan to recover from beneath his robe three time-worn parchments which he presented to the priest. The latter skimmed through the evidence authenticating the relic, made the sign of the cross and, with considerable veneration, covered the holy bones with the same piece of linen that had become another relic because of its contact with the hand of the saint. He then invited the two Arabs to accompany him to the Archbishop's palace where they were brought before his Grace and kissed the hand that he languidly offered.

Father Joseph informed the Archbishop, who gradually became more and more interested, about the miraculous recovery of the relic; when it was displayed before him with the authenticating documents, he became fully awake, excited and animated.

'Praise be to God,' he said with authority. 'The Holy Relic has to be solemnly taken to the cathedral and presented to the entire population for devotions. More important than that, I see its return to the Holy Land as an unmistakable sign from the Almighty telling us that He has not abandoned His people.' Turning to the two Arabs he said, 'And you, my sons, what are we going to do with you? Is it true that you wish to be baptized?'

The reply came from Nasir. 'We both made a vow under oath that if our mother were cured, we would become Christians. St John restored her to health; how could we fail him after he has answered our imploration?'

'Good, good. But what do you do best, because we have to provide you with work once you are settled among us.'

'We served at the palace of Constable Simon Mansel, the commander of Antioch. I was attending to his own person and Hasan to his horses.'

His Grace, unwilling to be responsible for two more mouths

to feed, issued his orders to Father Joseph. 'Instruct our two sons here in the Christian faith and give them baptism, as that is their wish. Then take them to Lord Philip's palace to resume the same work they used to do at the Commander's.'

Nasir and Hasan easily settled in the midst of Tyre's cosmopolitan communities, where Genoese, Venetians, French and other Christians from Europe mixed with Eastern Christians of different persuasions and Moslems belonging to a number of sects. They were rapidly adopted by the Lord of the palace, as well as by his staff, for they were always willing to accept the most cumbersome tasks during the most inconvenient hours. Philip even agreed to be their godfather, a political gesture meant to encourage the conversion of other Moslems. The two new converts were a model of piety; every morning, at the first hour, they attended mass in the small chapel connected with the palace and regularly took communion. Their profound devotion and impeccable behaviour were highly appreciated and praised.

They were given lodging in the servants' quarters, where they shared one tiny room with a valet from Beirut. The three men got along well together. A short time before summer, the Beiruti had to quit the Lord's service, as his father had died suddenly leaving no other adult male to take responsibility for his household. A new occupant replaced him, who turned out to be none other than Touma, Abdallah's Syrian correspondent.

Suspicious and inquisitive as he was, Touma seized the first opportunity to search the meagre belongings of the new converts. Nothing unusual was found, so he extended his thorough inspection to the room itself. In his own straw-filled mattress he dug out a bundle of strong material which concealed two frightening daggers, the sort used by the Assassins. He had heard accounts of blades being poisoned to ensure that the intended victim died from any wound received, however superficial. With trembling hands and a deadly fear in his heart, he replaced the daggers where he had found them. He had no doubt in his mind that his companions were *fidais* who had infiltrated Tyre on a murderous mission. Who were they going to sacrifice? And why two daggers? He had his suspicions that Philip was to be their target, but he could not be sure. It could well be the king during his next visit to Tyre, the Patriarch, the Archbishop or any knight who might have offended the sect.

What was certain for Touma was that if ever the two Assassins came to realize that he had discovered their secret, his life would not be worth a *fils*. If he denounced them, their brethren would slay him, no doubt about that. After all, why should he bother? Were the Franks treating him and those of his religion better than they treated the Moslems? Not at all, they took the Syrian Christians for granted and tried to win over the Infidels with further concessions; moreover, they looked at his Church with contempt, losing sight of the fact that it was much older than their Roman Church. Eventually he took the decision not to utter a word.

It was relatively easy to remain silent, but much more difficult not to let fear show up in one's face and affect one's whole demeanour by rendering it stiff and artificial. In no time, the two Ismailis realized that they had been unmasked and found themselves in a dilemma. If they got rid of Touma their mission would be in jeopardy, but if they let him live he could denounce them at any moment. After careful consideration, they resolved to spare his life but to implicate him in their plot, or at least one aspect of it, so that if he denounced them, he would go on to incriminate himself.

So one night before they all went to sleep, Nasir took Touma by surprise. 'Before we set out for Tyre we agreed with our eldest brother Nizar that he, after the lapse of a few days, would follow us to make sure that we are safe and sound. Our meeting point is the village of Batiole which belongs to the Sultan and is close to Tyre, and the agreed time is in two days. We expect you to go there in our stead, for we have no relatives in the vicinity, and leaving our work soon after arriving here to roam the countryside with no real purpose will necessarily cause suspicion. You don't have that problem yourself, for Kanah, your native village, is nearby and it is only natural that you visit your relatives; you've done that before. In the village you will look for Abu Ali's house and there you will find our brother Nizar. All you have to do is to convey to him our greetings and the following message: "The sword of the Sultan will strike soon." We entrust you with that simple mission; don't fail us.'

Terrified to death, Touma was unable to say a word, so he nodded his head several times in quick succession.

Just after sunrise on Sunday 17 August 1270, Philip of Montfort and his son John headed for the palace chapel. The order of the day was that straight after mass, celebrated by Father Joseph with little ceremony, they would go hunting. Owing to the early hour and the informality of the occasion, the Lord of Tyre's companions and retinue numbered only a handful. In the chapel next to Philip stood the Knight of Picquigny and behind them, their respective trusted servants, Touma and Abdallah. Prince John, Philip's son, was in the choir next to the altar, making preparations for serving the officiating priest. Nasir and Hasan, on their knees in one corner, were absorbed in prayer; few other people were around.

In the middle of the ceremony, Hasan grasped the collection tray and slowly headed towards Philip; he presented him with the tray and, quick as lightning, savagely plunged a poisoned blade into the Lord of Tyre's chest just as he was about to make his donation. Philip fell on to his back, mortally wounded, yet managed to gasp, 'Rescue John.' Simultaneously, Nasir ran towards John with raised dagger.

All those in attendance were petrified, incapable of making a move, except the Knight of Picquigny who, having already drawn his sword, delivered a deadly blow to the Ismaili next to him and ran after the other. Before he could reach Nasir, one of the guards standing at the chapel door rushed inside drawn by the commotion and saw the assassin's dagger raised against Prince John, who had instinctively extended his arms in a futile bid for protection. Without a second's hesitation, the guard nailed the assassin to the ground with his *pique*; other guards followed and finished him off.

Assured of John's safety, the Knight raced back to the dying Philip and knelt beside him, raising the dying man's head to let it rest on one of his arms while the other still held his sword dripping with blood.

In a corner, where Hasan had been dragged, several men who had by then come out of their state of shock plunged their swords in his now inert body.

In a whisper Philip asked, 'John?' The Knight put his Lord's mind at rest about the fate of his son.

As if Philip had gathered all his remaining strength to stay alive just to hear the reassuring news, he slowly turned towards the altar, painfully raising his hands in a sign of thanks, and passed away.

Carefully the Knight rested Philip's head on a cushion and covered his body with a cloak. Then slowly rising to his feet he said in a whisper to the attendants who had formed a circle around them, 'Our Lord is dead.' They looked at each other in disbelief; the three bodies lying in pools of blood on the white marble floor of the chapel bought them back to the harsh reality.

John was still in the choir, surrounded by guards, who

prevented him making a move lest there were more than two Assassins. Sitting on one of the steps leading to the altar, he buried his head in his hands and silently wept.

All of a sudden, Touma, who had been shuddering with fear as the dramatic events unfolded before him, looked left and right and realized that the two Ismailis were dead. Letting out a terrifying shout, he fell on the terrorized Abdallah and plunged a knife into his heart, in a cold-blooded attempt to dispose of the last witness of his plotting and spying. Out of breath, Touma stared at the stunned audience then shouted in a frenzy, 'These converts cannot be trusted; this man was probably one of the killers and would have finished the odious deed that these two couldn't complete.'

CHAPTER NINE

DESPAIR AND JOY

'The beast is dead; I have to celebrate this happy event,' exulted the Knight de Castre, addressing Aimeric Maurel and Arnaud de Foix in the intimacy of the latter's home.

'Don't let anyone know your true feelings, otherwise expect trouble and unwelcome attention,' came the immediate reaction of the cautious blacksmith.

'Not to worry,' replied the Knight with a roar of laughter, 'the celebration I envisage will be in Manon's arms.'

As soon as de Castre left them to join his favourite prostitute, Aimeric anxiously asked his older companion, 'Does the monster's demise at the hand of a non-Cathar atone for the crimes perpetrated against our Church?'

Arnaud was not prepared to let his exhilaration be deflated by speculative thinking about who had brought death to Montfort.

'God's wrath makes use of any instrument to establish justice; this instrument could well be a natural calamity or the murderous Ismaili with his poisoned dagger. Stop asking yourself meaningless questions and rejoice, but quietly.'

The young Cathar reluctantly followed this advice and ceased speculating about the matter which troubled his mind; but he was incapable of rejoicing because of the guilty feeling he was unable to dispel.

The account of Tyre's bloody Sunday had spread across the Holy Land like wildfire and brought with it consternation and despair. The strong man of the Kingdom of Jerusalem was no more and his loss was sorely felt in Acre, as it was everywhere. Misgivings were further heightened by the simultaneous news of the death of King Louis IX of France while on his way to the East at the head of another crusade.

If anything, Syrian Christians felt even more dejected than the Franks for, having no other place to retreat to if the Crusaders' territories were further reduced in size, they had no illusions about their fate. They would be exposed to Mameluke vindictiveness, accused of having sided with the Latins. In short, Montfort's death was a terrible blow to all the Christian inhabitants of the Holy Land.

As for the Moslems living under Frankish rule, they concealed their true feelings for fear of the mob's reaction, always unpredictable when fuelled by a combination of anger and panic. At any moment, and for any trivial reason, the rabble might have turned against them to avenge the murder of the Prince of Tyre, so they kept very quiet and avoided leaving their lodgings.

A few days after the news of Montfort's assassination had reached Acre, a Druze from Tyre presented himself to Gerios, carrying a letter from a fellow Druze who must have dictated it to one of the many professional writers found at the doors of courts and public offices. The letter was intended for Shams, but it would have been improper not to address it to her husband. The contents were painfully deciphered by Gerios and read to his wife, prostrate with grief on learning of Abdallah's murder. The letter related the circumstances of his death and named his assassin who, according to the sender had gone free and undisturbed because of his apparent loyalty.

Once the dreadful news had sunk in, Shams roused from her initial state of shock, lost her habitual composure and openly showed her grief and distress by crying and weeping aloud, tearing her hair and beating her breast. Deeply distressed by the anguish of his wife, Gerios did not know what to do or say; it was Zeinab who took control of the situation, trying to calm her mother and appealing to her to regain her self-control before neighbours flocked to the house. She also talked about revenge. Before long, the people were alerted and men gathered in the shop, with the women in the room above, to comfort the family and get details of the tragedy. When Arnaud and Aimeric heard of their friends' sorrow, they hurried to bring them solace, accompanied by the Knight.

As dictated by local custom they were unable to see Shams and Zeinab and had to be content with embracing Gerios, now a very proud man indeed, for now it would be possible for him to boast in front of his countrymen of his friendship with the three Franks who had taken the trouble to pay him a visit and commiserate with him.

The Maronite took heart from their presence, which seemed to exonerate Abdallah from false accusation. 'The murder of my brother-in-law will not pass unnoticed; a requiem mass will be celebrated next Sunday at St Andrew's Church for the repose of his poor soul. The office will be celebrated by a Latin bishop...you see, no Maronite is available at such short notice. It doesn't really matter, does it? For we all belong to the same Church.'

None of those present contradicted him and he was able to pursue his discourse while watching the faces of his visitors to detect signs of wonder and approval.

'That is the least I can do for my brother-in-law, even if it is going to cost me a fortune.' Heartened by the tacit support, Gerios moved on to threats. 'This dog, Touma, this Greek; he will have to pay for his odious crime and false accusation. He may have escaped the justice of the *Franj*, but he cannot avoid the vengeance of Abdallah's brothers. His days are numbered, I assure you.'

On their way back home, the Knight left his fellow Cathars for some business of his own and Aimeric was then able to tell de Foix what was in his mind.

'This is so sad; I wish I had never known Abdallah. I feel that we have, in some way, a share of responsibility for his death; for my part, I pressed him hard to contact Touma again.'

Slightly irritated, Arnaud nevertheless calmed down his anxious companion. 'We all knew there would be a price to pay, and poor Abdallah was aware of the danger he got himself into; let's hope that his God, the God of his own people, will accord his soul the grace to transmigrate to a superior body and a better new life. You should realize that with the death of Abdallah, our involvement in the earlier plot to kill Philip has now disappeared, with no trace left.'

Although not fully reassured, and somewhat shocked by what he had just heard, Aimeric changed the subject. 'I don't understand why, knowing his modest means, Gerios is prepared to hire one of the biggest churches of the city and to pay a bishop, and presumably two or three priests, for a requiem mass intended for the soul of a deceased who is not even from here.'

Arnaud smiled and teased him. 'Apparently, my dear young friend, you need to learn a lot more about your future parents-in-law. Let me tell you. The native Christians wait for an occasion like this to trumpet their grief, to manifest their love for the deceased and to boast their means. The more they spend, the louder the messages. By the way,' he stopped walking and looked at Aimeric with a twinkle in his eye, 'are you still serious about Zeinab? If you are, you should be prepared to spend a lot of money on the wedding ceremony to prove your elevated station, the extent of your love for the girl and your high esteem for her family.'

'What do you mean?' Aimeric enquired nervously, knowing that the modest sum of money given to him by his father would not allow any extravagant spending.

Arnaud realized the need to reassure the anxious young man. 'Of course, there is another solution; she can elope with you, with the blessing of her parents, then all these expenses can be avoided. But we will talk about that once you tell me of your plans now that our mission has been accomplished.'

'My feelings towards Zeinab are stronger than ever. I love her dearly and I cannot envisage life without her; the moment the period of mourning ends, I will propose. There are my studies of medicine too; I want to pursue them with Samuel, no one else; for these reasons I will not be going back to Milan for the time being.'

'What about your parents?'

'I am depending on your good advice on at least two counts: what to tell them, without hurting and disappointing them too much, and how to behave regarding Gerios and his family. As you made me aware, I am not fully acquainted with the local customs and traditions, and I want to avoid shocking them by the wrong attitude or words.'

'You can certainly count on me,' said Arnaud.

As if talking to himself, Aimeric continued, 'I fully realize that my decision to stay in the Holy Land will be a blow for my parents who have raised me, their only child, with the hope that I will not desert them during their old age. On the other hand, I sense that my destiny is here in the East and not in a country which, after all, is not truly ours. When I came to Acre I was certain that death was all that I could expect; now that I am given a new lease of life, I see things differently. If you allow me to stay a little longer with you and benefit from your generous hospitality, I will certainly not abuse your kindness for too long and will move to another lodging the moment I take Zeinab for my wife.'

The older man seemed vexed by what he had just heard. 'Don't be a fool. This house will be all yours one day; I know of no relatives of mine in the whole universe and you are like a son to me, so stop making plans of this kind.'

Back home, Aimeric locked himself in his room and sat on a coffer behind the wooden plank set up on trestles he used for his studies. He went into deep reflection, trying to find the right words to start a letter to his parents and convey to them with the least possible pain the momentous decisions he had taken. Whenever his resolve wavered, Zeinab's image came to the rescue and restored his determination.

Exhausted and gradually sedated by fatigue and the flickering light of the candle, he dozed off, his mind invaded by phantasmagoric people running around in front of him on the makeshift table. In his dream he saw himself reflecting on how such a small surface could accommodate so many people: here was Zeinab, lying down on her side, her head resting on her raised hand, her elbow supporting it on the table. She was undressed, but seemed very relaxed and was smiling – not at him, but at Marco Polo, the young man he had met in Venice some two years previously. In one corner of the magic table sat his mother and father, their lips tightly sealed with a disapproving look, again not at him, but at the girl. In another corner, Samuel was talking to his parents who did not seem to be listening. Abdallah suddenly appeared and splashed blood on everyone, then vanished with a terrifying laugh – which awakened the young Cathar.

The candle had long burnt out and the sun was already darting its first rays; his whole body ached and was stiff, but his mind was clear of any faltering. He seized a quill pen, dipped it in ink and put on paper some very resolute words which informed his parents of the decision he had taken, as well as reassuring them about his well-being.

Arnaud was shown the letter; he approved its contents and added a few words of his own with a coded message intended for the *Perfecti*. The letter would remain with him until he found a trustworthy person travelling to Milan and willing to carry it; failing to find such a person within a reasonable time, he would entrust it to a Genoese or Venetian ship, for a fee.

Having discharged a duty which had been weighing on his conscience, Aimeric decided to return to his studies, somehow neglected as of late. Samuel, as congenial as ever, readily accepted his apologies, put a finger to his lips to show he did not want to hear more and also, it became clear, to get a promise of secrecy from his pupil. He took him to the back of the house and into a small room where, on the floor, lay a body covered by a thick cotton sheet. As the physician felt the need to prepare his young student psychologically before he made him face a dead body with open incisions, he gave the following explanation.

'The dissection of human bodies was forbidden from the

time of Erasistratus, at Alexandria, centuries ago. The ban was never fully complied with, as one might expect, because the human thirst for knowledge is stronger than any edict. Nowadays, autopsy is tolerated and the ban is in the process of becoming obsolete; but it is still something technically illegal. No one, however, deserves the name of physician unless he has already dissected at least one corpse and examined the internal organs with his own eyes; no chart can be a substitute for observation.'

The physician leant over the form on the floor and unveiled the body of a young man, killed by a blow to the head apparently delivered with a sharp blade. Out of the corner of his eye Samuel saw the look of disgust that Aimeric was unable to hide and pretended not to notice it. 'My young friend, you must understand and believe that diseases are not punishments visited upon people by God for their sins, and act accordingly. Diseases are the imbalance of the four humours of the body, and wounds are inflicted either by accident or by man's devilishness, not by any vengeful hand from above. This is why we need to see what is inside the human body. Do you accept what I have just expounded?'

'Yes, master, and please forgive my unintentional reaction of disgust. From now on you will not find a more attentive pupil, I promise.'

After the shock of seeing and helping dissect the corpse, Aimeric gave himself up entirely to his studies, waiting for the period of mourning for Abdallah's death to pass. He wanted to propose to Zeinab straightaway, but had been told that he could not do so for at least six months, which would take him until the end of February of the year of Our Lord 1271. In the meantime, he paid regular visits to Shams's food stall which she reopened after a period of forty days, and where he could see Zeinab and exchange amorous looks, but not talk to her.

Finally, the period of mourning ended, word was sent to Gerios through a Maronite priest in preparation for the official visit, the purpose of which was disclosed in advance. At the arranged time Aimeric, wearing a new *pourpoint,* very tight fitting as dictated by the fashion, together with Arnaud and the Knight de Castre, were warmly welcomed by their host and the priest. For the convenience of his visitors, Gerios had borrowed three chairs; two were used, but the young Cathar ignored the one intended for him and sat on the floor opposite the two Orientals who beamed with delight.

Shams and Zeinab were in a corner, their heads covered with white veils, which also served to hide the lower part of their faces, but revealed eyes that were quietly loquacious. Normally the two women should not have partaken in the ceremonial visit, even though the future of one of them was at stake. It was Gerios, however, who had made the exception and invited them to stay in honour of the Frankish visitors.

Several minutes were devoted to civilities, then Arnaud opened the subject of the visit, using the Arabic tongue that all the Franks present had had to learn for practical purposes.

'The Knight and I are, in the Holy Land, the only relatives of our young friend here. Were his father and mother present, they would have been delighted to convey to you what I am about to say; in their absence, I pray that you accept us to speak for my nephew.'

'I, too, wish Aimeric Maurel's parents were with us; it would have been such a great honour,' said Gerios, full of the importance acquired by the occasion; then he added with feigned innocence, 'but tell me, how can I be of service to you?'

The Knight, unable to restrain himself, turned towards Arnaud and whispered, 'He surely knows why we are here.'

The older Cathar gently put his hand on the Knight's arm,

cautioning him to let him do the talking, and regained control of the conversation.

'Aimeric Maurel, here present among us, is a young man with a great future. He is being taught medicine by the most eminent of physicians and soon he will qualify as a full doctor; his art will allow him to earn a good living indeed, and he will be highly regarded in this land and beyond. This young man of such golden prospects has heard of your daughter Zeinab, of her great beauty, her modesty and of the way she has been brought up; he has asked us to convey to you his deepest desire to marry her, with your blessing.'

As if taken by surprise at the proposal and in need of some time to absorb what he had just heard, Gerios remained silent for a moment.

The priest took advantage of the respite and, fearing interruption, hurriedly said a few words for the sake of taking part in the matchmaking for which he had been promised a reward by both sides. 'I can vouch for the young man; he is very promising. As for Zeinab, I have known her since the day she was born. I baptized her and I pray to God to keep alive His servant so that he may bless her wedding as an assistant to her uncle *Bouna* Elias.' The intervention was ignored.

Because his words would not endanger the matchmaking process, Gerios nobly and emphatically said, 'I am not like those fathers who force their daughters into marrying against their will; if Zeinab is willing, Aimeric Maurel is welcome in my family, the more so that I have no son of my own. That was God's will and I don't reproach Shams.

'What was in your mind, girl? Speak up,' he said, turning to Zeinab, who uttered a timid, 'I am willing.'

The father was not a person who would leave the last word to anyone and therefore he made a concluding comment. 'Zeinab is treated in this house like a queen; I don't have another child and I expect the wedding ceremony to be a magnificent one – no less than the requiem for Abdallah, God have mercy on him.'

Incapable of keeping her patience any longer, Shams, who had remained silent until now, firmly intervened and to do that she removed the part of her veil covering her mouth. 'These are mere formalities. O husband, surely you and your future son–in–law will have plenty of time to discuss all the details of the ceremony. Why don't you offer our guests a glass of the brandy sent from Jbail?'

Aimeric and Zeinab gave Shams extremely grateful looks.

Afterwards, the two women took advantage of Gerios' leaving the room to bid farewell to the visitors to engage in a candid talk between mother and daughter.

'I know that you want to marry him, but until now you haven't had the occasion even to have a proper conversation together – you with the little Italian you know and he with the limited knowledge of Arabic that he's teaching himself – and that is assuming that propriety allows such a conversation to take place. Do you think that you will love him despite all that separates you?'

'I love him already and I know I will make him very happy!'

'Yes, yes, but I want *you* to be happy as well,' interjected Shams.

'We both will. I know how to handle a husband. After all, I have had you as the perfect teacher – just watching how you get anything you want by making my dear father believe that it is exactly what he wishes,' laughed Zeinab, looking tenderly at her mother.

'Your father is a good man; it is just that sometimes he needs to have his eyes opened. That is all I do.'

'But you have a way which makes him feel that he is always in control,' said Zeinab, with a perception beyond her years.

'Listen, you light of my eyes. Remember constantly to show respect to your husband, especially in front of other people, whether family or not. Now, between you and him, in moments of privacy and particularly when he wishes to approach you, you may be more bold.'

'Don't worry, mother, I will know what to do.'

CHAPTER TEN

HOPE AND FRIENDSHIP

'They're here! They're here! They've come to rescue us.'

'Let's see what Baybars can do now!'

Shouts of relief, joy and defiance were all that could be heard in the streets of Acre on 9 May 1271, as masses rushed towards the harbour.

This exuberant jubilation followed a sombre period of fear and despair, prompted by the fall to Baybars of the Krak des Chevaliers, the mighty Hospitallers' fortress which commanded the passage from the seashore at Latakia into the hinterland.

The Sultan's next move had been expected against Tripoli for, immediately after the surrender of the Krak, he had stormed the advance defences of that city, the two forts which crowned the Jebbel Akkar. It had been only a question of days before Tripoli would be besieged and taken; thereafter it would undoubtedly have been the turn of Acre.

Except that it did not happen; as a result of one of those sudden turns of events that had become frequent in Outremer, the Franks of the Syrian coast were to be given a new lease of life.

The banners of Henry III, King of England, and of Prince Edward his son, streamed out from every building and along the main streets of Acre. Edward was about to land at the head of some one thousand militant pilgrims. This providential rescue force had sailed from Palermo, where it had spent the preceding winter after the death of Louis IX, King of France, at Carthage, cause of the abandonment of the planned crusade.

The English force arrived in separate companies headed by some fifty barons and knights. The ships' bellies also brought from Sicily oil, wheat and salted foods, all essential commodities which had recently disappeared from city stores as a result of hoarding by unscrupulous merchants. They immediately reappeared, offered at a reasonable price, which made people's joy more complete.

The three Cathars and Gerios were among those who hurried to the port, summoned by the bells joyfully ringing and the majestic spectacle of the ships about to enter the harbour, banners flapping. When Prince Edward and his wife, Eleanor of Castile, disembarked from their ship, their renown as a strongly united and deeply religious couple had preceded them. They were officially received by the heads of the military orders, the civic authorities, the religious and secular dignitaries and representatives of privileged groups of Italian traders. Yet it was the reception of the exhilarated crowd which moved the noble visitors and their companions. The princely couple were escorted to their quarters by rejoicing men, women and children of all ages and standing.

Now that there was no immediate danger and peace of mind had been restored, in particular after the signing of a ten-year truce between the Mameluke Sultan and BohemondVII, titular Prince of Antioch and Count of Tripoli — a truce eagerly demanded by Baybars who was too clever to fight on several fronts — Aimeric could actually envisage taking Zeinab for his wife. Officially betrothed, the two deeply in love young people had been allowed to meet and talk to each other, but always in the presence of a chaperone. Physical contact remained out of the question, hence, amorous looks were more ardent than ever. Most of the time it was Shams who kept them company, and it was as a result of her tactful influence that Gerios had agreed to such encounters, which were not customary and could have been wrongly interpreted by his coreligionists and other Orientals. In actual fact, there was another reason for Gerios' tolerance; he was also willing to demonstrate to his future son-in-law that he was as broadminded as the Franks could be. Such broadmindedness made the Orientals wonder about the Franks' curious lack of jealousy regarding their women, allowing them to converse even in public with men who had no family connections with them. More amazing was a story going around that a newly arrived Frank husband had taken his wife to the public *hammam* and asked the male attendant to shave her pubic hair because he had heard that Oriental women did the same. It did not occur to this husband that they should carry out this intimate operation themselves, and if they were to be assisted it would certainly not be by a man.

The one condition that Gerios had made was that the meetings of the two lovers should always take place indoors and as discreetly as possible. His favourite saying was, 'If you are an ass, don't bray in public and don't give the whole world confirmation of what you are.' Most of the time, the lodgings above the shop were where Aimeric and Zeinab met.

One evening, after opening hours, Gerios joined the young couple who had been under Shams's watchful eye absorbed in apparently innocent discussion, interspersed with deep sighs and long moments of silence. Undoubtedly the Maronite loved his only daughter very dearly, yet he was terribly keen to keep up appearances at the expense of his purse and at the risk of casting a shadow over the happiness of his family. He poured himself and his guest a glass of wine from the vineyards of Tyre, settled comfortably on the floor and steered the conversation towards their forthcoming wedding. He reiterated his wish for a sumptuous celebration which would be proof of his deep love for his daughter and of his rightful standing. While the two young lovers were with them, Shams said nothing which might contradict her husband, but it was when Aimeric had left and Zeinab had gone to sleep that she reopened the subject.

'Dear husband, your wish for a grand wedding is also mine; how could it be otherwise if that is what you want? But, as they say, if the eye is foresighted, the hand is short. All that you describe takes money, much more than we can afford. I don't believe our future son-in-law has a fortune, and the little money we have we had better keep for bad days.' She paused and, with a sigh, added, 'Bad days can't be far away.'

'Woman! I have to keep up appearances, whatever the cost, otherwise I couldn't look any of my friends in the face.'

Shams chose her words carefully. 'There is something else as well – the death of my dear brother, Abdallah. It isn't that long since he was cruelly murdered. Damned be his wicked assassin! What would people say if, after a requiem mass that you so thoughtfully arranged and that remained the talk of the town for weeks, we go back to the same church, only after a short interval, to attend a joyous ceremony?'

'Wife, you may be right; but tell me, what else can we do? I refuse to attend a miserly ceremony which would badly reflect on me.'

Shams guessed from her husband's latest response that her words had made an impression on him and that he was about to give up, so she pressed her point. 'No need for that. Zeinab and our future son-in-law may well elope, unwilling to wait any longer for the end of the mourning period. For a little sum of money they will find more than one priest who will agree to marry them. For a while you will indicate that you are very upset, then you will forgive them and all will be for the best.'

Gerios remained silent for a moment. He eventually realized that Shams's subterfuge might give him a reason to boast about, for his seeming disapproval would be interpreted as an indication that he was not, after all, so terribly eager to see his daughter married to a Frank. Conveying that impression would necessarily improve his standing, and the idea contributed to winning him over.

'If they elope, how could I ever prevent it, having no advance knowledge of their arrangements?'

After this half-blessing, a plan for the elopement was concocted between Shams and the two lovers.

One night during the following month of July, just before dawn, while Acre was still asleep and the heat bearable, Aimeric rode towards Gerios' lodgings on the mule he had borrowed from Arnaud for the occasion. Mother and daughter were waiting for him in the shop, with the door ajar once they heard the rhythmic sound of the mule's hooves on the beaten ground and caught sight of the young man approaching. They waited until he got close before discreetly making their presence known. They hugged and kissed each other for what seemed to Aimeric an eternity; he urged them to hurry. At last a tearful Zeinab was released from her mother's embrace and helped by her future husband to get on the back of the mule; he took the mount by the bridle and they all advanced in the direction of the English Tower where the gate was manned by burghers responsible for the watches. The Cathar had chosen this precise night and gate as one of Samuel's patients, whom he too had attended, was on duty. When Aimeric was recognized, orders were shouted to let him pass with his veiled companion.

Outside the city walls, Aimeric took the direction of *casal* Imbet, located some twelve kilometres to the north. The *casal* had one church, St Cosme, and a priest who was renowned for being very broadminded. He would be prepared, for a proper fee, to join in wedlock a man and a woman who would not normally be allowed to marry – because one of them already had a spouse, was below the age of consent, or had been excommunicated by the Church.

It was around ten o'clock when the two travellers reached the first cottages of the *casal*; Aimeric asked for directions to the church and was advised that he would find Father Andreas in the adjoining presbytery. Having arrived at their destination and made known their presence by knocking on the door, they were taken inside by a young, attractive Moslem girl who did not take the trouble to veil her face in front of the two strangers and seemed totally at ease. Summoned by her shouts, a barefoot Father Andreas appeared wearing a robe similar to an Arab garment; it had once been white but was now covered in dirty stains and bulged indecently over an enormous belly.

In no time a deal was struck; Zeinab and Aimeric were taken to the well in the backyard so that they might wash, while the priest summoned his two customary witnesses and the half-witted boy who regularly served the mass for him. The whole wedding ceremony took no more than half an hour, at the end of which a gold coin was exchanged for the certificate of marriage bearing the seal of St Cosme's Church, the priest's signature and two crosses in lieu of witnesses' signatures. The young couple turned down an offer of hiring a room at the presbytery for the night and hurriedly set off in the direction of Acre, where they arrived exhausted at nightfall.

At home, they were welcomed by Arnaud and de Castre, both in an emotional state. The old man felt like a father to the young Cathar and deplored that he had been unable to attend the wedding. Had he done so, Gerios would have been extremely hurt and the charade of the clandestine marriage would have been exposed. As for the Knight, he was of a sensible nature; he could well kill a man in anger without blinking an eye, but would weep at the sight of a wounded horse. Besides, he was very fond of his young fellow countryman and did not miss an occasion to thank him for saving his life. The two men left the young couple alone after a glass of wine or two in their honour, the host on the pretext of a visit planned in advance and the Knight having insisted on moving to new lodgings, unwilling to be in the way now that Zeinab shared the house.

Once alone, Aimeric took Zeinab by the hand to his room, now crammed with a large, elevated four-poster bed which he had ordered in anticipation of the marriage. The bed came as a total surprise to the girl who, for the first time in her life, saw a mattress not directly resting on the floor. Being still so young, she sat on the edge of the bed and acted the way she imagined a Frankish lady would have acted in these circumstances, giving herself airs and mimicking the noblewomen she had met in the streets of Acre. Americ laughed heartily and joined in the game, inciting Zeinab to give her imagination free rein. For both, the game was also a pretext for delaying the moment they longed for and dreaded too, but nature quickly compensated for inexperience.

The morning after, Zeinab was too ashamed to face Arnaud and requested her husband's permission not to leave the room. He laughed, kissed her and ran downstairs in search of the blacksmith whom he found in his workshop. The cheerful, newly wed young man thanked his older friend for his thoughtful retreat the previous night. Arnaud did not need to ask Aimeric if he was happy; he could plainly see that written all over his face and he was able to guess much more from the young man's demeanour. An indecisive person had given way to a man in full control of his words and behaviour. Arnaud was delighted to witness that transformation, but tactfully said nothing, to spare his companion's modesty.

As Aimeric was not the kind of person to overlook his duties whatever the circumstances, he took the decision to write to Samuel and to Gerios; cutting short the friendly conversation with Arnaud he went back to his room where he found Zeinab asleep. In the letter to the physician he told him about his marriage, apologized for having missed some lessons and repeated his resolve to pursue his medical studies. More than ever he intended to qualify as a physician, trained by none other than his present teacher.

What this teacher was unaware, they had in common, because the pupil had never mentioned it, was that they both belonged to persecuted peoples. The young Cathar wondered whether one day he would be able to open his heart to Samuel and tell him all about himself, because he felt he was cheating the old man by hiding such an important aspect of his psyche and background.

He was brought back to the real world by Zeinab who had woken up sobbing behind the bed's curtains. Leaving the writing plank, he went to the bed and took her in his arms. 'What's the matter? I am here and I love you.'

'I miss my mother. I want to see her,'

Aimeric, aware that his wife was no more than a child, caressed her face, wiped away her tears with just a hint of impatience, but tenderly reassured her. 'Tomorrow is your mother's day here and I am sure she will not miss it even if that is going to anger your father; so in a matter of hours you will be in each other's arms. In a matter of days your father will forgive us and all will be just like before. You will see your parents as often as you want; that is a firm promise. Now, calm down, and let me write to your father.'

He gently disengaged himself from Zeinab's embrace and, after reflecting for a short time, wrote:

Most esteemed uncle, I throw myself at your feet and beg you to forgive me and to forgive your loving daughter. I give you my solemn word that nothing improper took place between us before we were joined in matrimony by father Andreas, the saintly priest of St Cosme. We are now husband and wife, as attested by the certificate of marriage which is with this letter. Only your blessing will make our happiness complete. I beg of you please to send word with the bearer of this message that you forgive us.

Your servant and loving son,

Aimeric, son of Guillaume Maurel and Blanche de Durfort.

The letter he had written to the physician was sent with Abdel Malek, the apprentice, but the one intended for Gerios was entrusted to Arnaud, who promised to take it in person to the ostensibly outraged father.

All went as predicted, and indeed as Shams had arranged; in a matter of days the young couple were warmly welcomed by Gerios, no longer able to play the role of the offended father or willing to deprive himself of the company of his only daughter. His alleged anger had lasted long enough to be widely advertised and admired.

These were days of bliss; Zeinab, as loving and loved as ever, was now in charge of the household. She had requested to be taught how to keep the accounts and her father had been a good teacher for such a gifted pupil who, although unable to read and write, had conceived instead a system of symbols comprehended by her alone. Aimeric devoted most of his time to studying medicine. Some of his spare moments were spent in Arnaud's workshop talking to the old man, but not giving him a hand, for after the enthusiasm at the beginning, the art of making swords appeared to him tedious, as it required no intellectual involvement. It did not mean that his regard for Arnaud as a human being had in any way diminished; on the contrary, it was now coupled with filial affection and a deep sense of gratitude. One reason for the latter was that his host had insisted on giving him, and promising every month, a sum of money enough to cover household expenses and to allow him to complete his studies. Although Americ had protested that he could not take advantage of such generosity, the reply was firm and final.

'I have no family, neither here nor elsewhere; you and Zeinab are son and daughter to me; you take care of me more and better than any of my own blood would have done. It is I who should be grateful to you and for that I only have to imagine what my life would have been without your affectionate attention and Zeinab's smile and loving presence. So, no more nonsense and allow me to take advantage of your company.'

With worries about daily subsistence taken care of, Aimeric spent part of the day either visiting patients treated by Samuel or giving his full attention to the teaching that was so altruistically bestowed upon him.

One beautiful morning during the month of October, nothing unusual for the region where seasons were well defined, the young student of medicine was getting ready to leave for his teacher's house when church bells started ringing to announce the arrival of a ship. The young man left his route and headed towards the port to check on the colours the ship was flying. When the harbour came into view he could see the proud banners of the Republic of the Doges high on the mast and the passengers about to disembark. He stood there on the quay, keeping his eyes open for any familiar face who might have brought a letter for him. Minutes later, Aimeric could not believe his eyes. Among those leaving the ship he recognized the young lad, Marco Polo, whom he had met in Venice and with whom he felt strong bonds of friendship despite the brevity of their association. The handsome young man that Marco had become in the years since they had met immediately recognized Aimeric and ran to hug him. Both seemed equally delighted by the chance encounter. After the first joyful reunion, the Venetian introduced his young friend to his father Nicolo and to his uncle Matteo, busy watching the unloading of their many bags.

It was hard to conduct an uninterrupted conversation amidst the hustle and bustle which accompanied the arrival of a ship. Disembarking passengers, welcoming parties, porters bending beneath incredibly heavy loads, all trod a hesitant path along the narrow quay, fighting over any space which happened to appear for a brief moment before being swamped by the flux of crowd and cargo. Marco made his rediscovered friend promise to follow them straightaway to the Consul General's *palazzo* where the Polos would be staying.

Aimeric was warmly received and found out that his name was already familiar to the elderly Polos, who had heard it not only from Marco, but also from Signor Carlo Favretto, who had returned to the city of the doges singing his praises. However, his most pleasurable moment came when he heard the young Polo assert that, had they not met by pure chance, the first thing he had intended to do in Acre was to seek him out at rue de la Carcasserie.

The news about the landing of the already fabled Polos spread throughout the city and a number of well-wishers gathered at the *palazzo*; the two young men, in need of privacy, discreetly left the assembly and retreated to a veranda overlooking the waterfront. The view was so breathtaking and soothing that they remained silent for several minutes, unwilling to interrupt the magic of the moment; finally they started talking simultaneously and burst into laughter.

Thereafter Aimeric was quick to give his friend, eager to listen, an account of his recent marriage and of his interest in medicine, and concluded, 'Tell me what blessed circumstances have brought you here? You know, when we met in Venice you mentioned to me that we may one day meet in Acre. I thought these were fanciful words, ideas that would never materialize; nevertheless, they have made our separation less painful; now that you are here I still can't believe what my eyes tell me.'

'You recall my permanent watch of the sea when we first met? It was the return of a father I barely knew that I was waiting and longing for. You see, he left us when I was little, and while he was far away my mother died. You brought me luck; a short time after I came to know you, my father and uncle returned home. They still hold a commission from Kublai, the Great Khan of the Mongols at Cathay, as ambassadors to the Pope of Rome; but when they left Cathay, heading for Rome, the Pope died and no one has been elected since then, so they are unable to discharge their commission. They are greatly concerned that the Great Khan might suppose that they have failed him and they have decided to go back to him to explain the situation; and here I am, going with them.'

'What a marvellous story! And how lucky you are to be part of the expedition.'

'Signor Favretto's account of the events of your journey together confirmed your impeccable behaviour all along. My father had in mind to ask you to join the expedition; that couldn't have pleased me more. Knowing now that you have married and you are about to qualify as a physician, I myself will dissuade my father from even raising the subject with you. I don't want you to abandon your studies, be lured into the prospect of adventures and riches and desert your wife. My mother suffered a lot, as indeed I have. Forgive my frankness, but that is the way I feel. If you are not too angry with me, I want your promise that you will accompany me wherever I go until I sail.'

'All I need is a few hours a day for my studies; otherwise, I am all yours,' replied Aimeric with a broad smile, showing his forgiveness.

The following day, he was reminded of his promise and invited to accompany the Polos to pay their respects to Monsignor Tebaldo de Visconti, the Pope's legate. Despite his instinctive reluctance and loathing for anything Roman and anyone who had to do with its see, he could not refuse the invitation and so was part of the delegation received by the prelate at his *palazzo*. Once in the presence of the legate, Aimeric experienced a sense of detachment and indifference he had never felt before when casting an eye on a prince of the Church. He tremendously enjoyed this newly acquired freedom from prejudice.

The aim of the Polos' visit was twofold. They would request that the legate write a letter to the Great Khan confirming that the see of Rome was still vacant. They would also request that he use his good relations with Arab princes and Mameluke governors in order to secure a safe passage for them to Jerusalem, where they intended to obtain some of the oil belonging to the lamp of the Holy Sepulchre. The oil had been formally requested by the Great Khan and he would not be able to understand why his ambassadors had failed to bring it back with them. They now had to face the dangers of travelling through enemy territory if they wanted to avoid returning to Cathay completely empty-handed.

Monsignor Tebaldo promised full assistance to his visitors, who then gratefully took their leave; while waiting for his signal to proceed, they could start preparing for the journey to Jerusalem. Aimeric diplomatically declined an invitation to join them; he did, however, introduce the Polos to Jacques de Castre who, as a warrior, would be useful for their protection; the Knight had no particular employment for the time being and was delighted to be given the opportunity to do what he did best and earn some gold.

A few days passed and the legate sent word advising that all contacts had been made, so the journey to Jerusalem might now proceed. These contacts were faithful to the assurances they had provided and the Polos safely fulfilled their mission. Back in Acre they lost no more time, having by now persuaded the Knight de Castre to accompany them also on their more adventurous journey. After an emotional farewell from Aimeric and Arnaud, who was warned of de Castre's imminent departure for the unknown, they boarded the vessel which would take them to the port of Laiassus in the Gulf of Alexandretta. Alone on the quay, the two Cathars looked at each other with the same question in mind: Are we going to see them ever again?

Fate occasionally plays tricks and had decreed they were to meet once more and before long. Just after the Polos sailed, word reached Monsignor de Visconti that he himself had been elected Pope. A courier was sent after Kublai's ambassadors, who were found in Armenia on their way to the Great Khan's court, summoning them to return to Acre. They were ceremoniously received by the newly elected Pope, given a papal letter for the Mongol and laden with valuable presents. Two learned friars were ordered to be part of their expedition and were bestowed with the authority to ordain priests, consecrate bishops and grant full absolution.

When the Polos and the Knight left Acre for the second time, Aimeric once more found himself on the quay saying goodbye, somehow convinced that this time he would never see them again.

CHAPTER ELEVEN

ANOTHER CONVERT

'Dear husband, I think that I'm carrying your child,' announced a blushing Zeinab. It was a joyous moment for them both as they had now been married for a few months and were anxiously waiting for their marriage to be blessed. Zeinab knew that this was the fulfilment she had been praying for to secure her marriage, especially if she gave birth to a boy.

Their joy and that of the rest of the family seemed tame, however, compared to Gerios' exuberance.

'Allah has deprived me of a son, but now He will most certainly give me a grandson to be the staff of my old age.'

'Don't say that, husband,' intervened Shams. 'You might

appear to be challenging whatever His will is.'

'And what if it is a girl?' Arnaud added teasing. 'Surely you should contemplate this possibility.'

Gerios looked at the killjoy with great pity, as if feeling pain at this show of ignorance. 'Talk, talk. There is no tax on talking,' he sententiously stated.

Majestically and without another word, Gerios turned away and left, followed by Shams. Together they walked through the city and, leaving by St Anthony's Gate, out into the countryside where they found soldiers of the Mameluke and Frankish armies gathering for a friendly tournament.

The only reason the Maronite and his wife, as well as a number of other people from Acre, were able to leave the security of the city walls at that time was because a truce had been negotiated between the Mameluke Sultan and Hugh III, King of Jerusalem and Cyprus, with Charles of Anjou, King of Sicily, mediating between the two. After lengthy negotiations, the parties had agreed on the terms of a ten-year-and-ten-month truce concerning Acre alone; but Acre was nearly the whole pathetic remnant of the Kingdom of Jerusalem anyway.

The ceremony of the signing of the agreement confirming the truce was, in itself, an intimation of its fragility and of the prevailing mistrust among all concerned. Frankish knights, together with representatives of the military orders, reported to the Sultan's headquarters to witness his taking of the oath to respect the agreed truce. The gifts they brought along were passed through two fires for purification and the removal of any magic or poison. It was then up to Baybars to send three emirs to Acre to witness Hugh's oath.

The Sultan, however, had his doubts about Prince Edward's wish to end the fighting. He was not convinced that the plan to form a new crusade had been abandoned; he suspected that Edward might take advantage of the respite offered by the truce to gather more armed forces against him. Pressing questions were also on the Mameluke's mind; could the English Prince curb the bellicosity of his barons and militant pilgrims? Did he really want to? The Sultan was not the kind of man to leave the resolution of problems to chance, particularly where military matters were concerned; thus he took the decision to remove Edward for good. He called in the master of political murders, the Lord of the Assassins, and commissioned him to carry out the deadly assignment.

It so happened that Ibn Shawur, the governor of Ramla, a town about a hundred and fifty kilometres south of Acre, had befriended Edward, lavishing on him and Lady Eleanor sumptuous gifts, and passing information to the prince about the Sultan's army. Baybars had been informed by his ever diligent spies about this treacherous relationship and he passed the intelligence on to the Ismailis.

Given the choice between dying at the hand of an Assassin or collaborating with a plot to kill the English lord, Ibn Shawur did not hesitate long and offered his full co-operation. All that was required of him was to introduce into Edward's entourage a self-sacrificing Ismaili devotee in the guise of one of his servants. Henceforth, gifts and information were invariably brought to Acre by the same so-called servant, and before long his face became familiar to the Prince's entourage. Having confided in one of the Oriental Christians in Edward's service that he wished to convert to the Christian faith but he did not know how to go about it, the Ismaili was brought before a priest and baptized. Thereafter, he gained everyone's trust and could go wherever he wished without being stopped or questioned.

He chose 16 June 1272 to carry out his criminal deed. He arrived at the English Prince's palace very early in the morning, greeted the guards and told them that he was bearing an extremely urgent message from his master to the

Prince and that the message had to be delivered in person. Prince Edward, still in his apartments, was advised of the messenger's pressing request to see him; he ordered that the man be brought at once to his bedroom with a translator and signalled to everyone else to leave them. Once the door closed behind the last person, the Assassin came nearer to the Prince, as if the message he was carrying had to be delivered *sotto voce*; suddenly, he jumped upon him, produced a dagger from beneath his robe and plunged it five times into his victim. Prince Edward fell back on to his bed, his legs giving way beneath him, partly because of the surprise attack but mainly because he had been instantly weakened by his wounds, which were now bleeding abundantly. Gathering what strength was left in him, he shouted for help, but the translator had already picked up a stool and prevented the Ismaili from finishing off the wounded man by striking him repeatedly on the head. At the same time, he yelled at the top of his voice to attract the guards' attention. The attacker was distracted for a few seconds, enough time for the two soldiers who rushed on to the scene, swords raised, to cut the Ismaili to pieces.

Alarmed by the commotion coming from her husband's apartments, Lady Eleanor ran in to find Edward collapsed on his bed, bleeding and shivering with fever, and a dead Syrian on the floor nearby, one hand still gripping the hilt of his dagger, surrounded by onlookers in a state of panic, not knowing what to do. In a matter of seconds she grasped the situation, realizing that her husband had most probably been wounded with a poisoned blade. Losing no time and without a hint of hesitation, she threw herself on to the bed next to her husband, looked frantically for his wounds, sucked at them and spat the poison out. She repeated this operation several times then, exhausted and probably having swallowed some of the poison herself, Lady Eleanor lay beside him out of breath, the smears of blood round her mouth making her look like a lioness who had fended off danger from her cub. Edward's life was saved thanks to her prompt and unselfish action; he would, nevertheless, spend the next few months convalescing.

The news of the attempted murder spread like wildfire and left the city in deep shock. 'Is this the truce that was so painfully negotiated?' was the question on everyone's lips.

Not allowing themselves to be overburdened with problems of that sort, a party of Edward's companions, armour-clad and fully armed, mounted their war-horses and rode towards the Arab villages and hamlets scattered throughout the nearby countryside. Many peasants were taken by surprise in their fields and slaughtered without pity, others were massacred inside their humble shelters, which were then burnt with no regard for any infants, women or old people who might have been inside and still alive. When at the end of the day the avenging party returned to Acre, they left behind them a hundred or more innocent people dead.

Baybars dissociated himself from the assassination attempt and sent Edward his congratulations upon having escaped death and his good wishes for a prompt recovery. To the innocents massacred in the aftermath of the attempt, there was no reference. The sacrifice of their lives served to reduce the immediate tension, but nothing could restore confidence once the dream of a real truce had been shattered.

The Franks, in particular those of Acre, were apalled, dismayed and concerned about what could happen next and how it could affect their future in the Holy Land. As for the Eastern Christians and for the Moslems who had taken the Frankish side, they in addition had worries about the present, lest they became the target of revenge attacks by the newly arrived pilgrims who could easily mistake them for enemies because of their Oriental garb.

Needless to say that life in Acre became bleak for one and all; more disquiet ensued when the English Prince, his lady and most of his retinue left for England from the city harbour. The day was 22 September 1272.

One event, which took place at about the same date, brightened up the life of a handful of people. Zeinab gave birth and Gerios' expectations were fulfilled as it was a boy, to be called Tanios. He was in good health and delighted all around him. What is more, Zeinab gained a new measure of confidence as she was now the mother of a baby boy.

Because of the scepticism shown when Gerios was predicting that Zeinab would most certainly produce a boy, Arnaud was now looked at by the shopkeeper with the air of someone who knew better. The Frank laughed at that and teased Zeinab's father by reminding him that *he* saw the baby more often than Gerios, as they lived under the same roof. Indeed, several times a day he left his workshop to have a quick look at baby and mother, before going back to what he had been doing with renewed good spirits.

A family, although a small one, had become Aimeric's responsibility; his mind and conscience were no longer burdened with a mission awaiting to be discharged; moreover, he had taken the decision to settle in the Holy Land, at least for the forseeable future. All these reasons combined to make him throw himself into his studies more zealously than ever. His aim was to start making use of his skills, the sooner the better, in order to earn money and reimburse Arnaud for the sums generously given to him.

At last came the day when Samuel told his pupil that he did not need his lessons any more. The two men were in the Jew's house, seated on the floor, either side of a brazier; they were wrapped in heavy cloaks as the weather was bitterly cold, and from time to time each extended his hands above the fire in search of warmth. For the benefit of his respectfully attentive pupil, the physician delivered his long-awaited verdict.

'My dear young friend, no more lessons for you. From now on you may see patients on your own, for I am confident that they will receive the best treatment at your hands. You are one of the most gifted students I have ever had and to delay your certificate of qualification would be wrong. Tomorrow it will be ready.'

The two men remained silent for some time; each had more to tell the other, but neither was willing to start. Eventually, the impulsiveness of youth drove Aimeric to speak first.

'Master — I will always call you Master — I have to confide in you. With your great generosity, you have passed on to me all your knowledge; for me to keep anything back from you would be wicked.'

He hesitated for a second, which was enough for the old physician jokingly to intervene, 'And what would be this secret of yours? Is it something terrible?'

'Contrary to what I let you believe, I am not a Catholic. My parents-in-law don't know that, nor my wife; they will not understand what it means and, if they do, they will regard me with horror as a heretic.

'I came to the Holy Land as a Cathar, entrusted with a mission by the elders of our Church. Soon after that, I discovered that I didn't have to carry it out after all; fate had intervened on my behalf. I must admit I was greatly relieved, but also ashamed of that feeling. After all these months in Outremer, that sense of shame has disappeared and with it any sort of religious faith. Here I am, in this part of the world that has seen the birth of most religions, realizing I have lost mine. The reason is that I have been the witness of too many atrocities perpetrated in the name of God and it seems that the infernal circle will never end... I feel relieved because I have told you what has been on my mind. Please forgive this late confession.'

'Not that it is of any importance now,' replied the old physician, 'but from the start of our association I found in you a certain aspect of sincerity unrecognizable in other Gentiles. I appreciate your sharing with me your secret and your most intimate thoughts and feelings; rest assured no one will ever hear from me a single word of what I have just heard from you. But be careful, not everyone may be that discreet; don't provoke the Church of Rome or worry your new family.'

'I won't. From now on I will take on the mantle of a Catholic. It doesn't cost me a thing any more. Tanios will be baptized exactly as Zeinab's father wishes and we will all go to Jbail for the christening.'

'What about your inner self and the sense of belonging to a community? Why don't you, my friend, revert to the source of religions? I am prepared to be your teacher one more time.'

'For the time being I am content to be in the state I am. Maybe later, or maybe never, I don't know. Content? I am not so sure after all, for a deep-rooted terror of the gods and of the unknown strikes me occasionally.'

'Anyway, leave it for now; don't make a rash decision,' said Samuel. 'Come tomorrow with Arnaud's mule; you will need it because, with the promised certificate confirming your qualification, you will receive books and medical instruments from me, as well as my pharmacopoeia.' For the benefit of Aimeric's enquiring look, he disclosed the reason for his unexpected and generous gift.

'Most dear friend, I have taken the decision to retire, knowing that there is a good physician in Acre. Another reason is that I am old and tired; I wish to devote what is left of my life to the study of the Torah, to elucidate the inner meaning of the text and to pray. I must also assume new responsibilities. I recall that you have met the learned Moshe ben Nahman at my place. The poor man recently died and I am told that no one but I, humble Samuel, is up to pursuing the Kabbalistic teachings that were his. I cannot undertake them as a layman. All my time will be needed for the task, so I have taken the decision to devote to it what time I have left.

'I will not be divulging any confidential matter by telling you that in Acre there are several Jewish sects: the groups of the northern French and Ashkenazi Tosafists, the Jews from Spain, the anti-Maimonides and other factions. And each sect is at odds with the others.' Samuel's voice had begun to rise in exasperation. 'All of them spread the wrong teachings of the law and they must be stopped! I believe that my duty lies just here.'

Never had Aimeric seen his teacher in such an agitated state, nearly shaking with anger. He was assailed by thoughts which made him feel ashamed, and which he was unable to dismiss from his mind. *If a usually tolerant and genteel man, such as this old physician, can get that upset and show such prejudice about matters which touch his beliefs, what is to be expected from other, normally less tolerant, human beings?*

Bewildered, Aimeric thanked Samuel for his kindness and generosity, promising to come back the following day.

CHAPTER TWELVE

A MOST PECULIAR JUSTICE

Vengeance purges shame
Arab proverb

Nestled in the hills overlooking the sea, between the towns of
Beirut and Sidon, but closer to the former, lay the village of
Aramoun. The village was part of the Mameluke province of
Damascus and populated by Druzes, including Shams's family.
Since news of Abdallah's assassination by Touma had been
reported to them, the father of the victim, Abu Khodr, his
mother and his three remaining brothers, Khodr, Jamal al-Din
and Saad, all nurtured the same obsession – to avenge their son

and brother. Even if they did not want to, a thought which never crossed their minds, every single inhabitant of their village would make them mindful of their duty, either by a subtle hint during a conversation or by a sidelong glance when paths crossed. Were a lengthy time to elapse without revenge, the whole family would be shunned and eventually ostracized.

Not once had the idea of forgoing retaliation occurred to any member of Abdallah's family, in fact, quite the opposite. After a hard day working in the fields, when they assembled either in the kitchen or in the garden, depending on the season, the sole topic was how to find the murderer. It took them about two and a half years to gather all the information they needed to make their move; Saad was the one chosen by the family to devise a plan of action and execute it.

As a Druze native of a Mameluke village, he had to have a good reason for visiting Tyre without causing suspicion. That reason had been easily found. In Tyre he would simply sell olive oil produced from the orchards surrounding Aramoun as far as the eye could see.

Shortly after the harrowing news of his brother's assassination had been reported to the family, Saad filled a few jars with olive oil, secured them in the saddle-bag on his mule and set off for Tyre, which he reached three days later. Once in the city he had started making some very cautious enquiries. Only repeated visits, with plenty of time between them, had enabled him to get a complete picture of what had really taken place that bloody Sunday. To his total dismay, he had found out that far from being looked on as a victim, Abdallah had been branded a traitor, while his assassin was being treated as a hero. Obviously the difficulty of the assignment was now compounded by this other element which needed to be addressed, too – namely, the clearing of his brother's name. Eventually a comprehensive plan was drawn up and agreed to by the whole family.

And so, most probably for the last time, jars full of olive oil were loaded on to the mule. Saad bade farewell to his parents and brothers, no one showing any sign of emotion, although they all realized that he might never return from the fateful journey. He took the route south, not once turning his head to exchange a last look with his family, and not for one moment beset by any scruples or hesitation about what he intended to do. He was fully aware of his duty and would carry it out whatever the consequences; when honour was at stake, no price for upholding it was too high.

On his way, the young Druze went over the intelligence he had gathered from his previous trips to Tyre; namely where his brother's murderer lived, his usual moves and habits. Thus he had learnt that every Sunday, when not on duty, Touma went to the Church of St Nicholas to attend mass in the company of his younger brother, Alexis. After mass, the two strolled on the beach if the weather permitted; otherwise. they would spend a couple of hours in a café and then separate until the following Sunday.

Saad made sure that he entered Tyre at first light one Saturday. With no time to lose, he sold the oil to his regular customers and took the mule to the market-place, where he rapidly found a buyer. He entrusted the proceeds of all the transactions he had just completed to a fellow Druze who ran the inn where he would be staying for the night, and gave him the following instructions. 'Keep the money for me. If I am not back in exactly thirty days, send it to my family at Aramoun.' Having dealt with his possessions, the young Druze went to sleep.

The following day, Sunday, Saad lay in wait near the entrance to the Church of St Nicholas. He did not have to wait long for Touma and Alexis to turn up. As they were about to enter the church, the young Druze seized Touma from behind and held him steady. Then, with one hand he pulled back Touma's head, throwing him off balance, but prevented his falling by using his own body as a wedge. With the other hand, he cut Touma's throat with a knife, then allowed him to fall to the ground in a pool of blood, watching as the man gave his last strangled gasp. He then dropped his knife and stood erect, motionless and impassive.

Alexis and other stunned members of the congregation recovered from their shock and hurled themselves on the murderer, savagely hitting and kicking him. During his ordeal, Saad did not utter a word; he did not even moan, despite the injuries being inflicted on him by the frenzied crowd. At that moment, a patrol of soldiers passed and Saad was pulled out from the mob and thrown into jail to appear before the Cour de Bourgeoisie which sat every Monday, Wednesday and Friday.

Early next morning, a Frank who spoke good Arabic presented himself as an attorney to the barely revived Saad. He offered his services, explaining that the assistance of a lawyer was required by the court for the defendant adequately to present his defence. The young Druze was glad to accept the offer and put the other's mind at rest by promising payment from the purse left with the innkeeper. As if yet more were needed to indicate how desperate was the case the attorney was about to defend, instructions to the innkeeper for payment of his fees were put in writing by him and marked with a cross by Saad.

This formality completed, the prisoner revealed to his attorney the motive behind the killing of Touma and the reason he did not flee once it had been carried out. The lawyer's attention became more intent as the account continued.

Shortly afterwards, Saad was brutally dragged by soldiers before the court of twelve jurors, chosen from among the town's burghers and presided over by a High Sheriff. Also present was Alexis as plaintiff, with a supporting crowd. Losing no time, an outraged Alexis accused Saad of the murder of Touma and requested from the court that he be tortured and hanged and that his corpse be exposed in the market-place.

It was now the turn of the attorney to address the court. 'My Lords, my client does not deny that he killed Touma. However, he had good reason for what he did; he formally accuses the dead man of being a traitor who took part in the murder of our Lord, Philip. God have mercy on his soul. It was not Abdallah, my client's brother, who conspired with the two Ismaili assassins, but Touma; and Touma killed Abdallah because he was about to unmask him.'

'That is a monstrous lie,' exclaimed Alexis. 'I strongly deny it.'

'If that is so, then my client will challenge Alexis in a judiciary duel. The Almighty will be by the side of the person who is telling the truth. That is the only way to find out, now that Touma is dead.'

Alexis, ashen-faced with fear, cried out, 'This man has confessed to a heinous crime perpetrated in front of many good people ready to testify; what else is needed to see justice done?'

'Indeed a man was killed, but Saad, here present, maintains that he had good reason for killing him; he accuses Touma of high treason. The two crimes are closely related. If Saad is hanged for one crime, the truth about the other will never be known. Moreover, if Saad is right about Touma's treason, he wouldn't deserve any punishment for he would have acted as the Prince's executioner. Only a judiciary duel can disentangle the two cases and indicate who is lying and who is telling the truth.'

The High Sheriff deliberated with the jurors for a while, then decreed that a duel would take place in three days' time in the square next to the cathedral, and that Alexis had the right to fight in person or appoint a champion.

At the set time and place Saad, who had now regained some

of his strength, was brought to the square in chains; then Alexis appeared along with the champion he had chosen. The champion, a butcher by profession, was a huge, muscular man who had accepted to fight in place of Alexis for a handsome sum of money. He seemed as confident as his employer about the outcome of the fight.

The Prince's representative, the High Sheriff and the members of the Cour de Bourgeoisie were all seated on a raised platform erected for the occasion. In the background loomed the silhouette of the gallows, awaiting the losing side.

The soldiers herded the dense crowd which had gathered into a circle, while at intervals a crier shouted a warning that any member of the public who came to the assistance of either fighting man, even by just a cheer or a sign, would be mutilated or put to death and have his assets confiscated.

Saad, freed from his chains, and the over-confident butcher were brought into the middle of the circle; each was given a cudgel, reinforced with iron plates set in the head, and an oval shield similar to the one used by Arab soldiers.

The signal to start the duel was given by the Prince's representative amidst a deathly silence. The more slender and agile Saad pounced on the butcher, pressing him backwards until he reached the edge of the circle, at the same time delivering a torrent of blows with his cudgel, most of which landed on his opponent's shield. Rapidly the butcher counter-attacked and the two men came struggling back into the middle of the arena.

The fight dragged on; neither of the opponents was about to give up, although both men were by now covered in blood. At this juncture, the High Sheriff shouted, 'Hurry on! Hurry on!'

As if galvanized by the shout, quick-as-lightning Saad skirted round the butcher, came up behind him where there was no shield for protection and delivered a formidable blow to his head. The butcher fell to the ground in agony, his head crushed by the iron-plated cudgel that Saad had wielded so well for that one last attack.

Upon the High Sheriff's order, Alexis and his champion were dragged to the gallows and hanged.

Divine justice had vindicated Abdallah and absolved Saad of Touma's murder. The young Druze was immediately released and helped by his attorney on to the back of a mule, a deed prompted not only by merciful compassion, but also by the wish to collect the money promised to him. Saad was then taken to the inn run by his fellow Druze, who dressed his wounds and helped him to lie down. He would need at least a week before he would be fully recovered and strong enough to withstand the hardship of the journey back to his village where, undoubtedly, a triumphal welcome would be his reward.

Justice had been done in a very peculiar way indeed.

CHAPTER THIRTEEN

FAMILY REUNION

The events which took place in Tyre were promptly reported to Shams and for a moment made her feel elated; not only was Abdallah's murder avenged and his name cleared of the malicious charge which had followed his treacherous death, but also her brother, who had carried the sword of justice, was safely back in his village. She herself, however, was unable to take part with her own people in the festivities which would without a doubt be held to celebrate shame having been washed away; and this realization cast gloom upon her joy. Because she had married outside her religion, Shams was still in fear of her family's wrath which, although not forceful any more, had certainly not abated. Despite the length of time which had passed since her elopement with Gerios, it remained risky for her to meet up with members of her immediate family. Justice having been done for Abdallah's slaying could remind them of another matter of honour which still needed redress. The slightest argument which involved one of her relatives could bring on him the blame for the failed duty to punish her and so revive a desire for shedding her blood.

Joy mitigated by sadness seems to be Shams's lot; Gerios wanted her to travel with him to his brother *Bouna* Elias's home in Jbail for Tanios' christening. Of course she would have loved to be there when her grandson was baptized, but she turned down the invitation because of her dislike of her sister-in-law Hanneh. She was not slow to realize that the feeling was reciprocated; the mere fact of their both staying in the same house would be an unbearable ordeal. Shams put forward several excuses for not going, but the one with which she scored most success was when she pointed out the need to attend to the shop and the kitchen stall. Money matters convinced Gerios of the soundness of the argument.

The month of October, when the weather was usually pleasant and the sea at its safest, was chosen for the expedition. Tanios was by then a little over a year old and strong enough to stand up to the sea trip to Jbail, a trip which required three days of coastal navigation, with two halts for the night: one at Tyre the other at Beirut.

The journey went as planned and on arrival Gerios, Aimeric, Zeinab and their little son were helped by two sailors from their hired sail to set foot on Jbail's natural jetty. It was shortly before sunset, a time when the last rays of the sun, now at sea level, tinted the waters and the city walls with magical colours and created new shades every few seconds. Minutes more and the sun would turn into a fireball with no rays to squander and would rapidly disappear behind the sea after a final metamorphosis into an overturned giant red bowl.

No one was at the port to welcome the visitors as Gerios had not sent word to warn his brother of their arrival, knowing that he and his party would always be welcome in the family house. Darkness would soon fall, so Gerios quickened his step, forcing the others following to do the same, in the direction of Elias's house, located between the castle and the Church of Saint John. A short walk from the harbour and the new arrivals surprised the family enjoying the last of the daylight in their garden in front of a one-storey construction of humble but well-kept appearance. In reality, the garden was tiny, but took the guise of something much larger from its dense vegetation and the citrus and fig trees which hid from the eye its actual limits. Sitting in a semi-circle round the entrance to the house were Father Elias, his wife Hanneh and their five children, Dawud, Yusuf, Zahra, Ghantus and Mariam – three boys and two girls whose ages ranged between eighteen and eight.

The visitors were received with cries of joy, in particular from Hanneh as soon as she realized that Shams was not among them. Aimeric and Tanios were fêted, the baby passed from hand to hand. Showered with kisses, frightened by the unfamiliar faces of his handlers and the commotion, he started crying and was saved from the ordeal by his mother who took him inside the house until he calmed down.

In a matter of minutes, the whole town was aware of Gerios' arrival, accompanied by his Frankish son-in-law. A number of relatives, neighbours and friends, and onlookers drawn by curiosity, filled the small garden, even crowding the narrow passages of the maze of houses, to express their welcome. Aimeric in particular was the subject of much attention, for his reputation as a physician had preceded him and more than one well-wisher had it in mind to get a free consultation about a real or imaginary ailment.

Eventually the family was left on their own and free to discuss more personal matters. They remained outdoors and enjoyed the soft blowing sea breeze which carried a delicate jasmine fragrance collected from the few surrounding gardens; in the sky, myriads of stars glittered. Unlike Acre, overcrowded, cosmopolitan and noisy, Jbail was quiet and peaceful. Both Frankish and Oriental communities lived there in more harmony than anywhere else in the Holy Land. The reason was that the Lord of Jbail, Guy II, who belonged to the Genoese Embriaci family, but had been born in the Holy Land, looked with distinct favour on the half-castes (*Poulains*), the Franks born, like himself, in the East, and the Oriental Christians.

This Lord of Jbail had married Marguerite of Sidon whose mother was an Armenian princess; the alliance had partly contributed to a temporary end to the deadly feud between the Principality of Tripoli and Jbail, its powerful fief, because Sibylle, the wife of the former Prince of Tripoli, Bohemond VI, was Marguerite's aunt. Besides his native inclination, Guy's policy was also based on expediency, for most of the inhabitants of his fief were Maronites, Oriental Christians, who, in spite of his conciliatory efforts, remained resentful of the superior attitude of the Franks and of the Roman Church's supremacy that they had been obliged to acknowledge. A recent resurgence of a powerful movement within the Maronite Church and the faithful had made a large faction revert to their old belief in the one Will and Energy of Christ, a belief that was condemned by the Catholic Church as a heresy and that their forefathers had to forfeit for political convenience soon after the Crusaders settled in the Holy Land.

The discontent of the Maronites was not only triggered by a sudden outbreak of religious fervour and interest in theological intricacies. In reality, they had always harboured a basic wish to revert to their initial religious practice which contrasted with the sumptuous ceremonial of the Latin ritual and the princely pomp of the Latin clerics. Maronite priests were much the same as their congregation – simple, peasant people – and their liturgy had none of the Roman grandeur. The patriarchs elected by the Maronite bishops led an ordinary life, unlike the Roman princes of the Church.

Guy had succeeded in gaining the confidence of the mutinous Maronites, who would not challenge his authority now strengthened by the truce concluded with Baybars for a period over ten years. What would happen after that was not something for the ordinary people to worry about.

Elias, his family and their visitors were but ordinary people and, with no threat looming, they should not have had any worries of a political or existential nature. Listening to what the priest was about to say might have confirmed that assumption; but soon it would appear that his optimistic view was not shared by all. Elias broke the sort of intimate silence that only close people enjoy by broaching a subject dear to his heart.

'Dear brother, you can't imagine my delight in having all of you among us; there is also sorrow in my heart knowing that you will not be staying for good. I can't understand this for you could have your shop here instead of having it in a foreign city; you could be among your family and brothers instead of being far away. Your son-in-law, a much valued new member of the family, will be perfectly able to practise here the art of curing and make good money out of it. In Jbail there is one physician only, and he is ignorant to the point that he could be a danger to his patients.

'Our newly arrived little angel will be raised among his cousins and will learn his religion the proper way. Where you are, you don't even have a Maronite bishop. And what about danger? Have you ever thought about the deadly peril you and your entire family are exposed to in Acre, where foreigners of all kinds and races land, pass through or settle? These people mean trouble; they know nothing of the East and they may well give the Sultan good reason to capture a much coveted city. Have you considered what would happen to all of you if the Moslems take Acre by force? I myself don't even dare think about it.

'Here we live at peace with all our neighbours, whether good Christians or Moslems; our Lord has restored trusted relations with the Prince of Tripoli as well as with the Mamelukes. And assuming that the worst happens, we can always take refuge in the mountains among our people. No one would come against us there.'

To this long monologue, Gerios' reply is a mere, '*Inshallah*, maybe one day.'

Gerias was no fool and fully realized Shams' strong dislike for Hanneh. He did not want to force her to move to Jbail and live in the same house as a sister-in-law she could not bear; he still loved his wife dearly and would not consider for a moment making her unhappy. Besides, the shop was earning him good money and he did not see why he should challenge his good fortune, which might turn away from him, given new surroundings.

Aimeric uttered a conciliatory, 'I have no family in the Outremer except Arnaud de Foix and you, and I wouldn't wish to leave Arnaud on his own. If, however, Zeinab wishes to follow her parents to Jbail, or anywhere else, I will certainly comply with her wishes.'

Gerios changed the subject by turning back to Elias. 'Tell

me, dear brother, is it true what I heard about the existence of a movement within our community which is directed against the Franks and the union with the Church of Rome? Is it a rumour spread by malicious people, or a real fact? If what I have heard is true, that would be most unfortunate, even disastrous. It could well breach the peace that you enjoy for now.'

Having sought and obtained his father's permission, Dawud intervened in the discussion; with a firm voice, not devoid of emotion, he answered his uncle's query. 'My revered uncle, no one has lied to you. You haven't heard rumours, but facts. The Maronite mountain is in turmoil and discontent is very high.' Dawud's voice rose and the discourse that he pursued had a more vehement tone.

'I fail to understand why, for so long, we have stood up for a foreign people who despise us; why should we remain allies of those who allegedly come to rescue us from our local enemies and treat us worse than we ever were treated before. It is time for us to realize that we have to count on ourselves and not on anyone else.'

Unwilling to hurt his son's strong feelings, but nevertheless realizing that the young man had gone too far in his outburst against the Franks, the priest firmly intervened, 'Oh, Aimeric, I apologize for my son. Be assured that his harsh words aren't meant for you; far from that. Now that you are one of us Dawud felt free to speak his mind. Please forgive him.'

'Don't apologize, I beg of you. I don't believe for a second that I am the one intended by Dawud. On the contrary, I wish to learn more from him about the actual situation in the district and the true feelings of the people. Please tell me all about it.'

None of those present could ever realize how genuine Aimeric was by expressing his broadmindedness and by distancing himself from the Catholic Franks, and how unconcerned he was about their future in the Holy Land – except when it came to the safety of his family.

Nevertheless, Elias did not allow his son to take command of the discussion; instead, it was he who obliged Aimeric. 'People living in the highest parts of the mountain above Jbail have expelled the priests who refused to revert to religious tenets abandoned years ago. Our venerable Patriarch was forced to move his residence from high ground to a place close to the coast seeking Frankish protection. My heart bleeds to see our community divided owing to hot-blooded youngsters.'

While talking, he had been looking at his two elder sons with sadness, yet not devoid of bewildered admiration. After a short pause he continued. 'Wisdom dictates that we stand by the Franks, our religious allies. Now it is too late to abandon them and, in any event, we will never be accepted by the other side; whatever we do we will be persecuted for religious reasons.'

'But we *are* now,' exclaimed Dawud. 'With due respect, father, are we not? In our own country we are but guests, tolerated by foreigners so long as we accept their rule. The lowest of the Latin deacons has precedence over you. Forgive me father, forgive me, brother Aimeric, for being so forthright, but I have to be. As for persecution, isn't it something we suffer despite, no…because of, the presence of our alleged allies? Remember, only five years ago the Mamelukes stormed the highest villages of our mountain, destroyed them and killed many of their inhabitants. And tell me, I beg of you, what did our "allies" do? Nothing. They made no move to help us, even though we suffered on their account.'

The priest was annoyed by the harsh words he had just heard; nevertheless, he did not seem to be entirely hostile to the ideas they conveyed. But what else could he do, except appease feelings which were running high among the young and demonstrate to his visitors that he was still in control of his own household. He looked at Dawud, then softly but also firmly to indicate that what he was going to say would be the last word on the subject, declared, 'I understand the reasons for your anger but, believe me, we can't do a thing; it is too late to change camps now. Patience is what we need. Across the seas there are innumerable Christians who will one day come to the rescue of the Holy Land as they did so many times in the past. If we don't stand by them now, what can we tell them then?'

Intending to add his own word of advice, Gerios rather loftily stated, 'Your father is absolutely right. Moreover, I see it as in our interests to keep allegiance to Rome, for otherwise we would be facing alone not one hostile party, but two. The Byzantines were never our friends, quite the opposite. If we took refuge in these mountains it was to escape their persecution. Listen to your elders, they know a little more.'

Dawud had too much respect for his father and uncle to pursue the discussion after they had decided to put an end to it. Although he remained silent, he did not seem convinced by their appeasing words, nor did his brothers who, including the youngest one, had been following the discussion with a passionate interest.

Aimeric jumped at the opportunity of a minute's silence to change the course of the conversation and said, 'Tell me more about your physician.'

'Nothing much to say,' Elias enlightened him. 'He is the only person who knows a little about the art of healing. In fact, he is the barber of Lord Guy and good at one thing: bleeding, whether you need it or not. Only in a case of emergency do we seek his service; otherwise we go to Tripoli. A doctor lives there: a Moslem, but a good man. He is always prepared to take care of those who knock on his door, with or without the means to pay him. Come to Jbail and in no time you will be rich.'

Aimeric smiled but said nothing. He glanced at Zeinab and found her deeply asleep with their baby in her arms, her head resting against the wall of the house, and the child's on her chest; they presented such a lovely sight that a smile appeared on his face and on the face of everyone else who had followed the direction of his eyes. That acted as a signal to bring the gathering to an end. Aimeric lifted Zeinab and the baby in his arms and took them straight to the mattresses that Hanneh had prepared for them for the night.

CHAPTER FOURTEEN

THE PHYSICIAN FROM ACRE

The following day Tanios was carried by his mother into the Church of St John which stood in the middle of the town, a few metres from Father Elias's house. The church was a beautiful Romanesque building, with an elegant outdoor baptistry adorned with three Italianate arches. Dawud and a distant cousin stood as godfathers to the baby, whilst a Latin priest and *Bouna* Elias officiated. Tanios was admitted into the Church by aspersion, baptism by immersion having been prohibited by Rome a few decades before.

After the ceremony a joyful procession made its way back, preceded by a flute player who drew strident sounds from the reed instrument and by another musician who excitedly beat a tambourine and, at intervals and after a series of beatings, frantic-ally shook the instrument to make its girdle of tiny bells tinkle.

A merry crowd took over Elias's small garden and energetically consumed whatever sweets were offered by Hanneh. Unaware of his recently acquired saintly state and the reason for all this commotion, baby Tanios, still in Zeinab's arms, looked with astonished, wide-open eyes at the giant creatures who caressed his face with enormous fingers; but this time he showed his utter disapproval with a big yawn, followed by a deep sleep. Zeinab took him inside the house away from the visitors' chattering voices and remained with him for a while delighting in contemplation of his angelic face and savouring a moment of quiet.

The last guests were about to leave when a man rushed into the garden, went up to Elias and out of breath said, 'Venerable man, my master, the Knight Baudouin, needs the art of the physician from Acre. He has been wounded by mistake with an arrow shot by one of his hunting companions; he was hit in the leg and since then his situation has worsened, despite his being cared for by the court physician. Your guest is required at the castle and I have orders to take him back with me.'

'The wounded Knight is the brother of Guy, the Lord of Jbail,' Elias explained to Aimeric, who seized the small coffer containing some of the pharmacopoeia he had brought with him from Acre and followed the servant's quick steps. A short walk and the two men came in sight of the castle, which comprised a high massive keep, surrounded by a square fortification enclosing a courtyard. A square tower defended each of its corners, while a fifth stood in the middle of the north wall to offer better protection to its only gate. A moat completely encircled the castle and a drawbridge gave access to the entrance.

They quickly crossed the bridge and were given permission by the soldiers guarding the gate to enter the castle. From there Aimeric was taken to a room in the keep where he found the Knight lying on a bed, shaking with fever and obviously in great pain. He was surrounded by several men and women who looked anxiously on. One man, who seemed more composed than the others, proceeded towards the newcomer, presented himself as Nicolo, the court physician, and declared in a tone which left no room for contradiction, 'The wound has formed an abscess which is badly infected; if the leg is not amputated forthwith our Lord will certainly die.' He then added dismissively, 'There is nothing else that can be done and any further delay will be fatal. I have tried everything.'

At the same moment, Aimeric realized that in one corner of the room stood a giant of a man holding a terrifying axe. The young physician glanced at the wounded Knight and his eyes met the latter's imploring expression. He gave him a reassuring nod and smiled as if to tell him *don't worry*; then turned to Nicolo, who seemed ready for the fight he could see coming, 'I want to examine the leg.'

Without waiting for anyone's permission, he bent over the injured man and thoroughly investigated his wound. Then, ignoring Nicolo, he said for the benefit of the patient, 'My Lord, I believe I can cure you; no amputation will be necessary.'

The court physician was not prepared to give up so easily, for too much was at stake for him. If the newcomer proved to be right he, Nicolo, would lose money and prestige and thereafter would inspire even less confidence. Therefore he, in turn, ignored Aimeric and addressed the Knight, 'My Lord, which would you prefer; living with one leg or dying with two?'

Realizing that he had to be just as cunning, Aimeric retorted, 'If my cure doesn't work, I will know in a few hours; if that is the case, then I wouldn't oppose the radical treatment recommended by my learned colleague. On the other hand, if amputation is carried out now, we will never know whether my remedy would have worked; my Lord will be disabled for life and have lost a good chance of keeping his leg.'

No hesitation was conceivable after these sound words; the Knight ordered Aimeric to proceed and administer his remedy. Nicolo's first impulse was to leave the room in anger; he stayed, however, hoping that this optimistic young physician from Acre would ignominiously fail in his attempt to save Baudouin's leg and he himself would be triumphantly restored to favour.

Aimeric opened his coffer full of medicinal plants and herbs and prepared a concoction from carefully selected ingredients. He then thoroughly cleaned the wound and the abscess, made a poultice out of the prepared mixture and applied it to the abscess, holding it in place with muslin. Having completed the treatment, he advised his patient to rest and asked the anxious people around him to leave the room, as he was not going to check on the progress of the treatment for another few hours at least. Once alone with the Knight, he sat on a chair as comfortably as he could, for he was not prepared to lose sight of his patient, knowing how desperate Nicolo was to regain control of the situation. He might well take advantage of Aimeric's absence to remove the poultice and allege that it did not work, or he might even carry out his odious treatment without further ado.

Six hours later Aimeric untied the muslin and examined the abscess and the wound; he seemed very satisfied and applied a fresh poultice, all the while reassuring the Knight with words of comfort. After further similar treatments, the abscess opened; once more Aimeric cleaned it as well as the wound, bandaged the leg and announced to a grateful Baudouin that his leg had been spared.

Aimeric reached home early in the morning of the next day. News of the miracle he had performed at the castle had spread throughout the town, and so a fair number of people had gathered to see him, begging for his treatment. Despite extreme fatigue, due to nervous tension and a sleepless night, he obliged them all, but not before giving his father-in-law, who had offered to help him, firm instructions to take no money from the poor or from close relatives. When the last patient had left he very quickly ate some lentil soup prepared by Hanneh and got some rest; he then returned to the castle to check up on his patient, whom he found on the mend and in high spirits. He was fêted by all those who had crowded into the room and showered with gifts, including a gold goblet and pieces of silk, brocade and taffeta. Nicolo was nowhere to be seen.

While Aimeric was still in Baudouin's room, a servant approached and informed him that the Lord of Jbail wanted to see him immediately. He took leave of his patient and followed the servant into a vaulted hall where he was announced. In the half-light he was able to make out a man and a woman reclining in armchairs upon an elevated platform; around them, sitting either on stools or casually on the edge of the platform, were several courtiers. When Aimeric got closer, Lord Guy left his chair and took the physician in his arms, thanking him warmly for having saved the leg, and even possibly the life of his brother.

Guy was fair-haired, extremely handsome and had exquisite manners; he complimented Aimeric saying, 'I hear that you live in Acre, that hateful place; I wish you were with us instead. We need people with your art and knowledge; if one day you decide to accept my invitation, you will always be welcomed.'

Aimeric was profoundly touched by this open display of appreciation; he thanked the Lord and took leave of him.

Everyone in Elias's home was excited to see the gifts brought in by a slave. Zeinab coquettishly wrapped herself in the piece of silk given to her husband, so he told her to keep it for herself; her childish joy was the best reward he could ever have hoped for. Out of the corner of his eye Aimeric could see Hanneh looking at them; he went over to her and gave her the piece of taffeta. The poor woman could not believe her eyes; she had spent her entire life raising a large family, all the time battling with poverty and deprivation. No one had ever given her a token of appreciation and she did not expect any, for she believed it was her lot to do exactly what she did. So when Aimeric told her that the taffeta was for her to keep, she grasped hold of it and ran to the kitchen, where she could cry with no one around to see.

Early the following morning, before the household had woken up, Aimeric strolled in the garden on his own, elated by the scent of flowers still heavy with dew and by the birdsong which timidly started up with a few notes at the first rays of the sun. Moments later he was joined by Hanneh, who apologized for her sudden disappearance the night before and expressed her gratitude for the gift she had received; she then went into the kitchen to start her usual early morning routine by preparing the family's breakfast.

Next it was Dawud who turned up and interrupted Aimeric's solitary stroll; together they silently paced up and down the tiny garden until the younger man opened his heart to his companion. 'For the third night in a row I haven't been able to enjoy a peaceful sleep; the discussion with my father keeps coming back to me – and there is something else.' He hesitated briefly then continued, 'I need your help, for I want to follow the path dictated by my heart and by my faith, and I don't know how to do that without bringing too much grief upon my father whom I dearly love and deeply respect. You are held in such high regard by him and, indeed, by the whole family, that you alone can convey to him what I am going to tell you, without breaking his heart.

'Until this morning I wasn't sure whether I should bother you with my problem, not because I have no confidence in your wise judgement, but to avoid involving you in a matter which will distress my father whichever way it is presented to him. Then, when I was watching you on your own in the garden, it seemed to me a sign and an opportunity to unburden my mind to you and seek your advice.'

Talking about his dilemma seemed somehow to have comforted the young Maronite, who mustered up all his courage and rapidly came out with, 'I want to be a priest.'

The other looked at him as if silently asking, *So, where is the problem?*

Dawud replied to the unspoken questioning, 'I want to join our real Church, the one of our fathers, the one which remains independent from Rome. I wish to be taught the true religion by Bishop Luke of Bnahran.'

'Indeed we have a problem here,' commented the physician, adding, 'Your decision will most certainly break your father's heart – that is, besides the embarrassment you will cause him. Dear cousin, as much as I want to be of help, I am afraid I don't have to hand any practical advice which will allow you to follow your inclination and at the same time spare your father distress and chagrin. But let me ask you: what does your mother think of it? You haven't mentioned her once. Does she know what you have in mind?'

'Yes, she is aware of my choice and she blesses it. She can't be of any help, however, with regard to my dear father, and most probably her interference could make things worse. From the bottom of my heart I thank you for listening to me with much greater sympathy than I deserve and I now realize that

I shouldn't have troubled you with a problem for which there is no happy solution for all concerned. I now realize that I have to wait and pray that circumstances will change and bring an end to my dilemma. I am really grateful to you for allowing me to unburden my mind and, please, please, forgive me for the inconvenience I may have caused you.'

Aimeric reassured him that nothing of the sort had happened; he felt somewhat liberated from the burden of trying to find a satisfactory solution when apparently there was not one.

CHAPTER FIFTEEN

SAD NEWS FROM MILAN

Six most unhappy men in their late thirties were languishing in a tower by the sea, in Acre, where they were being kept prisoner. Their only contact with the outside world was a high, barred window which meagrely lit the few square metres which had been their prison for the last four years. Through this small opening they could hear the incessant battering of the sea against the rocks surrounding the tower and they allowed their minds to travel on the waves to the Egyptian shores, and freedom.

These men were prominent Moslems and war leaders whose luck had deserted them during a daring but unsuccessful attempt to invade the Frankish island of Cyprus, with the help of a fleet of seventeen galleys camouflaged as Frankish ships which had sailed from Alexandria and other ports of the Egyptian delta during the month of May 1271. The Mameluke fleet had evaded the Italian ships on patrol and headed for Limassol. Their objective had been to disembark in that port and take the island by surprise while King Hugh was in Acre.

A combination of bad manoeuvring and fierce winds had caused eleven of the galleys to run aground. The Cypriots captured some two thousand sailors and men-at-arms, among them the six prisoners who included the commanders of Alexandria and Damietta.

When the news of the disaster reached the Mameluke Sultan, he told his familiars, 'We angered the Almighty by painting our galleys with the infidels' colours and by displaying banners bearing their cross. The price we paid could have been much heavier, except for Allah's mercy.'

Five long years had elapsed since the disastrous raid and nearly all the prisoners in Frankish hands had died, escaped or been exchanged for Franks taken captive by the Mamelukes. The only ones who remained alive were the six locked up in Acre, where they had been moved from Cyprus as a guarantee against a Mameluke attack. A very heavy price had been asked for their release, a price that Baybars had refused to give, declaring, 'I have dispensed with them.'

That had been his official reply to the numerous mediators who were busy trying to secure a deal. In reality, the Sultan left no stone unturned in his secret yet sustained efforts to have his commanders released. His latest attempt had been to summon to his court in Damascus one of the deputy governors of Safed, a man by the name of Seif al-Din, and put him in charge of the rescue operation with the following instructions:

'Bring them back to me, whatever the price, whatever the means.'

In turn, Seif al-Din called together his own spies operating in Acre. They came separately, so as not to arouse the suspicion of the Franks, which would doubtless happen if they were all to leave at the same time. An informant by the name of Ismael, reported to the deputy governor that one of the jailers in charge of the six prisoners detained by the Templars, was a Frank who paid regular visits to a house in Acre's brothel district and seemed to be infatuated with one and only one girl, Margherita.

'That is a lead worth following,' commented Seif al-Din to himself, adding for the benefit of Ismael, 'You have at your disposal an unlimited amount of money. Give, or promise to give, whatever sums you deem necessary. I want only one result and that is the liberation of our brothers. I will not tolerate failure.'

Back in Acre, Ismael's first step was to meet Margherita in the presence of her two protectors, Pietro and Sergio. He promised them large sums of money if Geoffren, the jailer besotted with the girl, were made to co-operate. This appeared to be within Margherita's capabilities, although some sort of planning would be needed to overcome any hesitation or scruples her lover might have. A scheme was rapidly drawn up and immediately put into action.

Margherita played the part of a woman madly in love with Geoffren and no longer able to stand other men's company. Her utmost desire, as she pleaded with him, was to move from the house she shared with other lodgers and go to live with him. The only obstacle was money; she owed money to Pietro and Sergio and, until she had discharged her debt, Margherita had to do whatever she was ordered to. The first objective was to find the money which would free her from the clutches of the two awful men who 'protected' her.

This was where Ismael came in; she introduced him to Geoffren, who obtained from the Arab a substantial loan, enough to pay off Pietro and Sergio and to set up home with Margherita. On the date of maturity, the jailer was unable to redeem the loan or any part of it. To his astonishment, Ismael seemed very understanding, even satisfied with his short-coming as he put the following offer to Geoffren.

'Two of my relatives are imprisoned in the tower. I want to send them food and clothes. Deliver these to them and I will consider part of your debt as paid.'

Margherita was at hand to encourage Geoffren to accept the proposal. Not being able to refuse her, he did whatever she wanted and started, without even realizing it, the descent towards treason and treachery. The two lovers needed more money to pay for the extravagant lifestyle that the girl had now begun to demand, and that Geoffren would be unable to give her without more loans. Fortunately Ismael was always ready to oblige without asking questions, until one day he disclosed his real objective, namely the freeing of the six Moslem prisoners.

It was now too late for the jailer to refuse to co-operate or go to the authorities, for he was already an accomplice, having smuggled Frankish clothes, food and messages to the men in the tower. In addition, he still owed Ismael a great deal of money, while Margherita continued to spend even more,

Yet, all was not lost. Geoffren was promised the redemption of all his debts and the sum of one thousand dinars when the prisoners were freed. He and Margherita made a plan to leave Acre the same night as the escape and take refuge in Safed, awaiting payment of their reward. From there they would decide where to go and settle for good.

Files, saws and ropes were given to the prisoners and a date fixed for the breakout. When the time arrived, they sawed through the bars of the window and, one after the other, all wearing the smuggled-in clothes, climbed down the rope secured around the stumps of the bars. Waiting for them at the foot of the tower was a man ready to row the small boat being tossed around on the waves, and who would direct the way. Silently he steered the boat southward and after a while drew into a small creek. There the escapees found horses, fully harnessed, and another escort. A short ride took them to the safety of Moslem territory.

Meanwhile, unseen by the other guards, Geoffren deserted his post and fled towards the lodgings he and Margherita had taken close to the 'Accursed Tower'. The plan was to get away before the breakout was discovered, as his part in the escape would soon be uncovered. He raced along the deserted streets but before he reached his destination a man who had been hiding in the shadows suddenly jumped on him from behind. Geoffren's hands were violently pulled behind his back, forcing him to stop and stand still, completely helpless; simultaneously, a second man plunged a dagger into his chest. As he collapsed, dying, he recognized the man as Sergio.

Leaving their victim, the two assassins forced their way into Margherita's room. When the young girl saw them armed with a knife, and with no sight of Geoffren, it did not take her long to realize what their deadly intention was. She gave a feeble shout and ran towards the window in an effort to escape; but stricken with mortal terror she was not quick enough and was murdered before she could utter another cry.

Their evil deeds completed, the two killers felt safe, as there were no witnesses left to link them to the escape. Were Geoffren and Margherita still alive, they would doubtless have disclosed their names under torture. Now the situation was different; at least that is what they believed. Obviously Pietro and Sergio could not forsee the furore which was to take hold of Acre when the breakout was discovered and the bodies of the two lovers were found. The jailer's being from France caused accusations of treason to be made against all his compatriots by the Italians in Acre. The Frenchmen swore to bring the whole matter to light and find out who had been Geoffren's accomplices.

Margherita's connection with Pietro and Sergio was reported to the Templars who were now conducting a thorough investigation into the circumstances of the escape. The two men were brought in chains before the investigating Knight and swore their innocence, insisting that Margherita had forsaken their 'hospitality' long before she was found dead. The Templars needed to establish an Italian connection with the jailbreak; in that way, Geoffren would not be the only traitor against his faith and race. The Knight took the decision to submit his two prisoners to a terrifying ordeal by water and fixed the date for it.

In the meantime, Gerios and Aimeric with his wife and child returned to Acre which they found in turmoil and on the verge of civil war. Greater distress awaited Aimeric, however, when he read in Arnaud's face that he was the bearer of sad news. His friend took him in his arms and pressed him against his chest.

'My poor son, I have terrible news for you. Your dear father has passed away.' He released Aimeric from his embrace and handed over a letter from his mother. Incapable of uttering a word after what he had just heard, Aimeric took the letter and went to his room

Zeinab left the baby in Arnaud's care and joined her husband. She realized that Aimeric needed all the attention and comfort she could give him and that no one, not even their baby, should share this moment. Silently, she sat on the bed next to Aimeric as he read his mother's letter telling him that Guillaume had died peacefully in his sleep and that it was only when Blanche had woken up in the morning that she had discovered his body cold and still. A physician, hastily summoned, confirmed his death and a Cathar *Perfecto* prayed for a better transmigration of his soul.

Aimeric dropped the letter into his lap and put his head in his hands, feeling great remorse for his long absence from home, particularly during such a trying time when he should have been close to his mother. In spite of her tender age, Zeinab was able to guess what was going on in her husband's mind. She moved close, hugged him and whispered words which immediately lifted him from his brooding, 'If it is another boy, we will name him Guillaume; that is a saint's name, isn't it?'

Aimeric was delighted to learn that Zeinab was expecting another baby; joy and sorrow alternated in his mind. The impact of the announcement was plain to see and Zeinab persuasively added, 'If you decide to leave us for a while, you will find Tanios and me waiting for you with the baby... and when you return, he will get accustomed to your face in no time at all.'

Indeed, the idea of going back to his mother, even for a few months, had occurred to Aimeric as soon as he had learnt of his father's death; on the other hand, the fact that Tanios would soon have a brother or sister had made him change his mind almost immediately. How could he leave his son and pregnant wife on their own in turbulent Acre? They needed his protection; his duty was to remain with them.

'I will be here with you when our child is delivered.'

Zeinab's joy had no limit, she nevertheless contained herself. 'Any decision of my husband's, I shall obey.'

There was no falsity or hypocrisy in her behaviour or words. Her attitude and discourse were the fruit of experience transmitted from mother to daughter in a time when a woman had very little say in the affairs of her husband.

On the day fixed for the assassins' ordeal by water, Gerios and Arnaud, both tough men, well acquainted with death in its numerous forms, met as previously arranged and went in the direction of the Venetian quarter near the Arsenal where Pietro and Sergio would be forced to submit to God's judgment. Aimeric had declined accompanying them, claiming he had to make a number of visits to his patients. In fact, he refused to witness a barbaric spectacle which was supposed to distinguish between innocence and guilt, having no doubt whatsoever that God had nothing to do with any cruelty perpetrated by men against other men, particularly in His name. The two Italians might well have committed the odious crimes of which they stood accused, but there must have been another way of discovering the truth.

A big crowd had assembled in the square, eager to see a drama which in all probability would end with the actors being put to death. But one never knew, and the unexpected might well occur...

The accused were brought under heavy guard to the foot of a huge cask filled with water. Upon a sign made by the investigating Knight, two soldiers seized Pietro, bound his arms behind his back and secured a rope around his chest. They then lifted him under his arms, forcing him up a ladder which took them to the top of the cask; once there, they tied the rope to the cask and dropped Pietro into the water. If he sank, it meant he was innocent and the soldiers would immediately lift him out with the help of the rope. If he did not sink, that meant he was guilty. The accused did his utmost to sink, but failed. At once he was taken down to await execution, too weak to struggle or shout his innocence. The same operation was carried out on the terrified Sergio, with the same result.

Minutes later, the bodies of the two men were dangling from the gallows.

CHAPTER SIXTEEN

FEAR AND TRAGEDY

Happiness is a dream,
sorrow lasts for ever.
Arabic proverb

'Dear husband, you can't carry on like this; slow down with
your work, otherwise you will pay with your health.'

With a good head for business – she took after her father –
Zeinab also meant that her husband should stop seeing the
destitute for nothing. They flocked to his door every morning,
drawn by his growing reputation, not only as a good physician
but also as a compassionate and generous man who, in

addition, provided them with the necessary medicines free of charge.

Aimeric grasped what his concerned wife was implying; hence his indirect reply, 'The more people I treat, with or without payment, the more my reputation spreads; besides, as you well know, I can't leave a sick person unattended over a question of money. Don't forget that I receive my reward from the well-to-do, often with sumptuous gifts. Those pay for the others and so everyone is even.'

Not wholly convinced, Zeinab left the matter at this point, knowing full well that she could say no more than she had already said.

Acre had now more or less recovered an air of normality after the turmoil which had followed the escape of the six Moslem prisoners. The commotion had died down with the killing of nearly all of those who had organized the escape. The one exception was Ismael, who had disappeared from Acre, leaving behind much bitterness for his unpunished role in the spiriting away of the invaluable hostages. His disappearance, however, could not be exploited by one Frankish community against another, for as a Moslem he had done what for them was understandable, if not admirable.

Surrounded by affection and attention, Zeinab reached the full term of her pregnancy and gave birth to a baby girl, helped by her mother and a woman from the neighbourhood who had some experience as a midwife. While his wife was in labour, Aimeric was not allowed in the room, for childbirth was deemed a matter which should be dealt with by women. He nevertheless stood by the door, ready to intervene if necessary.

The mother was very disappointed by the sex of her new baby; she had wished for and even expected a brother for Tanios and was unable to hide her frustration, despite the partly contrived manifestation of joy displayed by all. Not even the promise carried in the aphorism quoted by Shams and repeated by many others, 'With a girl comes her share of wealth,' could bring a smile to her face. None the less, it took Martha, the name chosen for the baby, less than a week to make her way into her mother's heart. As if aware of being unwelcomed, she multiplied smiles and gurgles and was a most well-behaved baby. Eventually, Zeinab clasped Martha to her heart and there she remained most of the time afterwards.

All the fuss about his sister deeply dissatisfied four-year-old Tanios and because of his odd behaviour he was taken to his grandmother's away from the cause of his unconscious jealousy. There he was utterly spoiled by Gerios who, in appearance at least, refused to bow to the 'operation of charm' deployed by Martha and maintained a determined preference for his grandson.

The extreme laxity shown towards Tanios by his grandfather worried Aimeric, who eventually took the decision to expose his son to a more enriching influence and, above all, provide him with an education. The education given to Aimeric by his parents had allowed him to learn the art of medicine away from home, earn a decent living and acquire a respected status in a faraway country. However, he was too busy to teach his son himself – even had Tanios not been asleep most of the time when he returned home late in the evening. And Zeinab, being illiterate, could not be of help.

The matter was resolved by Arnaud, who had made the acquaintance of an Italian friar prepared to teach not only Tanios but also Zeinab for a modest fee the art of deciphering the mysterious handwritten letters of the alphabet, of reproducing them and forming words. It was also arranged that during the lessons Martha would be in the care of her grandmother.

Friar Bonifacio was a middle-aged man with a reputation for piety. He had come to the Holy Land from Ravenna, his native town, some twenty years before and had stayed there, becoming fluent in Arabic.

Arrangements were made for him to call at Arnaud's lodgings every Monday and Thursday. The lessons took place at the workshop in the presence of Arnaud and Abdel Malek, his young apprentice, for it would have been improper to leave a young woman on her own with a person of the opposite sex, even if that person belonged to the Church.

Zeinab's joy knew no limits when she started recognizing the letters of the alphabet beautifully written on a time-worn scroll. Bonifacio was a dedicated teacher and his two pupils made good progress.

During one of the morning sessions, Arnaud unexpectedly left the workshop on urgent business, fully reassured that the proprieties would be observed due to Abdel Malek's presence. No account was taken of the devil inside the friar's mind, the lust he had secretly nurtured since Zeinab had first unveiled herself, having become accustomed to him and her trust in the man having slowly developed.

No sooner had Arnaud turned his back, than Bonifacio peremptorily commanded the apprentice to go to the tailor, Abraham the Jew, and take delivery of a garment he had ordered. Abdel Malek obeyed without a second thought.

Alone with Zeinab and Tanios, the friar turned his attention to the young woman and tried to take her in his arms to kiss her, paying scant attention to the child who looked on with big astonished eyes.

Zeinab endeavoured to free herself from his embrace and shouted for help, but Bonifacio put a strong hand over her mouth, nearly suffocating her. At the same time, he tried to force her on to the floor, but she resisted and bit the hand covering her mouth as fiercely as she could. The man screamed with pain and hit her in the face, which had the opposite effect and galvanized Zeinab into action; she cried out louder than ever and kicked her attacker. Tanios started crying, frightened by his mother's obvious distress.

At that moment, Arnaud returned and for a few seconds remained motionless, confounded by the appalling scene taking place in front of him. Quickly he got a grip on himself, seized an iron bar and struck the friar on the head; one blow was enough to send him to the floor, motionless.

Realizing the man was dead, Arnaud reacted swiftly. He bolted the workshop door, took Zeinab and Tanios by the hand straight to their room, instructing them not to leave it until he told them to do so. He then went back to the workshop and hid Bonifacio's body behind a pile of wood, unbolted the door to allow Abdel Malek in when he came back and sat down to get his breath back

He did not really know what to do; if he went to the sergeants in charge of maintaining peace and order, he would have to tell them why he had killed the friar and that would necessarily involve Zeinab's name, with all the inconvenience, to say the least, which would ensue, and the malicious gossip which would unavoidably be spread around.

The other choice was to transport the body somewhere close, without being seen, and maintain that the friar had left the workshop very much alive when he had finished his teaching. Arnaud favoured the latter, which had the advantage of sparing hardship to the dear ones he considered his family. He decided to wait until Aimeric returned before making any move — which, anyhow, would have to take place during the night.

He resumed his work as if nothing had happened, and when Abdel Malek reappeared he was told by his master that

Bonifacio had gone, leaving instructions to keep the garment at the workshop until the next lesson. From time to time, Arnaud went to Zeinab so she was not left too long on her own after her ordeal.

Once Aimeric was back and told about the circumstances of the friar's death, he raced to his wife and son to make sure that they had not been harmed. Both Tanios and Zeinab shed silent tears, afraid of making any noise which could attract attention. Aimeric gave them solace the best he could and asked Arnaud to take him to where Bonifacio's body was lying. He was not prompted by any morbid curiosity, but wished to verify that there was no sign of life in that body. When Aimeric had confirmed that the friar was indeed dead, he and Arnaud made preparations for the removal and disposal of the corpse. They decided to wait until late at night and take advantage of the respite to devise a good story in case they were stopped on their way and the nature of their load uncovered.

Every now and then Arnaud argued, 'I am the only one responsible for the killing. I don't want you to compromise everything you have achieved so far by giving me a hand. Go to Zeinab and Tanios, they need you.'

'Do you really expect me to leave you? Am I that brainless not to realize that what you did was for the sake of my honour? In case we come across any inquisitive person, leave the talking to me.'

'What could you convincingly say about two men carrying a body in the middle of the night?'

'You seem to forget that I am a physician. While I was on my way back home after my round of visits, I found the poor friar dead; he had had a bad fall and his head had struck a rock. I rushed to you, asking for your help to transport the poor man on your mule to a church where he could repose awaiting burial. That is all that I would say.'

In the event, the group formed by the two men and the mule carrying Bonifacio's body encountered no one. Aimeric stopped the mount next to a rocky place by the sea and indicated to his companion where and how to lay down the body. He then soaked a piece of material with the dead man's blood and pressed it against a protruding rock beside which the corpse had been made to lie.

Back home, Aimeric spent the rest of the night trying to reassure a shivering Zeinab and to comfort Tanios, who was unable to sleep.

'Forget about the whole incident,' he said. 'The body of that despicable man has been removed and his death will be blamed on an unfortunate fall.'

'What if I were to be taken to jail, what would happen to you and the children?'

'Nothing will happen to any of us. You have nothing to do with Bonifacio's death. Promise me, however, that you will not say a word about what took place here, not even to your mother.'

'I said nothing to her when she brought back Martha and I promise that I will say nothing to her or to anyone else.'

'What about Tanios? Will he keep quiet?'

'It is amazing; he seems to have forgotten all about the dreadful experience. Still, I am afraid that if he is questioned, he might suddenly remember and start talking.'

As Aimeric had anticipated, Bonifacio's death was put down to an unfortunate misadventure; not by everyone, however, for another friar, who belonged to the same confraternity as the dead man, started being inquisitive about Bonifacio's last hours. Where had he been after teaching Zeinab and Tanios? And why did he go to the seashore where he had his fatal 'fall', knowing that he had no business whatsoever in that part of the town? These were the questions which puzzled the friar.

Seeing him around the house made Zeinab very nervous, so it was decided that she and Tanios should be taken by Gerios to Jbail for a short stay with her uncle and his family. In her absence, Shams would take care of little Martha while Aimeric went about his professional activities which he could hardly desert. Although it was Arnaud who should have been more concerned, having delivered the deadly blow, his nerves, toughened by years of struggle and ordeal, allowed him to confront any unpleasant situation.

Understandably, Zeinab's parents were concerned about her unexpected trip to Jbail. Her mother took her daughter aside and asked, 'Are you sure all is well between you and your husband?'

'Of course, everything is fine.'

'I carried you in my womb for nine months. No one loves you more than I do. If there is any misunderstanding with Aimeric, it is me you should confide in.'

'I assure you there is nothing of the sort. We love each other very dearly. All I need is a little change; my husband is more busy than ever and cannot accompany us. That is all.'

Shams was not convinced by what she was told, but wisely decided not to pursue her questioning. Preparations for the journey were speedily made amidst increased tension in Acre between, on the one hand, Templars and Venetians, and on the other, the Hospitallers, the Teutonic Knights and the party of King Hugh.

After the departure for Jbail of Gerios and his daughter-in-law and grandson, riots broke out on the streets of Acre between Moslem merchants from Bethlehem and Nestorian merchants from Mosul. The former had placed themselves under the Templars' protection and the latter under the Hospitallers'. The riots spread and took on a serious dimension precisely because of this support. It was not only the merchants who were fighting each other but, in addition, their protectors had joined in the fight as well as the usual rabble of criminals. Peaceful citizens stayed indoors and the majority of the shops remained closed most of the time as everyone was afraid of being caught in the middle of frenzied violence. Even inside their homes and behind their locked doors no one was safe, because looters and robbers, more daring by the day, had realized they could go about their wicked business with total impunity. Anarchy it might have been, nevertheless the acts of despoliation were well organized. Criminals had their informers who told them where to find valuables or an easy prey.

Word had come to a gang of particularly vicious felons that a woman, Shams as it happened, stood alone between them and a shop full of merchandise. On that account, the gang made a forced entry into Gerios' shop during the night and started piling all the goods that they could get their hands on into large, strong bags.

Shams was awakened by the noise that the thieves made. She hid little Martha in a corner of the room above the shop, making sure the baby could not roll out across the floor, and cautiously went down the stairs to find out the cause of the noise. She found herself face to face with the members of the gang.

One of them threatened her with a knife, while placing a forefinger on his lips to make her understand that she must remain silent. She obeyed and stood still in the middle of the shop, which was now almost empty of merchandise.

Their job almost completed, one of the criminals had another look at the woman standing in front of him and found her to his liking. He came close to Shams and started fondling her. She struggled with her assailant, shouting for help. He took fright and savagely stabbed her with a knife. The blow went straight to Shams's heart; she fell to the floor and died instantly.

The gang fled, but not without taking their bags full of the loot. Despite the commotion which had most certainly been heard by their neighbours, no one dared come straightaway to investigate. Fear had taken a grip on the whole town and everyone kept to themselves.

With the first light, a few people plucked up enough courage to make their way to Gerios' shop. They found the door half open and cautiously entered. One woman, aware of Gerios' absence, called out Shams's name; her shout was transformed into a shriek of terror when she stumbled on her body.

Fortunately, she remembered that Martha had been in the care of her grandmother and rushed upstairs looking for her. Finding her fast asleep, she took her in her arms and silently wept.

CHAPTER SEVENTEEN

TO GIBELET

Grieve for the living
not for the dead
Turkish proverb

'How did it happen? How *could* it happen? I don't believe I won't see her ever again. She was more than a mother, she was the one I always turned to for advice and solace.' Zeinab buried her face in her hands, sobbing. Tanios came close to her and rested his head on her knees, his lips trembling.

They were both sitting on the floor of the room above the ransacked shop; with them were Aimeric and a prostrated, broken-hearted Gerios, unable to say a word — he who was usually so loquacious. One more time Aimeric patiently explained, with slight exasperation in his voice, 'I had to bury her before your return. Arnaud and I made all the necessary arrangements for her to have a beautiful funeral.'

Aware of how much appearances meant for his father-in-law, he added, 'All the neighbours, horrified and in mourning, attended the church service and accompanied her to her last resting place. The Grand Master of the Templars and the Communes each very graciously sent a representative who stayed until the end of the ceremony.'

The last part of Aimeric's address was intended to bring comfort to Gerios who would have been thrilled to hear such names had the circumstances been different. This time he did not stir from the depths of his despair and prostration, which Aimeric broke once more.

'Come and stay with us until we all move to a bigger house. This place is full of both happy and terrible memories, you shouldn't remain here on your own.'

'I will not stay in Acre one day more than necessary after the mass which I intend to see celebrated to mark the fortieth day following the death of my beloved wife.'

Zeinab raised her head and looked at her father with an alarmed and enquiring expression.

He looked determined. 'I have made up my mind. I am going to move to Jbail; you will come and visit me as often as possible. Once there, I don't believe I myself could stand coming back to Acre.' Unexpectedly, Gerios lost control of himself and burst into tears. His daughter hugged him and joined in the crying, followed by Tanios, unable to hold back his own tears any longer.

Extremely moved by this sight, Aimeric impulsively exclaimed, 'I have a better idea. Why don't we all settle in Jbail?'

As his wife and father-in-law stared at him, not believing what they had just heard, he repeated, 'Yes, why don't we all settle in your native town, where we have a loving family and friendly surroundings. I am truly disgusted with the behaviour of the people of Acre. I need a more peaceful environment in which to raise my family and practise my art. Yes, let's all go there. Arnaud might even be convinced to come and live with us.'

In the early part of 1277, Aimeric and his young family, moved to Jbail, the major town of Guy's principality. They went by road, which took a little longer than by sea, but was more comfortable in winter. Gerios had preceeded them to buy a house large enough to accommodate them all.

Parting from Arnaud, who had been steadfast in his refusal to leave Acre, had been highly emotional for everyone. Although they promised each other to stay in touch at least once a year, they all knew that the best of intentions could be defeated by adverse circumstances impossible to disregard, knowing the ever-volatile situation in Outremer. At first Arnaud had intended to accompany them part of the way, but then he changed his mind, overcome by strong feelings of emotion.

So he bade them farewell, watching them with their hired mules, overloaded with belongings and human charges, leave town from its northern gate with their guide and escort. He stood on the wall walk, waving goodbye, as they all waved back.

Gradually, before his eyes, Aimeric, his family and their party faded and disappeared from his view. That was too much for the old man. Head bent, he trod heavily in the direction of a home which, only a few days before, he could not wait a minute more than necessary to regain and be reunited with a family he considered his own. God only knew how much he was going to miss Aimeric's company, Zeinab's freshness of youth and the laughs and cries of the two little ones, in particular Martha, who needed more of the attention taken away by her brother.

In a matter of a few months he had lost all the friends dear to his heart. First had been Shams, the only woman he had ever really loved; neither finding the courage nor having the will to show her his feelings out of respect for her and her husband, he had been satisfied to revere her in secret as long as he knew she would always be around. But now that she had gone for ever, his earlier reserve appeared pointless and he could not help feeling a sense of bitterness and regret.

Then it was Gerios who had left Acre, probably never to come back, and he would certainly miss him. The two of them were very different; nevertheless, the Cathar had grown fond of the Maronite, once he had discovered behind the superficiality and ostentation an extremely good-hearted and hospitable man who would never knowingly do harm to anyone.

His entire life was shattered and he did not deem that the pieces left were worth reconstructing. He felt like someone waking up from a delightful dream to be confronted with grim reality. After all, were not the last few years a passing dream? Now that he thought of it, he had no one and nothing legitimately for himself; his love had not been his to hug and treasure and Aimeric was his old companion's son, not his own. Zeinab loved him like an uncle and from time to time would have a heartfelt thought for him; as for Tanios and Martha, they were too young to indulge in sad and nostalgic reminiscence.

Being on his own most of the time now, except when he worked at the forge with Abdel Malek or when he saw a client, Arnaud became almost a recluse, living in the past with his memories. As for the present, he only allowed his thoughts to travel to Jbail to share the new life of his adopted family, which he saw as peaceful and joyful. Exhausted after a hard day's work, he would take a little rest, absorbed in the contemplation of the fire at his forge or of the stars on a warm evening.

Unfortunately, peace was not to be enjoyed at Jbail, but Arnaud had no means of knowing that or of having any hint about the war which was being prepared for by Guy of Gibelet and his Overlord, Bohemond of Tripoli, one against the other and each one sweeping along with him a faction of the Maronite community, thus divided into two feuding camps.

This division within the community had reached families; sons stood against their fathers and brothers against brothers; wisdom and restraint were branded treason and pusillanimity. Instead of the peace and harmony that Aimeric and his family had expected to find in Jbail, they encountered gloom and discord. Elias's family was not spared the disease of dissension, and if its members loved and respected each other enough to prevent open hostility, they had divided loyalties, nevertheless.

Dawud had become a priest, a follower of Bishop Luke of Bnahran, unlike his father who had remained a priest loyal to the Church of Rome. The Bishop and a large section of his flock, recruited especially from among the inhabitants of the mountains, had reverted to the forsaken belief of the Maronite Church in Christ's one Will. This religious revival was coupled with fierce nationalism, fuelled by the excesses and arrogance of those Franks who remained immune to anything Oriental and of the Latin clergy, both being a source of suffering and great disillusionment for the local Christians.

Guy of Gibelet, who presented himself as the champion of the *Poulains* and of those Christians, supported the rebellious movement. What he expected to achieve was peace in his lands and local backing against Bohemond, Overlord of Tripoli, and his Roman faction.

Dawud, his brothers and sisters, and even Hanneh their mother, all favoured Luke's movement, whereas *Bouna* Elias and Gerios were more cautious.

Since the time the immigrants from Acre had taken up residence in Gibelet, an uneasy climate had prevailed whenever the young members of the family met with the elderly ones. Aimeric was caught in the middle and tried hard to find a subject of conversation which was not controversial.

The news of Baybars' death, which occurred during the first summer the two families had spent together, was a welcome digression which abated internal quarrels. Franks and local Christians were overjoyed by the demise of their feared enemy, which they saw as a sign from Heaven telling them they had not been abandoned, and for a time they savoured their common joy. What they did not realize was that a more deadly danger was looming before them.

One afternoon, the Lord of Gibelet summoned Aimeric and Dawud to present themselves immediately at his castle. The two men were startled and slightly worried by the command, which did not seem related to the art of healing either body or soul.

Brought to Guy's presence by two pages, they listened with growing nervousness to his instructions.

'Signor Aimeric, I am going to entrust you with a secret mission of the utmost importance. I would like you to go to Acre as speedily as you can. There you will see the Templars' Grand Master, Guillaume de Beaujeu; request from him, in my name, armed forces for the defence of Gibelet.

'Father Dawud, go to my good friend Bishop Luke of Bnahran, and request from him as many Maronite archers and fighters as he can mobilize. I will meet them with my own fighting forces at Ma'ad on the first day of the last week of July.

'I count on you both during these trying days. Don't fail

me.' These last words the Prince pronounced half pleadingly, half threateningly.

The two young men left the castle more bewildered than before. The priest, with the optimism of youth, interpreted Guy's words the way he wanted them to mean. 'I'm sure our Lord is preparing a punitive raid against those who claim to be Maronites, but are Rome's lackeys and a thorn in the side of our Lord.'

'I'm afraid the matter is more serious than that. Otherwise, why should the Templars be summoned to the rescue?'

'What do you think, then?' asked Dawud, disquieted.

Aimeric looked at him gravely. 'There are rumours that Bohemond has gone back on his earlier promise to give the hand of the heiress Aleman to John, our Lord's brother. I wonder whether the intended gathering of armed forces is not the prelude to a war with Tripoli.'

'You may well be right, for I heard, only yesterday, that not only was the girl kidnapped and married to John, but in addition, all her lands and assets were seized by her husband.'

The two men looked at each other with increased concern and walked home to prepare for their respective missions.

On horseback, on his way to the capital of the Kingdom of Jerusalem and accompanied by one servant, Aimeric had ample time to reflect on this new turn of events in his life, 'Why am I involved with the quarrels between these Catholics? I don't even hate them any more, despite the sufferings they inflicted on my family and people.'

The last thing he wanted was to become embroiled in these wranglings, yet he had to be, whether he liked it or not. The momentous events which he could see coming made him wonder whether moving with his family to Gibelet had not been a mistake. Most probably it was, but it too late now to do anything about it. He promised himself to keep aloof from the coming storm after he had fulfilled the mission entrusted to him.

The only advantage he could see in being a most reluctant messenger was the opportunity to press Arnaud to his heart much sooner than he had ever dreamed. With that pleasant prospect in mind, he spurred his mount on and continued his journey in a better mood.

In the meantime, Dawud, on the back of a mule, had started his own journey towards the village of Bnahran, the seat of Bishop Luke who led the Maronite separatist movement from Rome.

Bnahran lay nestled in the highland, half-way between the coast and the valley of the Qadisha. The valley was situated high in the mountains, at the foot of a forest of cedars several hundred years old, and had been the early refuge of the Maronites fleeing Byzantine persecution. It was now inhabited by monks who led a solitary and godly life in the dozens of caves which riddled its flanks. In time of danger, the people of the villages that crowned the surrounding peaks took refuge in these impregnable caves. The visitor who looked at the panorama from a high vantage point was given the impression, amplified by the majestic backdrop of the mountains, that he had surely reached the end of the world.

The young priest followed the coastline northwards until he reached the town of Boutron, from there he started the ascent towards his objective, following a steep, narrow path. From time to time, he had to dismount to relieve the mule of its burden, particularly when the path skirted deep and frightening gorges. But he eventually reached Bnahran safely and, at his request, was taken to the Bishop.

Bishop Luke was a middle-aged man of short stature, indistinguishable from other people around him except for the attention accorded him by others. Dawud went straight to the man he had come to meet, bent over his hand and kissed it. When he straightened up, he could see the Prelate's piercing eyes assessing him.

After the exchanges necessary for the observance of proprieties, and to allow the traveller to introduce himself and rest, the bishop signalled to Dawud to follow him to the privacy of an adjoining room. There he listened to the message brought to him, reflected for a long moment and, before giving any answer to be reported to the Lord of Gibelet, asked, 'Tell me, *Bouna* Dawud, how is the mood of our brothers of the littoral?'

His young visitor hesitated a moment between a polite answer and the truth; he decided on the latter. 'All the young people are with us; the others prudently wait to see which way the wind blows.'

Bishop Luke produced a quick smile instead of a comment, as if to say, I know the kind of people you refer to. He then invited his visitor to wait in an adjacent room and convened *muqaddem*, other chieftains and men of religion to join him to discuss Guy's request, which could have grave consequences.

After talks lasting several hours, the messenger was told to rest for the night, return to Gibelet the following day and convey the promise that a fighting corps of two hundred Maronites would be in readiness at the place and time indicated.

Aimeric was also successful as regarded his mission. A few days later he was back at Gibelet, accompanied by thirty Templars sent by the Grand Master for the defence of the town.

With the presence of the Knights from Acre, tension mounted in Gibelet; there was talk of war and rumblings of discontent abounded. The elders were not duped by the contrived explanations given for the prevailing tension with

Tripoli and were well aware that a private quarrel was about to degenerate into an internecine war of vast proportions which could draw to an end the Frankish presence on the littoral.

They were, however, unable to contain the young blood among the Maronites, including Dawud and his brothers and sisters, who interpreted the alliance between their Frankish Lord and the faction of their Church, which was trying to free itself from the subjection to Rome, as the prelude to more self-determination over their mountains.

A perplexed Aimeric did not know where to stand in the midst of what had become a highly controversial and endless issue. On the one hand, he was wary of anything religious and particularly any dispute rooted in religion; on the other, he could see the enthusiasm of the young Maronites around him for what he sensed they believed to be a struggle for more autonomy for their community. Was not that struggle much the same as the desperate combat conducted by the Cathars of older generations for the independence of their beloved Languedoc, which had ended so tragically?

Aimeric sank into deep melancholy, not knowing what to believe and how to behave. This worried Zeinab, who could not guess the reason for her husband's sombre mood. Then one evening in the privacy of their modest room, while the two children were asleep and Gerios was out chatting with his brother, she took all her courage in her hands and asked, 'Is there anything I have done which has displeased you? If that is the case, I am ready to make amends...to do anything to bring back a smile to your face.'

Those simple words, coming from her heart, deeply touched Aimeric, who felt terribly guilty for having conveyed the wrong impression to the woman he still loved very dearly. He suddenly realized how much he had neglected her these last weeks, being preoccupied with an obsessive dilemma. He held her in his arms for a long, silent moment, then their bodies became locked together in an unbridled, passionate embrace.

CHAPTER EIGHTEEN

INTERNECINE WAR

Under the walls of Gibelet castle and in the oppressive heat, a hundred knights waited to receive their marching orders. Among the colourful surcoats worn on top of their mail, the attractive lance pennons and the helmets with flamboyant crests carried by squires, a company of some thirty knights, in full control of themselves, stood out in sharp contrast with the surrounding clamour. They wore the same white coat, with a red cross on the left breast, and another on their distinctive kite-shaped shields. They were the dreaded Knights of the Temple who, when they joined the Order, swore to fight to the death, to accept every combat, even when outnumbered, to ask no quarter and to give none. The other Knights who would fight side by side with the Templars looked at them with unease, for their carefully cultivated reputation for ferocity had struck the hardest of men.

War-horses covered with leather and quilted trappers and protected by defensive metal plating formed with squires and sergeants another boisterous group.

All of a sudden the tumult died down as Guy, his two brothers and a small retinue stormed across the drawbridge on their mounts. With them rode Aimeric who was required to join the expedition in his capacity as a physician. Hence he was unarmed and not equipped for fighting. He carried behind him a box, carefully fastened, containing medical instruments, bandages and a variety of substances for medication.

Dawud had been sent ahead the day before to see with his own eyes that the reinforcement expected from the Maronite Bishop was indeed ready to march. Since the young emissary had not come back, it was assumed that Luke had been true to his word.

Bidding farewell to Aimeric and Dawud had been a painful but somehow restrained ceremony for their families. *Bouna* Elias and Gerios had shown their disapproval of Dawud's active involvement by remaining mostly silent the whole evening which preceded the young priest's departure to Ma'ad, while his brothers and sisters, full of excitement, had circled him untiringly, asking dozens of questions such as, 'Will you be armed?' 'Will you fight?' Their mother had rebuked them, requesting a little calm, and then had kept herself busy, unwilling to give herself time to reflect on what might happen to her eldest son whom she loved dearly and admired profoundly. Not for a moment, not even in her heart, had she reproached him for making a commitment she regarded as a sacred duty.

Contrary to her husband, who had lived all his life in Jbail, by the sea, and was endowed with a benevolence acquired by contact with all sorts of people, Hanneh had been born and raised in Hasrun, an isolated village overlooking the valley of the Qadisha and situated some two thousand metres above the sea. The people of the mountains were tough and hard, like their weather and their surroundings. Once they had made up their minds, no one and nothing could change them. Having, in their majority, adhered to the dissident movement started by their Church, they were ready to support the cause whatever the cost. Obviously Hanneh would not sacrifice someone she loved for just any reason, but it was a distinctive feature of people committed to a cause not to perceive its possible unpleasant consequences and, if occasionally they did just that, these disquieting thoughts were promptly dismissed.

Aimeric's inclinations were quite the opposite; he did not want to take part in the quarrels which opposed Gibelet to Tripoli, and the Maronites faithful to Rome to those against, but how could he refuse to accompany his Lord at a time when his skills would be much needed. He had tried to alleviate Zeinab's fears by telling her that he would have to stay away from the scene of battle, waiting for the wounded to be brought to him. 'Believe me, I will not be in any danger at any time.'

Zeinab had put her arms tightly around her husband. 'Please think of the children, think of me. For our sake, don't take any risks. You are more valuable to us than any belief, however dear it is to my heart.'

With these touching words in his mind, Aimeric followed the small army which had been given the order to march by the Lord of Gibelet, who placed himself at its head, immediately followed by the Knights of the Temple. Still restrained, yet as threatening as ever, their contingent presented a formidable fighting corps.

The troops journeyed along the coast, a ride of about two hours, until they reached the Madfoon river. There they dismounted to allow the horses to rest and drink, and to await and join up with the Maronite fighters.

A short while later, Dawud appeared on horseback, accompanied by three stern-faced mounted chieftains. Behind, and in tumultuous disorder, came archers equipped with short-bows, foot soldiers armed with axes and long spears, and slingers with a long knife inserted in the belts which held in their short tunics at the waist, leaving their bare legs unhindered and free to move quickly – some two hundred soldiers in all.

Almost at the same time, a local scout came at a gallop from a northerly direction and reined in his horse beside the Lord of Gibelet. 'Forces of about two hundred and fifty soldiers have left Tripoli on their way south,' he announced, out of breath.

'Is Bohemond in command?' asked Guy.

'I haven't seen him, my Lord. I believe Roger de la Colée is at the head of the forces.'

'Are there many knights among them?'

'I have seen with my own eyes and counted some one hundred of them; the rest are foot soldiers.'

'Good man. Have some rest and something to eat... Take this for your pains.' Magnanimously the Master of Gibelet threw a purse to the scout who, with great dexterity, caught it in mid-air. Guy then turned to his brothers and all of them made fun of Bohemond, whom they branded a coward for not having the stomach to fight his own wars.

With no more time to lose, orders were given to the knights and foot soldiers to prepare for battle; the former were handed their helmets and lances by their squires, while the rest checked their weapons.

Aimeric took advantage of the preparations to accost

Dawud, who appeared to be avoiding him. 'You aren't going to fight, are you?'

'What do you expect me to do? Watch from the sideline my brothers fighting and maybe getting killed for a cause I encouraged them to join?'

The order to march being shouted out prevented the two men from pursuing a discussion which, anyhow, seemed to be leading nowhere.

The knights were deployed in three divisions, each division consisting of three lines, each first line held by the Templars. The foot soldiers were amassed behind the mounted soldiers in more or less orderly fashion and given instructions for when the fight began. The small army then started moving, but at a slow pace, in order not to distance those who rode from those who were walking and to avoid tiring the horses.

The two opposing armies came face to face at a place between Boutron and le Puy du Connétable. Following their respective orders, the cavalry halted to allow the infantry to go ahead and deploy into two masses. At the front were the spearmen, who presented to the cavalry of the enemy a hedge of spear points; behind them, the archers and slingers started hurling their missiles, while at the rear stood the knights, seething with impatience but controlled by the commander-in-chief.

The missiles wreaked havoc among the Tripoli troops, which prompted Roger de la Colée to order the cavalry to charge. The horses in the first wave were confronted with the hedge of spears, and panicked; some unseated their riders while others held back, refusing to budge; the following wave crushed against the first and pandemonium ensued.

This was the moment Guy was awaiting; he ordered his cavalry to charge, compelling Bohemond's forces to retreat in great disorder, leaving behind many dead and wounded.

Roger de la Colée was captured, brought before Guy and beheaded; other illustrious prisoners who had fallen wounded during the battle were finished off without mercy.

Aimeric, who had witnessed from a distance the battle and the sinister deeds which followed, attended to the wounded from Guy's camp, while searching for Dawud with worried eyes. He was nowhere to be seen and Aimeric's concern grew. When at last he had finished dressing wounds and fixing broken bones as best he could, he started looking for the young priest on the battlefield. Eventually he found him, unconscious, lying face down on the ground. Aimeric carefully turned him over and a nasty chest wound came into view; it was a wound that must have been inflicted by a spear or some other pointed weapon.

The physician staunched the flow of blood, examined the wound and covered it with an ointment he deftly prepared. He sought the help of two passing Maronite soldiers, who lifted the priest, still unconscious, on to the back of a mule, then he asked one of the soldiers to take the reins of the animal. They cautiously made their way towards Hamat, the closest village. He himself controlled his own horse with one hand and walked beside the wounded man, his other hand extended over him to prevent a possible fall, while he lent an attentive ear to the rhythm of his breathing.

Eventually the procession reached Hamat, where Aimeric knocked at the door of the first decent dwelling they came across. An agreement was rapidly reached with the couple who opened the door. In no time, *Bouna* Dawud was laid down on a bundle of hay, still attended to by Aimeric. Expecting a long stay where they were, he despatched his companion to Gibelet to inform their family who, as was to be expected, would now be extremely worried about their fate.

After a few hours of Aimeric's constant and skilled

treatment, as taught by Samuel, his beloved Master, Dawud opened his eyes and painfully smiled at his delighted carer. The prospects of recovery seemed to be good, on condition that the wounded young man agreed not to move from where he was until he got back a minimum of strength.

On the second day, the young Maronite appeared eager to talk. 'What happened to me?' he asked.

'Don't you remember?'

'Not a single thing after the first clashes.'

'You have been badly wounded, but you are on the mend. By the way, your party won; Tripoli's forces were completely routed.'

The young priest raised his arms towards the roof and feebly uttered, 'Praise be! I knew that God would not abandon us.'

'Now that you've done your deal, no one can blame you for stepping aside.'

Dawud gazed at him in astonishment. 'Stepping aside? Never! The moment I can get on a horse I will resume what I consider to be my duty.'

Not willing to tire his patient, Aimeric shrugged his shoulders and urged him to rest and not to speak any more. In the afternoon of the following day, while the physician was outdoors talking to his hosts, three mounted figures appeared, silhouetted against the sun. As they got closer, he was able to make out Zeinab, *Bouna* Elias and Hanneh, riding mules. Before long, they fell into each other's arms. Dawud's parents were relieved to be assured that their son was still alive and, without wasting any more time, they entered the room where he was resting to see with their own eyes that it was true.

Having recommended that they did not tire him, Aimeric, took Zeinab outside. Unable to control herself she said, sobbing, 'My dear father has remained with the children, otherwise he would be here too. He wanted me to stay and he himself to come, but I refused. I was afraid that you might be wounded or, worse, dead. I wanted to see you and not just hear of your condition.'

He took her in his arms. 'You can plainly see that I am still in one piece. Don't cry any more.'

'Promise me that you will never again take part in an armed expedition.'

'I promise.'

Aimeric made the promise expected from him knowing full well that if he were ordered by his Lord to second him in time of war, he would have no choice but to obey. Sombre thoughts passed into his mind, casting a shadow on the joyful reunion. He mused how restricted his power was to decide the course of his life and he wondered whether he could ever be the master of his own destiny – if anyone could.

CHAPTER NINETEEN

FALTERING TRUCE

'Tell us, how did you receive your wound?'

Gathered around Dawud, his brothers and sisters, as well as relatives and neighbours, demanded to hear an account of the battle which had already been given to them dozens of times.

Dawud had come back to Jbail to a hero's welcome, but he was still convalescing. With the passing of time he had recovered his memory of all the events which had taken place the day he was almost killed, up until the time he fell. He obligingly responded to their request.

'We withstood the first assault of the cavalry and we routed them; another wave was thrown against us, and behind the mounted assailants crept foot soldiers, most of them Maronites, lackeys of Rome.' Pausing for a moment he then continued, more for himself than for his audience. 'I remember, as if the events were unfolding at this very moment, that one of those miserable wretches – I will most certainly recognize his dreadful face again – came running with a spear pointed straight at me. I could see him getting closer, but I could do nothing to prevent being run through: the strap of my shield was entangled with my saddle and I couldn't lift it for protection. The next thing I remember is falling from my horse – and then nothing.'

'Tell us in detail what happened before that,' urged his younger brother Ghantus, keen to hear about glorious deeds and not the hero fainting.

The young priest smiled and was about to work out an imaginary heroic feat so as not to disappoint his eager listeners, when Hanneh entered the room. She gave her son a quick, loving glance and promptly dismissed the visitors, fearing that they might have tired him already. He did not object and took her hand and kissed it. They exchanged looks of deep affection and tender understanding.

When Hanneh first saw her wounded son, lying in agony under a roof which was not his, her first thought had been of guilt for having supported his struggle, though mostly in silence, for that was all she was allowed in terms of support. Now that he was under her care, a sense of pride had taken over, fuelled by the many visitors who came to pay their respects and show solidarity.

She held back a smile and, as if Dawud was privy to her inner thoughts and needed no explanation, asked, 'Had we been defeated, would there have been as many?'

He immediately grasped her point and replied, 'No one wants to be a partner in defeat. Even Jesus Christ, when arrested, was abandoned by his disciples and disowned by Boutrus. Do you expect our cowardly and opportunistic fellow citizens to behave otherwise?' He then added, 'Can you imagine Istifan or Ayyub asking after me if I were taken prisoner by a victorious Bohemond?'

Hearing the names of the two most selfish persons in town, two opportunists totally devoid of any principles or scruples, she burst into laughter, joined by Dawud who winced and pressed his wound to ease the pain caused by his uncontrollable shaking.

Just at that moment Aimeric entered the room to visit his patient, as he did at least three times a day. Smiling, he enquired, 'What is the matter?'

Then addressing Dawud he gently rebuked him, 'You shouldn't get yourself into this state, although I am glad to see you happy. Happiness is a sign of good health.'

Mother and son shared their thoughts with him, bringing a smile to his face, which had something to do with the two persons named by Dawud, and also a little with his father-in-law and *Bouna* Elias who had shifted from tacit disapproval of Dawud's active commitment to open approval. In front of their lost-in-wonder visitors they described the sequence of events of the battle as if they had participated themselves; it could be that they would end up believing they had! Naturally, Dawud's role in the fighting was exaggerated to the extent that it became unrecognizable to him.

Aimeric did not dwell long on the strange behaviour of human beings and went on with the business of examining his cousin's injury. Satisfied with the progress, to raise his spirits he told him, 'I have just come from the castle. I learnt there that a truce has been signed between our Lord and Bohemond...a truce for a year.'

If the physician had expected to cheer up his patient, he was to be disappointed, for Dawud's reaction was vehement. 'We did not fight for such a result. What we are after is more autonomy from a Church that is treating us with contempt. Until we get it we won't, we *shouldn't*, cease the struggle.'

Hanneh was as disappointed as her son and made her disenchantment clear. 'If it is solely a quarrel between Frankish lords, why should we take part at all?'

'Mother, as soon as I feel better and I am able to ride, my first visit will be to Bishop Luke. He must know something that we don't and must have informed views on the future.'

'Let's hope you are right,' she said with a deep sigh.

Not expecting what he had thought to be good news to have such an affect on his relatives, Aimeric left them to continue his round of patients. The rich and powerful did not come to him, he had to go to them. Some of his visits were completely useless when the allegedly sick persons were no more than hypochondriacs, afraid of illness. However, he pretended to believe that they were affected by the ailment of their imagination and comforted them the best he could. Samuel of Scandalion had taught him that illness could be in the mind as often as in the body. Sometimes he was lavishly paid for the care he had provided, and at other times an offhand oversight left him without payment he could not claim for fear of offending. With time, he had acquired the sort of philosophy which prompted him to accept things as they came as long as they had no profound effect on him or on his family.

During the round, the truce which had been proclaimed was discussed and, in general, received with satisfaction and relief by the Franks he met. Only a few pessimists questioned why the truce was for one year only. Did it mean, in true fact, that the antagonists were tired and needed a respite before resuming warfare?

Normally the local people came to him at home to be treated. So he did not know exactly what their thoughts were about the latest events, but the gloomy ambience of the town could be read as a sign that they must have shared Dawud and his mother's views.

When he returned home late in the afternoon, Zeinab met her husband with a question which seemed to burn her lips. 'Is it true that a truce was proclaimed and that Bishop Luke was not even consulted about it?'

'What I know for sure is that there is a suspension of hostilities for a year. That is the good news. I know nothing about the other matter.'

Zeinab adamantly refused to be appeased or to question her own query, which was more of an outraged announcement. She pursued, 'It is unacceptable to stop the war at this point. What have we gained? Nothing.'

The whole atmosphere of Jbail, charged with religious excitement and intolerance, as well as the influence brought upon her by her young cousins, had eventually swayed Zeinab, who rallied to Luke's cause and was watched by Aimeric with gentle bewilderment.

Gerios, who had joined in the conversation, seemed to have lost his fighting spirit and regained his usual common sense. All bragging forgotten, he added to the discussion a comment which had the effect of infuriating his daughter. 'What do you know about politics...you are only a woman! At least we have peace, and business can be resumed.'

Aimeric changed the subject to avoid any argument developing. 'Last night I dreamed of my beloved mother. She and I were strolling in a splendid garden, an exact replica of the Garden of Eden. As we followed a most exquisite, flowery path, we met Arnaud, our dear friend. We did not seem to recognize each other and our paths crossed without a single word exchanged. But when I woke up I was bemused and wondered how could we have ignored each other as if we were perfect strangers? What does this curious dream mean? Can anyone tell me?'

'I pray to God that no mishap ever befalls Arnaud. But I am afraid what is meant by you and your mother not recognizing him is that he is gravely ill or, worse, that he is no more of this world,' replied Gerios.

'I do also hope that my mother is in good health. Maybe I should go back to Milan and see her,' muttered Aimeric to himself.

After the elapse of a few months, thanks to the skilled care dispensed by Aimeric, his young cousin was able to wander in the house and the garden for most of the day, even though his wound still troubled him. One morning he made known his resolution to visit the Bishop of Bnahran.

'My son, you are too weak for such a journey,' objected Hanneh.

'But I have to know why our community was prevented from gaining any of its objectives, why the war we were winning has come to an end and what the plans are for the future. All that I have to know.'

'At least let Yusuf go with you.'

What Hanneh did not disclose yet was that she also had it in mind to ask Aimeric to accompany them and be with Dawud in case the journey proved too strenuous for him or his wound reopened. It was a request the physician could not and would not refuse and so a few days later the three were on their way, travelling in easy stages to reach Bnahran.

They were welcomed by Luke, who received them surrounded by a number of other visitors. Invited to sit, the three newcomers accommodated themselves cross-legged on the carpet, which was the only furnishing in the room. Once they had settled, Dawud looked around and made an incredible discovery. Here, among those present, sat the man who had nearly killed him. He kept his composure and did not allow the turmoil in his mind to show. He did not even tell his two companions of this amazing coincidence, afraid that they might not have been able to retain their own composure in the same way.

Knowing that his visitors from afar had not come to him for a social call, Luke indicated to them to follow him into the privacy of another room. There, to his bewildered audience, the young priest revealed what he had found out.

'Are you absolutely sure that is the same man?' asked the Bishop.

'Positive. How could I forget the face and the eyes of my would-be killer?'

'Tell me exactly; where is he sitting?'

'He was the third person on your left.'

The Bishop remained lost in thought for a while and then declared, 'That is Sim'an from Duma and, on reflection, I am inclined to believe that you are not mistaken.'

Yusuf put his hand on his dagger and made a move towards the door. He was prevented from going any further by Luke's words. 'Let's be as cunning as this man. After all, we could use him to feed our enemies false information about future moves and lines of thinking. When he becomes useless to us, he will be all yours, my son.'

These words had the effect of calming Yusuf down and all present agreed on how to behave in front of the traitor, Sim'an.

The matter having been settled for the time being, the young priest turned to the subject about which he had come to see the dignitary. Choosing his words carefully, he questioned the relevance of a truce where nothing had been achieved. Having been wounded in battle gave him, to a certain extent, the right to ask questions.

The prelate's answer was to the point and apparently very candid. 'In our struggle, we are not on our own. We are supported by a mighty Frankish faction and we in turn give it our full support. Going to battle, observing a truce, making peace: all that needs a joint decision. Tremendous pressure was exerted on Lord Gibelet to stop the fighting; he had to comply after consulting with me.

'You, Dawud my son, were not aware of the consultation because you were lying wounded, and I didn't have the pleasure of knowing Yusuf, who is visiting me for the first time. But I and Lord Guy did have an exchange of views and I realized that there had to be a respite in the struggle for the time being.

'Prepare yourselves for another armed confrontation which may occur sooner than later. This time, I promise you, there will be no pause until we realize all our objectives. Come with me; let's go back to my visitors. Act normally with Sim'an. Leave the matter to me.'

CHAPTER TWENTY

THE WARRING PATRIARCH

After a night spent in Bnahran, the three men from Gibelet wended their way back on their mules, which made careful progress down the steep paths; they did not need close attention as they knew by instinct where to tread. Aimeric gave free rein to his thoughts.

Amazingly, while under the prelate's spell, he had enthused over a cause which was not his. However, during the night he had had time to reflect on the futility of actively fighting for any cause, however just it might be. True, he himself had been prepared to kill for an ideal, but a short sojourn in Outremer had been enough to make him change his mind.

He continued to reflect to himself how a place where all sorts of fanaticism grow like weeds can also incite deep scepticism. Abhorrent deeds which are inspired by one mental state may also prompt the other.

Aimeric's inner transformation had been kept to himself; no one had had to know about it, not even Arnaud. It would have been too painful for the old man to be told of more religious disaffection. He had shared with him his doubts and temporary irresolution about the mission, but he had never told Arnaud about his fundamental change of heart and his eventual loss of faith. The only person he had fully confided in, short of telling him the real nature of his mission, had been Samuel of Scandalion, somehow a stranger compared to his father's old friend and fellow Cathar. It was often the case that one found oneself confiding one's most secret thoughts to a perfect stranger encountered during a chance meeting.

In reality, Aimeric was not proud of himself for being no longer able to grow zealous over an ideal; he nevertheless promised himself to give his support and assistance to his cousins during their struggle, without any deep involvement. He considered it a duty towards his adopted family, as well as a means to redeem himself for his lack of commitment.

'He is remarkable, the Bishop, isn't he?' Dawud's comment roused him from his meditation.

'Oh, yes. He was quite impressive,' Aimeric felt compelled to reply.

'Did you see how he behaved towards Sim'an, once he knew the miserable wretch was a spy planted by our enemies? His behaviour remained exactly as before,' added Yusuf admiringly.

'This Sim'an is from Duma, a *casal* located east of Batroun in the interior. The village has been recently fortified by the Count of Tripoli and a contingent of Frankish soldiers is stationed there to control the surrounding area. Sim'an fled his native village, not willing to collaborate with people who stand against his beliefs; at least that is the story he concocted to make himself welcome in Bishop Luke's circle.' Dawud passed on this information while they were drawing close to Gibelet.

They entered the town by the Land Gate and went straight to their families. Their father was received with shouts of joy by Tanios and Martha who ran towards him, informed of his imminent arrival, God knows how. Closely following them came Zeinab and Gerios, never too far from his little grandson.

Aimeric dismounted and, in turn, held the two children close to his heart, lifting first the boy, who had not yet fully overcome his feeling of jealousy towards his sister. Proprieties did not allow him to hug his wife in the street, so he refrained from any demonstration of affection towards her; instead, he kissed his father-in-law on each cheek and they all went inside the house.

Thereafter, Aimeric and his family enjoyed a few months of peace and quiet. The successor to Baybars was a weak son, who was kept busy trying hard to hold together the diverse pieces of the vast kingdom left by his father. The one-year truce with Tripoli was about to lapse and yet war seemed an unlikely prospect.

Then, in a matter of days during the month of August in the year of Our Lord 1279, the whole mood changed to one of gloom. The new Sultan abdicated and another son of Baybars, a mere seven-year-old child, succeeded him. The Templars took advantage of the confusion in the Mameluke camp and of the truce with Bohemond coming to an end to send twelve armed galleys to moor in the port of Gibelet.

The ordinary people of the town were rightly concerned, while the militants exulted; the small fleet was an undeniable sign of another war to come, and war was a chance to further their cause. Once more the young priest and the physician were summoned to the castle and given their orders. Dawud had to go to Luke with instructions to march with his forces against Duma. There he would assist a Frankish force to lay siege to and storm the fortified *casal*, while he, Guy, would attack Nephin, a baronial castle by the sea in the county of Tripoli. Aimeric would accompany the second contingent.

The priest asked the Lord's permission to send Yusuf to Bnahran in his stead, his health not yet allowing him to participate in battle. Permission was granted and a date and time for military action were set out and memorized.

At the head of a small contingent of Maronites assembled from Gibelet and its vicinity, Yusuf reached the Bishop's see late in the afternoon. Luke was holding court in the open air, chatting with his regular visitors and loyal followers, among them the duplicitous Sim'an.

The Bishop welcomed the newcomers with great warmth and cordiality. After a brief interval for the travellers to rest, he led Yusuf indoors and there, with no one else present, he was informed of Guy's plan to attack Bohemond's forces on two fronts. The Bishop went back to the gathering which was waiting impatiently to hear from him the news brought by the young messenger, for no indication could be extracted from his companions who, when questioned, had only replied, 'We came to fight, but we don't know where or when.'

Luke sat cross-legged on the ground beneath the branches of a venerable oak tree and delayed the moment of addressing his audience so as to increase the dramatic tension he sensed and enjoyed, knowing that he had the power to control it. Eventually he delivered the following speech.

'You wonder what's going on; why these courageous young men have left their loved ones to join us. You know in your hearts the reason. We and they have the same cause for which we are prepared to fight until victory or death.

'Victory is at hand. We will march with our ally, the Lord Guy of Gibelet, against our common enemies, and with God's help we will defeat them! Thereafter you will elect your own Patriarch, and your own Church will enjoy full autonomy...and away with slavery.

'Our immediate objective is to attack and capture the village of Majedlaya. There we will meet Lord Guy's army in five days' time. Go now and prepare yourselves for this decisive battle which will open up the way to Tripoli.'

The false information given about which village they were about to attack was intended for Sim'an, whose next move would undoubtedly be to inform his masters of the plan as it had been passed on to him.

On the agreed day a strong force, with Luke at its head, left Bnahran for Duma, in the opposite direction to Majedlaya, the alleged objective. The traitor, having carried out his act of betrayal as expected, was immediately seized, tied up and forced to march under guard, jeered at and goaded by his previous companions, who had instantly forsaken him as if he had never mattered.

Close to the real objective, the Maronite contingent linked up with the waiting Frankish forces. Thereafter, Duma was besieged then stormed after a fierce battle. The treacherous Sim'an was brought to its market-place, tortured in front of his horrified relatives and killed by Yusuf who thrust a dagger straight into his heart.

In the meantime, Aimeric rode to Nephin with Guy and his knights who laid siege to the fortress. Unless the castle, built on the edge of the sea and remarkably fortified with its twelve towers, were cut off from the maritime route which provided it with all the necessary supplies from Tripoli, no surrender could be expected. A complete embargo had been anticipated, but this was not to be. The Templars' fleet, instead of blocking Nephin, went straight to the port of Tripoli but could not enter; a storm scattered the galleys and three of them ran aground not far from Guy's forces.

A very disappointed Guy took the decision to withdraw and return to his castle. On his way back, leaning on his horse's neck, fatigued and despondent, he saw one of his knights, recognizable from afar by his pennon, coming down the hill at a gallop. He brought with him the good news of the victory won at Duma. Immediately invigorated, Guy made a triumphal entry into his town.

Amidst the hubbub and chaos which accompanied the army's arrival, Aimeric accosted the emissary from Duma, '*Mesire*, I am Aimeric, the physician.'

'I know who you are and I do hope I will never need your skills,' said the knight, with a hearty laugh.

Aimeric smiled and disclosed the reason for his approach. 'My cousin is a young Maronite from Gibelet who joined Luke's fighting force. His name is Yusuf. Do you know what has happened to him?'

'Look, I am not sure whether we are talking about the same man, but a young soldier from Gibelet by that name was assassinated soon after he had executed a traitor discovered amongst Bishop Luke's followers. The spy had also wounded and nearly killed the avenger's brother. That is all that I know,' finished the Knight.

'Sadly, I believe we mean the same person. Do you know the circumstances of his assassination?'

'Not really, because I had to leave in a hurry to report to Lord Guy and inform him of our victory.'

The Knight moved away, leaving a totally dismayed and bewildered Aimeric. Should he tell Yusuf's parents the terrible news, or should he wait until his death had been confirmed? He opted for the latter alternative, although he knew in his heart that the details given by the Knight could not point to any person other than Yusuf.

The physician returned to his family. Not a word about what he had just learnt did he utter, not even to Gerios, although he was tempted to confide in him. He anxiously listened out for the wailing which would certainly emanate from the direction of his uncle's house indicating that the appalling news had been brought home.

Always attentive to her husband's bearing, Zeinab became aware of his dreadful state. Out of the respect which operated even between husband and wife, she refrained from asking direct questions. She had available to her, however, oblique means, belonging to an art cunningly perfected out of necessity by the feminine gender throughout the years, which could lead to the result she was looking for.

'Let me bring you a cup of orange blossom water, it will do you good. Tell me where the pain is so that the meal I cook for you won't worsen your condition.'

'The pain is not in my body and I've no appetite for food.'

'Is it me, then? Are you angry with me?'

'Not at all, wife; there is something else, something dreadful I can't disclose at the moment.'

Their conversation was interrupted by screams and loud laments coming from somewhere in the neighbourhood. That was the confirmation that Aimeric had feared but anticipated. He knew that he must now reveal the reason for his distress to his wife and father-in-law, who were ready to rush outside the house to find out the reason for the sudden commotion.

'Wait, I know what's happened; it concerns Yusuf. I am afraid he's dead, killed in action.'

Thereupon, all of them, including Tanios and Martha, joined

Elias's family and the mourners. Yusuf's body had been brought back by his comrades and lay in his room. His prostrated father and mother were told by Yuhanna, his closest companion, of the circumstances of his death.

'No sooner was the traitor executed and justice done, than Yusuf was struck in the back by an arrow shot from one of the roofs. He died instantly and did not suffer for a moment.

'We immediately rounded up Sim'an's family and relatives and slew them. No one escaped our angered knife... Unfortunately, all the blood that was shed couldn't bring back our beloved comrade.'

The screaming and wailing of the mourners escalated in intensity when they heard what had happened; no one was able to hold back his tears. The confusion was at its height inside the house and in the garden, which was full of mourners who could not get in. Gerios took into his hands the matter of achieving some order. He directed the women to assemble in the room where Yusuf lay surrounded by professional mourners who kept enumerating the deceased's virtues, over and over again, in a prolonged and plaintive tone, bringing more tears to everyone's eyes.

During the afternoon, a knight called on the family to convey Lord Guy's condolences. He was received at the garden door by Aimeric, who guided him to *Bouna* Elias. Realizing that the representative was not one of the Prince's brothers nor an eminent nobleman, those present felt unhappy and dejected, for the dead and his family were not being honoured as they should have been. A few allowed themselves a murmur of protest, but the Frank remained unaware of the mood brought about by his visit. It was only after he had left that comments burst forth.

'They are all the same; they don't care about us or about our feelings.'

'We were on this land long before they came.'

One of the women commented, 'They don't honour those who have died for them.'

Hearing these words Hanneh came out of her prostration, raised her head and, gazing at no one in particular, said aloud but with no hint of bravado in her voice, 'Yusuf hasn't given his life for anyone, but for a cause. He didn't fight for the Franks, he fought side by side with Bishop Luke and fell for the resurgence of our Church. My other sons, Dawud and Ghantus, will do the same, even if they too have to pay with their own lives.'

Deep silence followed these words. Aimeric was very touched, knowing Hanneh's love for her children. He was again a little ashamed of his lack of commitment which, if ever exposed, could be regarded as selfish indifference in comparison to the over-excited prevailing mood. What he was unable to go along with was the prospect of the ultimate sacrifice on the altar of any cause.

CHAPTER TWENTY-ONE

ILLUSORY HOME

*Home is not where you live but
where they understand you*

'The Mamelukes have chosen a new sultan, an experienced
man-at-arms, as cunning and ruthless as Baybars.'

Back from the castle where he had gone to visit a bedridden
patient, Aimeric relayed to his relatives, gathered around a
comforting brazier, the news he had just heard from Lord Guy
himself.

'Do they believe at the castle that we are in any danger?'
asked a worried Gerios.

'They don't think so. The governor of Damascus refuses to place himself under the authority of the new sultan. It will take some time and many battles before one triumphs over the other.'

'*Hamdulillah*,' murmured Gerios.

'Does this sultan have a name?' inquired Elias.

'Yes. Qalawun, who wants to be known as *al-Mansur*, the Victorious; although the royal title seems a little premature.'

'Allah protect us,' muttered Hanneh, crossing herself.

Aimeric reassured his audience. 'We are not in imminent danger, that I know. Qalawun has to confront not only the Syrian rebellion, but also Mongol incursions into the north. I don't believe he will be that foolish as to look for more enemies.'

'It seems to me that the time is right for us to press for an advantage,' interjected Dawud. 'We should dismiss the present Patriarch who is a puppet of the Latin clergy and elect Luke as the independent head of our Church.'

His father gave him a worried look and sanctimoniously stated, 'In times of change, keep your head down.' Then he added for his son's benefit, 'Your ambitious ideas don't have any chance of succeeding without Lord Guy's active participation, and he cannot commit himself unless he first secures the Templars' assistance.'

'That is most unlikely,' intervened Aimeric, 'for peace between Tripoli and the Temple has been achieved.'

'And as usual, Luke was not consulted. They use us whenever they need us, but once they attain their own objectives, they forget all about us,' muttered the young priest with great bitterness.

Loud banging on the door interrupted the conversation and startled all those in the room. They looked at each other as if they might obtain the answer to who could be the caller at this late hour, and in such dreadful weather.

The door was opened from the outside by an impatient hand and a silhouette appeared in the doorway, bent over in the still raging storm. Aimeric's heart started to beat frantically, a mixture of anticipation and apprehension sweeping through his body as he seemed to recognize Arnaud de Foix. It was indeed him! One by one he embraced them and, having been urged to sit down, placed Martha on his lap, her tiny head trustfully resting on his broad chest.

Arnaud sensed beneath the warm welcome the anxiety of his hosts to know what had brought him to Gibelet. He realized that he could not leave them in the dark any longer, although what he was about to tell them would be a very sad message for at least one of them and might have a shattering effect on the lives of the others.

Turning towards Aimeric and choosing his words carefully he said, 'My dearest friend, I've news from Milan. It is about your poor mother; she is not at all well. In fact, her illness could be very serious but, of course, no one can know for sure.

'A relative from Milan wrote to me about her health, telling me that she doesn't want you to know how ill she is; she doesn't want to be a burden and, above all, her wish is to avoid putting you in any kind of dilemma or causing you any hardship. If her instructions were to be carried out, you would only have to be notified of her demise when it comes.

'However, my correspondent has been unable to handle the situation alone lest he is blamed for his silence when it is too late; so he shifted the weight of the decision on to me – whether to comply with her wish or to inform you straightaway of her illness.

'I felt I didn't have a right to hide from a son what I've learnt, more particularly when this son is himself a physician. So here I am.'

Ashen-faced Aimeric shook himself out of his torpor and

turned to Arnaud. 'I am most grateful to you for having taken the trouble to make a difficult journey in this weather. Please tell me, when did you receive the missive? Does it bear a date? And may I see it?'

'A pilgrim gave it to me five days ago. It was written a few months before that.' As the letter was handed over to him, amidst complete silence, Aimeric could not but feel guilty for not having interpreted correctly the premonitory dream about his mother and Arnaud; he now read for himself every word with extreme care, trying to find any clue or hint which might have escaped his older friend. Assured that he had been told everything and that nothing had been withheld from him, he looked up and said softly, 'I wonder if I've still time to give her proper care and try to cure her.'

Aimeric's final words left no doubt in Zeinab's mind of the decision that her husband had already taken. She was unable to refrain from throwing a black look at the one who had brought the sad news, a man she otherwise loved and respected, while reflecting, *He should have kept it to himself. My husband has already made up his mind to leave us to go to his mother. Only Allah knows when he'll return...*

In the intimacy of their bedroom Aimeric, who could not but suspect how worried his wife must be, took her in his arms to give her solace. 'I'll be back as soon as possible. The mere prospect of being far from you and the children is already an unbearable idea.' Zeinab rested her head on his shoulder and said with a tremor in her voice, 'I'll travel with you in spirit, following each of your steps, and from the day of your departure I'll constantly watch the sea, always hoping that the next boat will bring you back.'

These words moved Aimeric, who was otherwise too preoccupied to make love to his wife; yet he manifested the paroxysm of tenderness he felt for her at that moment by holding her tightly all through the night, listening to her regular breathing and lovingly contemplating her angelic face after she fell asleep. He himself had too much on his mind to do the same.

The day after, the physician was promised passage to Genoa on a boat which was expected to call into the port of Gibelet in a fortnight. He took advantage of the wait to put his affairs in order and to take leave of the Lord of the castle, who recommended him to come back the sooner the better, an indication how much his services were appreciated.

One other thing he did was to engage an artist from Livorno, who had made Gibelet his home and found much favour with the nobility. For a modest fee, a noble man or lady could be represented in a sacred painting either as the person who was offering the picture or as part of the background.

For this particular commission he was retained to paint miniature portraits of Zeinab and the two children. The promise of a handsome sum if the work were finished before Aimeric sailed overcame the painter's protest about such a short time being made available to him.

Another objection came from Gerios who was unhappy with the prospect of his daughter being alone with a perfect stranger. Aimeric won him over, however, by pleading with him to attend all the sessions needed to complete the portraits. The physician intended to take these portraits with him so that his mother, if she were still alive, could see how his family looked, and also for himself to contemplate whenever a nostalgic mood overcame him.

Neither of the children had reached an age which allowed them to realize the meaning of the preparations that had brought turmoil to the household. However, because of the sadness around them, they instinctively sensed that important events were unfolding.

Eventually the time came for the dreaded separation; a two-masted, round cargo ship berthed in the port. A few days were necessary to take on water and food supplies, then word was passed round that the vessel was about to sail.

Accompanied by his family, relatives and well-wishers, including Arnaud who had decided to remain in Gibelet until his friend embarked, Aimeric set off towards the port. It only took a little time to cross to where other groups of travellers and people bidding farewell were gathered on the jetty. For the last time Aimeric kissed his family and relatives. As he gathered Zeinab to him, she was unable to contain her tears, and her example was followed by Tanios, who had begun to realize that his father was really going away.

After short formalities Aimeric finally went on board. Upon recommendation from the castle, he had been assigned a bunk in one of the few cabins on the deck. Within the hour the lateen sails were hoisted and the ship moved slowly away from her berth; from the deck the physician watched the group of his family and friends gradually get smaller and smaller until they disappeared completely from his sight.

The ship, as he soon found out, carried in its hold some three hundred Kipchak and Circassian slaves intended for the Mameluke markets. They were disembarked in Alexandria, their next port of call, and replaced by a cargo of spices from India, China and the East Indies, which would be sold at maximum price to European consumers.

Leaving the choppy waters of the port of Alexandria behind, mixed feelings assailed Aimeric; he longed to see his mother, but with the possibility that she might have already passed away, he would rather that the voyage never ended. The distress caused by not knowing whether or not she was still alive was an uncertain condition yet better than the inescapable finality of death he might have to face on arrival.

After another call, at Palermo, the ship entered the harbour of Genoa, a large amphitheatre surrounded by high hills strewn with lavish villas. Straightaway Aimeric hired a cart for himself and his luggage and two days later he arrived at the door of his parents' home in Milan, his heart beating frantically. He hesitated a few seconds then, mustering his courage, stepped inside.

Nothing had changed since the day of his departure to Acre ten years before and more. The kitchen, with its huge fireplace, the shining copper plates and utensils, the tall chairs and massive table; everything was as when he left. Only his mother could have kept the house in such perfect order; she was certainly alive, were the thoughts which ran through his mind.

He climbed the stairs at a run and stopped at the doorway of his parents' room. Looking in furtively, Aimeric was overjoyed and profoundly relieved to see his mother in her bed, even though her hair was now white and her face emaciated. She had her eyes closed, so he tiptoed inside and found Agnes, the faithful servant, in a corner. He raised a forefinger to his lips, urging her to remain silent, then signalled her to follow him downstairs.

Once out of earshot, Agnes exploded, 'Master, master! I can't believe my eyes, you are back,' and then hastily added, 'My mistress's joy will have no limits. I am going to wake her up.'

'Wait. Shouldn't she be prepared before she is told I'm here?'

Agnes looked at him, unable to understand his concern. 'But master, she knew you were coming.'

'How on earth could she know that?' asked Aimeric bewildered.

'She didn't tell me how, but she was certain that before long you would make a sudden appearance, just like today.'

'How ill is she? Do you know what she is suffering from? Is

she being seen by a physician?' Aimeric anxiously questioned Agnes.

'Your mother has lost weight and complains of weakness all over. A physician visits her from time to time and causes her to bleed,' she replied. Then she added, mumbling, 'I know nothing about these matters, but each time he sees her she is worse…'

Aimeric left the servant mumbling and returned to his mother's room. This time he woke her up and took her in his arms, feeling with great dismay how tiny and frail her body had become.

'Are you happy?' These were the first words which came to her lips.

'I am much more so now that I have seen you. I will take care of you and soon you'll leave your sick-bed.'

She smiled gently as an answer and while he examined her asked him a lot of questions about his wife, his children and life in Outremer. He could find nothing wrong from his preliminary examination.

The following days were filled with a constant stream of welcomers, people enquiring about their relatives in the Holy Land, and the Brethren who had looked after his mother. Among the visitors was the physician who regularly visited Blanche. He came one afternoon as usual, wearing a long black gown, an indication of his high academic status, accompanied by an apprentice who carried a flask and beaker which they would need for samples. Aimeric introduced himself and felt that the visiting physician was immediately on his guard.

'I must thank you for taking care of my mother. Enlighten me, I beg of you; tell me what's wrong with her in your opinion.'

'Your dear mother, God bless her, is threatened with an excess of humours, causing her sickness. Blood-letting releases the excess and cures her for a time,' came the explanation in the most pompous tone.

'Don't you think that blood–letting, in her case, could weaken her constitution? I would, instead, start by giving her strength with a nourishing diet which fortifies her.'

'I have heard such nonsense from Sicilian physicians, but I would never experiment on my patients with what they recommend.' The voice was scornful. 'I am a man of science and will use only orthodox methods to cure them.'

'Then,' retorted Aimeric, 'I don't see how we can both take care of her.'

The other left the house very irritated, followed by his apprentice showing comical, accentuated signs of disapproval.

Having rid his mother of these two ignorant men, Aimeric devoted his time and skills to her welfare, and over the next few weeks her health slowly improved and she was able to wander, first in the house, then outside in the warm weather.

After several months spent in Milan, he started to consider going back to his family But how could Aimeric ever tell his mother about these thoughts? It was she who opened the subject, as if she had been aware of his predicament and wished to exonerate him of any feelings of guilt he might have.

'My dear son, I can't fail to notice that you look at the portraits of your loving family more and more often. You must miss them a lot; I believe it is time for you to go and join them.'

'But, mother, how can I leave you on your own?'

'I'm not on my own. I've Agnes and all the Brethren who take care of me. You must go; your first duty is to your family.'

'Why don't you come with me?' he quickly said, as if the question had been with him for some time.

'I don't want to leave my house, and anyway, I'm too tired and too old for such an adventure.'

Mother and son left their unselfish dialogue at this juncture, each promising themselves to promote their own point of view at the first opportunity. As it happened they did not have to, for an unexpected turn of events decided the matter for them. The physician who had been dismissed by Aimeric could not swallow the insult, and with time passing the insult had grown to become a grave offence in his mind. He went to the guild of medical practitioners and lodged a complaint against Aimeric, accusing him of being a charlatan who used unorthodox methods on his patients and, most outrageously, on his own mother.

The complaining physician was well known and well respected by his community, so the charge he had brought against a man who was relatively unknown in the town could not be ignored. Hence an investigation was opened and Aimeric was summoned to appear before a panel of physicians.

On the fixed day and at the appointed time, he presented himself in front of the ten judges who would decide for or against his healing procedures. He had no fear, but felt apprehension at encountering ignorance and intolerance. He was invited to enter a large, panelled hall and sit facing his judges, whom he had time to study before the proceedings started. His attention was focused on one of them who, he believed, was displaying a particularly antagonistic attitude. He was not mistaken for that man, Signor Laurenti Capello, was, in fact, in charge of the investigation, which thus started under unfavourable auspices.

'Aimeric Maurel...the name does not have a familiar ring to it. Tell me, Signor Maurel, from which country are you?'

'I was born in Milan.'

'But your father is not from here, is he?'

'My father is dead; he came from the Languedoc as a young man and settled in Milan until he passed away.'

Signor Laurenti paused for a while and then resumed the questioning. 'Where did you learn the art of healing?'

Maurel handed over the certificate of qualification he had received from Samuel of Scandalion.

'And who is this Samuel of Scandalion?' enquired Capello, with a scathing glance at the document he was holding. 'I presume he is not a Christian.'

'He is a Jewish philosopher, a scholar and a physician from Outremer.'

The judges looked at each other; one of them, a venerable man but unnoticed until now by Aimeric, took the floor. 'At the University of Salerno, where I studied and taught for a while, we had medical works translated into Latin from Arabic. Arabs and Jews have apparently achieved astonishing results by devising and following the directions found in these works. Maybe Signor Maurel would enlighten us by describing his procedure when he treated his mother.'

Capello quickly jumped to his feet, shouting, 'If you are willing to compare our orthodox ways of treating illness with the ways practised by infidels and enemies of Christ, then I strongly object.'

The judges discussed among themselves in low voices but with great animation, then they requested that Aimeric leave the hall while they engaged in further debate. When he was summoned back, he was told that another hearing would be held in three months' time. Obviously the judges had been unable to agree on how to proceed at present and had decided to postpone the problem and the solution.

Aimeric returned home in complete disgust at the intolerance shown by the judges, except for one as far as he could tell. What hurt him more was his examiner's inappropriate narrow-mindedness, which was not objected to by any of his colleagues, when his non-Italian origin was underlined. That painful moment in his interrogation had made him realize that he was more of a stranger here than he had ever been in Outremer, where he had been instantly accepted and even looked up to by the local people, simply because he was a Frank. No one had ever asked him where he was born.

At this point in time, Aimeric was determined to go back to Gibelet. If he could, he would sail even before the date of the next hearing, sparing his judges the predicament of a divisive investigation and the embarrassment of having to render a decision for or against treatments they knew very little about. All he had to do now was to wait for the appropriate time to notify his mother of his decision as gently as he could.

Blanche made the first move, as if alerted by a premonitory feeling. After welcoming him back she informed her son, 'I've enquired and been told that a ship bound for Gibelet leaves Genoa in ten days' time. You should be on that ship.'

'But, mother, you haven't asked me how the hearing went.'

'Never have I expected anything good from arrogant and bigoted people. Why should it be otherwise this time?'

'You're right, mother. I had a most disagreeable time, not for trying to extricate myself from their clutches, but for the degrading spectacle I was forced to take part in.'

'Tell me all the details later on, Aimeric. Now I want you to give me a firm promise that you'll take that ship. I need to know to prepare myself for our separation.'

Aimeric did not give her the spoken assurance she expected. Instead, he slowly nodded his head, showing his acceptance.

Three days before the ship's departure, his belongings, the gifts bought for his family and items given to him by those who knew of his imminent departure and had asked him to deliver to people living in Outremer, were all loaded on to the cart belonging to a Cathar who had insisted on driving him personally to Genoa.

At the doorway of the house Aimeric kissed his mother, then Agnes and the many friends who had come to bid him farewell. Suddenly he turned back to his mother, clasped her tightly and kissed her again for the last time before climbing on to the waiting cart. Slowly, painfully, the horse pulled its heavy load, taking away from Blanche her beloved son, most probably for ever.

CHAPTER TWENTY-TWO

ELUSIVE PEACE

'Tanios, my son, I barely recognized you. Two years ago I left behind a boy and now I find a man. And you, Martha, come here close to me. I want to see my little princess.'

Aimeric hid the emotion which overwhelmed him after being reunited with his family under a profusion of light-hearted words and jokes, but Zeinab could not begin to express what she felt, having her husband safely here beside her again.

When he had disembarked at the jetty at Gibelet, Aimeric had not expected to see any of his relatives. To his surprise and delight they were all there to welcome him.

'However did you know that I was on that boat?' he asked.

'We didn't, but every time a ship was announced by the ringing of the church bells and whenever she was flying Genoa's flag, we all came to see if you were on it,' answered Gerios.

They all went back to Aimeric's house, he leading the way holding Martha in his arms, with Tanios, Gerios and Elias proudly walking beside him. Close behind came Zeinab and Hanneh, followed by her children pushing a wheelbarrow loaded with his belongings. On their way, the returning traveller was welcomed by every passer-by who recognized him, as if he were a lost son. The warmth of their reception added to his already deeply felt emotions. Suddenly he realized that one member of his family was missing.

'Where is Dawud? How is he?' he enquired, slightly worried.

'Dawud is fine. He is with Bishop Luke and we expect him at any time, as from today,' answered his father to Aimeric's relief.

At home they sat comfortably on the floor to hear all the details he was prepared to give them about his journey and his stay in Milan. Then came the moment for the distribution of presents brought for each one of them. Outbursts of joy and amazement accompanied what was produced from the bag: the doll for Martha, a little painted wooden horse for Tanios, two hand-written, illuminated books of prayer for Elias and Dawud, and for the others there were leather shoes, belts and gloves, and woollen clothes from Flanders.

It was late in the evening when Aimeric and Zeinab were left on their own in the intimacy of their bedroom, Hanneh having thoughtfully proposed that Tanios and Martha stay with their cousins for the night, an invitation the children were always very keen to take up.

'Did you miss me, or didn't you have time to think of me

with all those lovely ladies around you?' asked Zeinab coquettishly.

'The ladies I've seen are my mother and her servant, Agnes. They are both nearly the same age,' came the answer, which was obviously intended to tease yet not satisfy her.

She fell for it and persisted. 'That's not who I am talking about, God bless them. I mean the young women who must have swarmed over you.'

Unwilling to keep the game going much longer, Aimeric took her in his arms and gave her the promise she needed to hear. 'There is only you. Nothing will ever change, whether I am with you or far away from you.'

She smiled and rested her head on his chest as a prelude to a night of passion which would completely reassure her.

The next day Dawud reappeared in Gibelet. He was over-joyed to see Aimeric, but looked otherwise deeply preoccupied. 'I've important news,' he announced. 'Patriarch Daniel has died. The next patriarch has to be Bishop Luke. We should seize the opportunity. I have to give Lord Guy an account of the situation. Please come with me.'

Aimeric was as reluctant as ever to take part in the struggle he could see coming. On the other hand, he did not want to appear discourteous and, anyhow, he could not delay going to the castle to pay homage, particularly as the news of his return must have already been reported.

And so the physician and Dawud presented themselves to Lord Guy, who gave a warm welcome to Aimeric and listened closely to what the priest had to say. Thereafter he retired to discuss the situation with his two brothers, Baudouin and John, his cousin Guillaume and a handful of counsellors, including a Templar Knight. After their meeting came to an end, the Seigneur of Gibelet announced his decision to the two visitors.

'*Bouna* Dawud, go straightaway to Bishop Luke and tell him to proceed from Bnahran to the Monastery of Our Lady in Mayfuq, accompanied by the bishops and other clergymen faithful to him, as well as by his armed forces. There he will meet with a corps sent from Gibelet.

'With Bnahran, Duma and Mayfuq in our hands, the whole countryside will be under my control; then Luke will be elected patriarch of your autonomous Church.'

The young priest's joy was clear to see, though it was soon replaced by a concerned alertness, shared by Aimeric, as more instructions followed.

'Tell Luke not to move from Mayfuq. I need him there with his forces so that Bohemond will not expect any assistance from the hinterland.'

Guy paused, looked intently at the two cousins, then continued, 'You both have my full confidence. What I am going to say you mustn't repeat to anyone except Luke, of course. I'm going to attack and take Tripoli. Signor Maurel, you'll accompany me. I might need your skills after all,' he laughed, then continued on a more serious note. 'The other vital mission I entrust you with, *Bouna* Dawud, is to inform Luke that I'll need reinforcements for the battle. He has to keep his own forces to control the countryside, so tell him to send emissaries in my name to the Moslem governor of the Krak des Chevaliers, promising that once I've taken Tripoli it will be partitioned off between me and the Sultan. All I want from him is to be given two hundred or, even better, three hundred Moslem fighters from the Mountain. I need them now. The governor has my solemn word that Tripoli will be ours to share. Go at once. May God protect you.'

The two men who left the castle could not have been in more contrasting moods. Aimeric was worried and reflective, while a jubilant and greatly excited Dawud was already making preparations in his mind for his departure to Bnahran.

The following weeks brought a succession of ominous events. To respond to the election of Luke as patriarch of the Maronites, a second patriarch, Jeremiah of Dimilsa, was elected at Bohemond's instigation, by bishops and other religious dignitaries who had remained faithful to Rome. Jeremiah took up residence in Halat, a coastal village south of Gibelet, controlled by the Prince of Tripoli.

If the split in the Maronite community conveyed an inauspicious message, the arrival at Gibelet of some three hundred Moslem fighters sent by the governor of the Krak des Chevaliers, together with a robe of honour meant for Guy, left no doubt in the mind that war was about to break out.

Eventually, what had been feared took place at the beginning of the year 1283. Guy and six hundred soldiers, half of them Christians and the rest Moslems, embarked during the night on a galley and four smaller boats and sailed towards Tripoli. On the bigger boat were also Aimeric and some forty knights with their war-horses; Lord Guy and his brothers' mounts had been sent ahead to the Temple's House located by the sea where the expedition was expected to land. So they would find their horses rested and fresh and, as promised by the Temple, they would be joined by a number of soldiers waiting for them.

When the expedition reached the meeting point, the Seigneur of Gibelet ordered that the smaller boats be run aground, to ensure they were no longer seaworthy. In that way his invading soldiers had no option but to fight most valiantly, knowing that there was no possible retreat. The Knights disembarked from the galley, leaving behind Aimeric, the crew and a handful of soldiers.

On the deck, Aimeric and his companions anxiously strained their eyes to penetrate the darkness, but they were unable to see anything. Several hours passed in silence, then just after daybreak they heard a clamour coming from the distance, followed by a menacing silence which made them very apprehensive. Suddenly, a small group of Knights could be seen galloping towards them across the beach to arrive in a state of great agitation. They dismounted, abandoned their horses and were helped aboard the galley. Lying exhausted on the deck, they rid themselves of their coats of mail, and one of them, apparently their leader, ordered the skipper to set sail at once. To the passengers assembled around him, he then related the tragic events which had taken place when the expedition landed.

'After we touched down, we went straight to the Temple's House. Neither the Templars' Commander nor the promised troops were there and we realized immediately that we had been betrayed. Our boats being broken and the capacity of the galley being far less than our actual number, the only solution was to negotiate an honourable truce. We all went to the Hospitallers' compound to put ourselves under their protection. Soon we found the compound surrounded by the entire population.' The Knight paused, drank a little of the wine given to him, and with a deep sigh resumed his dramatic account.

'After difficult negotiations undertaken on our behalf by the Commander of the Hospital, Lord Guy agreed to surrender himself and all his men on condition that he will receive only a five-year jail sentence, after which his land will revert back to him.

'Somehow I've no confidence at all that Bohemond would keep his word. Hence amidst the confusion and disorder which accompanied the surrender operation, I and my companions sneaked out unnoticed through a side gate.

'What's going to happen to all of us, I don't know. What is

sure is that Bohemond will occupy Gibelet with no opposition, for there is no one left to fight him.'

The Knight's account was received with total dismay by his increasingly panicking audience. Aimeric was the first to get a grip on himself. He addressed the skipper, 'Are you prepared to call at Gibelet for us to take our families and belongings on board and then sail to Tyre? I am sure that you will be handsomely rewarded by all willing to be part of the voyage, including me.'

Aimeric had made the proposal after thinking quickly that he and his family would most certainly be in great danger if – no, when – Gibelet was occupied by Bohemond. He had participated in too many battles against the victorious Prince, most unwillingly, but who was going to believe that, to be forgiven. The physician was convinced that he had no choice but to move back to Acre. Caution dictated that he should first land with his family at Tyre; its Prince, John of Montfort, was an ally of the Genoese and was expected to be welcoming. That would not be the case at Acre. There, the settlers from Pisa were the sworn enemies of the Genoese and might be more than unkind to the refugees from Gibelet. After a short stay at Tyre, as part of his plan to allow the upheaval to subside, Aimeric and his family would then go quietly to their final destination.

While Aimeric was thinking very carefully about what was best under the circumstances, he was unable to refrain from a brief, dry smile at the thought that he was about to take refuge with the man whose father he had come to Outremer to kill. Once more he thanked Providence for having spared him the ordeal of committing a murder and, even more, for having brought about in him a fundamental change which made him immune to any kind of insane fanaticism.

He shared with his companions the arrangements planned

in his mind and they all agreed that they were most suitable and expedient.

The galley moored at the port of Gibelet, where its sad passengers were met by the anxious population gradually succumbing to panic. Aimeric proposed, and his companions agreed, that they should not all leave the ship at once lest she sail without waiting for them to come back with their families and belongings or be commandeered by people desperate to leave the town. Nearly half the Knights volunteered to guard the ship; they had no families and their meagre possessions could easily be fetched by their comrades.

Aimeric gathered his family and relatives around him and informed them of the distressing situation and of his decision to leave Gibelet. He urged Zeinab to get the children ready and to pack their most precious possessions. While he himself crammed more medical instruments and medication into a box, he said, 'I believe that you, Ghantus, will be in danger here; either you come with us or you join Dawud and Luke. As for you, Uncle Gerios, I expect you to accompany us.'

'I'll join Dawud and Patriarch Luke. I wonder if they are still at Mayfuq, but I'll find out,' was Ghantus' reply.

'I'll stay here,' said Gerios. 'You, my dear children, go to Acre. I prefer the turmoil of Gibelet to the sadness of Acre where I lost Shams. Besides, I am too old to be troubled by Bohemond's men.'

Amid scenes of general panic, distress and sadness, Aimeric and his family embarked on the galley already full of passengers who had been allowed on board. Tyre was the next destination of those people who had to rebuild their lives one more time.

CHAPTER TWENTY-THREE

CURTAIN DOWN

Mercy is rare,
vengeance is common
Arabic proverb

'We will soon return to Gibelet...Lord John is riding with all his knights to take over the town. With God's help he'll occupy it and give it back to Lord Guy in due time.'

That was the optimistic prophesy of most of the refugees who had found precarious shelter in Tyre. Not all shared that happy assurance, however, and Aimeric was one of the sceptics. He realized the obvious, that Gibelet was much closer to

Tripoli than Tyre was, and that Bohemond had been on a war-footing and was ready to invade it long before John and his knights had started their march. Gibelet was like an open pomegranate, to be taken by the first arrival, and the Prince of Tripoli was the most likely one.

What the physician had expected, happened. Hardly had John of Montfort reached Beirut, than he heard that his intended objective was in the hands of Bohemond. He returned to his fief, to the despair of those who had had such high expectations.

In the meantime, and with greater difficulty, Aimeric had found refuge for his family in two rooms rented at three times the usual price. Tyrians were prepared to commiserate with the unhappy displaced persons, but when it came to business, they could be extremely shrewd. Charity was for them a few words of compassion, not interference with their purse.

After a couple of weeks, Aimeric and his family moved back to Acre and to an emotional reunion with Arnaud who, generous as ever, offered them the hospitality of his house. His kindness was gratefully accepted until permanent, suitable accommodation could be found.

The physician resumed contact with the people he had treated in the past and made several visits to the town's dignitaries, with a view to advertise his return and to try and recover the practice he had left behind. Among the people he had in mind to visit, for an emotional reason this time, was Samuel of Scandalion who, he was told, could not be reached at present, being out of town on a teaching tour.

The one person he thought he would not see was Jacques de Castre, who had left more than ten years before with the Polos for faraway exotic places. He could not have been more mistaken, for one evening the Knight unexpectedly turned up at Arnaud's house with his usual exuberance and loud cheerfulness, which frightened the children at first. He was and looked older, but he had lost none of his vigour and still remained the colourful character he had been.

After much hugging and kissing came the moment for the exchange of news and happenings since their separation. Alternately joyful and dejected, de Castre listened to the account of the birth of Tanios and Martha, Shams' assassination, the departure to Gibelet and the return to Acre in such tragic circumstances.

Asked about his own adventures, de Castre sat comfortably in an armchair and gestured to Martha, inviting her to draw close. When she timidly obeyed the summons, he took her on his knee and began his incredible story for a most attentive audience.

'As you know, I left with the Polos for the port of Laiassus, where we landed. From there, we started a long journey fraught with danger. We crossed several countries inhabited by Moslems, Hindus and Christians of various denominations, and finally we reached the Imperial Court of the Great Kublai who received us most graciously.

'If I only knew how to write, I'd produce a penned account of all the marvels and astonishing people I've seen and met.'

'You can always dictate to a scribe what you've experienced,' suggested Aimeric.

'I might do so, but only when I'm too old to go back to Cathay. After all, I don't want to disclose all the information I've painstakingly gathered to potential competitors,' replied the Knight with a crafty twinkle in his eye.

'What happened after you reached Cathay?' asked Aimeric, worried and impatient to know what had brought de Castre back to Acre on his own, without the Polos. Could it be they are all dead? he pondered sombrely.

'I was appointed adviser to the army of the Great Khan, to

make them aware of the ways we fight and our tricks of war. When he decided to invade Zipangu, I was part of the expedition which turned out to be a total disaster for the Mongols. The Samurais cut them down after storming our ships at anchor; our landing was delayed, you see, because of rough seas. Trying to fend off the attackers, who unexpectedly leapt on us from their small boats that had defied wind and storms, I was wounded and barely escaped with my life, with the few who were spared the Samurai sword. Back in Yanking, the Khan allowed me to leave with two camels laden with goods and spices.'

He then added, to Aimeric's relief, 'I bade farewell to the Polos – by the way, you have a letter from Marco – and joined a caravan with a number of camels and other beasts of burden as far as the eye could see. We crossed hazardous deserts, reached Samarkand, Tabriz, Lesser Armenia and, finally, Arnaud's house,' declared the Knight with a thunderous laugh.

Everyone joined in the laughter and congratulated de Castre on his safe return, asking him hundreds of questions about the lands and the people he had encountered.

'Would you stay with us?' The offer came from Arnaud in the form of a question. 'You will have to camp out in the workshop because the house is full.'

'I would rather keep an eye on my goods until they are sold. I've rented a room at the khan where they are stored,' he replied, then jokingly added, 'You see, I'm rich now! With wealth come worries and one of them at the moment is not to be robbed of what has been amassed in perilous situations.'

The same sort of friendly gathering took place on several successive evenings, during which the Knight narrated to his fascinated audience episodes of his travels and adventures. Then one evening he arrived at Arnaud's house not his usual cheerful and affable self but in a state of great bewilderment.

'You should see what's going on in the Pisan quarter. People are totally out of their minds and out of control.'

'What do you mean? Has trouble flared up again? Between whom this time?' they asked simultaneously, having gathered round him.

'Nothing of the sort; quite the contrary. People appear to be overcome by a joyful madness; their houses are illuminated, there is music, dancing and drinking in the streets, and plenty of food being given away. They've also erected a makeshift theatre, and when I asked around what was the reason for the celebration, I was told to see for myself the pantomime which is being performed there.

'Their reticence is most probably due to the fact that they realized by my accent that I'm not from Pisa. The next performance is about to start so I ran to take you back with me. I'm dying to know the cause for the Pisans' excitement.'

Engulfed by intense curiosity, Aimeric, Arnaud and the Knight hastily left for the Pisan quarter. Once there, they made their way through a joyful and unruly crowd and reached the newly erected theatre. Standing at some distance from the stage, because of the great number of turbulent and unrestrained spectators, they tried to see and listen to the actors, a difficult endeavour because of the incessant jeers and taunts from the crowd.

Gradually they began to realize that what they were watching depicted the dramatic events which took place after Guy's capture. One richly dressed actor, supposedly Bohemond, was sitting on a chair; before him were dragged four other actors who were forced to kneel before him. They were assumed to be Guy, his two brothers and their cousin.

'Am I not your Lord and are you not my vassals?' asked 'Bohemond'.

'Yes, sire,' answered the four 'prisoners'.

'*La Haute Cour* heard you confessing. You have admitted that three times you attempted to take Tripoli by force and three times you failed owing to divine Providence. Your confession is recorded by the public notary and witnessed by honourable men of our saintly Church. For your vile deeds there is but one punishment.' 'Bohemond' paused dramatically. 'You will be put to death like traitors!' he bellowed.

His last words caused a tempestuous clamour of approval from the crowd. When it abated he stared at each one of the prisoners' and emphatically declared, 'You will be thrown into a ditch and walled in, to die slowly from hunger and thirst. Take them away!'

The spectators roared like wild beasts and a thunderous applause burst out, accentuated by loud jeers, lewd taunts and strident whistling.

The three companions, disgusted and dejected, left for home without exchanging a word for some time. They did not doubt for a moment that the unfortunate prisoners had died the atrocious way depicted on stage. Aimeric was most affected as he knew Guy and his brothers personally. He had attended to them and they had shown him gratitude and kindness.

Even more disturbing was the unknown fate of Gerios and the rest of the family. Aimeric worried about what might have happened to them after the Lord of Tripoli occupied Gibelet. The lack of mercy the victor had shown and the barbaric death he had inflicted on enemies who belonged to his own people were ominous signs as to how he must have treated the locals who had sided against him.

While on their way back, Aimeric contemplated whether he should bring the news of the Genoese's atrocious fate to Zeinab, who was already agonizing over her father and the rest of the family. He decided to say nothing about the stage representation, to spare his dear wife unnecessary increased anguish, and urged his two companions to follow his example.

All worries were wiped out after a few days when Gerios arrived in Acre, the bearer of reassuring news. 'We weren't troubled in the least; when Bohemond's army entered Jbail, Ghantus had already joined his brother at Mayfuq. From there they took refuge with Luke, high in the mountains, at Hadath, where a stronghold had been secured.

'In Jbail, the old and the women weren't inconvenienced, they left them alone. My brother Elias easily convinced the commander of the garrison that he remained faithful to the Roman Church and had never shared his sons' rebellious views. As for me, I wasn't even questioned. When matters had settled, I took the decision to visit you to bring you in person the comforting news.

'But, alas! Those captured in Tripoli weren't that fortunate. You must have heard what befell Guy, his brothers and cousin. All the other Genoese taken prisoner with them were blinded; some have returned to Jbail, miserable wretches who must lament every moment of their useless lives for still being alive. As for our poor brethren captured with Guy, they rot in Bohemond's jail and will probably die in shackles.' Gerios fell silent, lost in his thoughts. Then he wiped away a tear and hugged Tanios.

The unbearable misery and the heartbreaking dispersion of his own family were not the only causes of Gerios' tears; he was also desperately worried about the future, not for himself but for Tanios, wondering what kind of prospects the child would have in Outremer.

One morning, a messenger handed over to Gerios a letter intended for Aimeric who was out visiting his patients. It came from the Venerable Samuel to tell Aimeric that he was back in Acre, that he would have wished to present himself to welcome him, except for a bout of illness which hindered his moving about, but did not prevent him from receiving his pupil if he would be kind enough to visit him.

Once more Aimeric made his way towards Montmusart to his old teacher's house. He reminisced about the time he took that road to attend his first medical lesson when, young and in love, he believed he could grasp the whole world in his hands and change the course of history without having to pay a price. He paused, feeling a sudden fatigue, and reflected with slight bitterness and a touch of irony, I was prepared to interfere in matters much bigger than my humble person, and I was prepared to do that without the slightest hesitation or any doubt ever crossing my mind. Now that I need to make a decision which only concerns me and my family, I'm incapable of thinking straight.

After a few pauses on his way, and more dispirited thoughts, Aimeric reached his destination. He found his old teacher lying down on his mattress, aged and having conspicuously lost weight. Aimeric leant towards him, hugged him and said, 'Let me examine you.' Then he added joking, 'That is, of course, if you have confidence in my skills – and why shouldn't you? You see, I had the best of masters.'

Samuel answered back in the same vein, but in a faint voice, 'Fate can make a fool of any physician. I'm too old to be bothered with my own body.'

Interpreting these words as an invitation to proceed, Aimeric thoroughly examined the old man. 'When did you last eat?' he asked, having finished his investigation.

'I don't know. Probably yesterday, when my sister Sarah brought me some chicken broth.'

'I don't see anything wrong with you, except your memory. Oh! I don't mean about numbers and letters of the Bible, but for more earthly things – like for example, eating.'

The old man feebly smiled. More recommendations on the need for him to take care of his health ensued, then Aimeric gave him an account of the events in his own life since the time they had lost sight of each other. He concluded with the dilemma over which he was agonizing. 'I don't know where to settle. In Milan I was treated like a charlatan by ignorant people; in Outremer I keep on running like a rabbit from one place to another, trying to protect my family from danger.'

'Ah! I know what running means,' interrupted Samuel. 'My people have done just that since the time of Abraham. You have to adapt to the circumstances of the moment. You are happy here? Then stay here. After all, have you thought how Zeinab and the children would cope in an environment unknown and probably hostile? Gerios is Zeinab's only parent and she is his only child; it would be cruel to separate them. Your mother, you told me, is in good health and surrounded by people who take care of her. Make up your mind once and for all, and don't think about leaving unless you are forced to. Here you are respected and loved by all the people around you.' Weary from the effort he had made, the old man closed his eyes and leant against the wall at the head of his mattress.

Aimeric asked thoughtfully, 'Shall I leave now? Are you too tired?'

Samuel nodded so the younger man left him with a few words of recommendation. 'Promise me to eat regularly, and whenever you feel the need for a physician don't hesitate to send for me, day or night. Anyhow, I'll come and visit you soon.'

A much more light-hearted Aimeric went back home. What Zeinab whispered in his ear as they lay on their old bed comforted him on the decision he had already taken. 'I may be bearing another child,' she murmured.

He hugged her, trying his best not to wake the children

sleeping in the same room. It was his turn to whisper back to her. 'If it is a boy, we will name him Yusuf, and if a girl, Shams.'

She kissed him tenderly to express her appreciation for his thoughtfulness and then sententiously declared, 'Aimeric Maurel, you are the best of men. My father will be so happy.' Zeinab belatedly realized that her voice had awakened Tanios and Martha. The result was that the two children, half asleep, left their mattress and slipped into their parents' bed. Husband and wife looked at each other helplessly, knowing that their deep, loving feelings of that moment could not be expressed more intimately.

Aimeric was unable to sleep, and for a while he affectionately looked at Zeinab and the children, who obviously did not experience the same difficulty; then, making sure not to awaken them, he went downstairs and out into the courtyard. He sat down on the bench by the well to savour the quietness of the advanced night. The weather was wonderfully mild; thousands of stars glittered in the sky and an indiscreet full moon radiated a bluish light which metamorphosed familiar objects into unrecognizable ones.

Before long a dark figure appeared in the doorway, remained motionless for a short while as if trying to identify who was by the well, took a step forward and Arnaud's face became discernible in the moonlight. He approached Aimeric and sat down on the bench next to him. Neither said a word lest the magic of the moment be spoiled. Eventually the physician broke the silence. 'It is most fortunate that you came to join me; we have to talk, and there is no better time than this. Zeinab and the children are asleep and I am not interrupting your work. Besides, words come more easily here and now than in the light of day.'

Arnaud's curiosity was much aroused, yet he decided to keep silent so that he did not unintentionally say something which could dispel the confidential mood of his younger friend.

'The love and care you gave me,' Aimeric began, 'and the financial support you so generously provided for my studies and my welfare make me feel that I have found the father I first left and then lost.'

Arnaud was about to interrupt the words of praise and appreciation that his nature and upbringing made him uneasy to hear and accept, but Aimeric gently raised his hand to indicate that he had not finished.

'There is also another kind of debt I owe to you, a duty of openness. I would be cheating if I didn't disclose to you the change that this son of yours has undergone since the time he first set foot in Outremer. I must do this, even if it demeans me in your eyes.

'Dear Arnaud, I am not a Cathar any more; I have lost my faith. Forgive me if my confidence makes you sad or angry; believe me, I am not proud of it myself. If, after this, you don't want us in your house any more, I cannot blame you. We will move as soon as we find a suitable dwelling.'

'What is this nonsense?' Arnaud vehemently interjected. 'You are the only family I ever had and you will always be welcome here, whether a Cathar or not. Tell me, I beg of you, have you converted to another religion? Is it Samuel who convinced you to adhere to his?'

'Nothing of the sort,' came the answer. 'There is no fibre of religiosity left in me and no other faith has lured me; certainly not Catholicism with its intransigence, nor Judaism, preoccupied with dietary law and the hidden meaning of obvious words.'

Arnaud was not about to abandon his quest, not out of curiosity, but for his keen interest in the spiritual life of his young companion. So he carried on.

'Doesn't it ever cross your mind that you may be wrong; that you are passing through a temporary stage of scepticism and that one day you will be more than happy to be restored in your faith? Don't you have some degree of doubt left?'

'Dearest Arnaud, when you have religious faith you are besieged with doubt; when you lose it, all you are left with is the ability to question.

'The disappearance of doubt is the result and reward of the disappearance of religious belief, although a sense of emptiness impossible to appreciate and difficult to dispel is the legacy of both vanishing.

'But enough of that. I have better news that I believe will make you happier. Acre is the place I'll settle in for good; I will remain next to you and, furthermore, Zeinab and the children will not be separated from Gerios.'

'That is the kind of news I'll take to bed now,' Arnaud replied joyfully. 'What about you? Aren't you going to sleep?'

'I'll stay a little longer and take advantage of the beautiful night.'

On his own and at peace with himself and his conscience, Aimeric looked back at the events of his life since he had come to Outremer and, overcome by spiritual feelings, thanked the Providence which had shown such benevolence to him and his family, and made of him a dispassionate sceptic.

I have lived an honest life, he reflected. *I don't fear death which could come at any moment, whether in Outremer or in Milan; eventually the result will be exactly the same: an equal amount of dust and ashes, whether here or there. Venerable Samuel, you were right; let it be the circumstances which decide for me. From now on, each day must be enjoyed.* Carpe diem.